THE LAST VAMPIRE QUEEN
BOOK TWO

# GUARDIAN OF BLOOD AND SHADOW

## LINDSEY SPARKS

Editing by Fresh as a Daisy Editing

www.freshasadaisyediting.com

Cover by Lindsey Sparks

ISBN: 9781949485370

# ALSO BY LINDSEY SPARKS

**ECHO WORLD**
ECHO TRILOGY
Echo in Time
Resonance
Time Anomaly
Dissonance
Ricochet Through Time

KAT DUBOIS CHRONICLES
Ink Witch
Outcast
Underground
Soul Eater
Judgement
Afterlife

FATELESS TRILOGY
Song of Scarabs and Fallen Stars
Darkness Between the Stars
Uncross the Stars

**LEGACIES OF OLYMPUS**
ATLANTIS LEGACY
Sacrifice of the Sinners
Legacy of the Lost
Fate of the Fallen
Dreams of the Damned
Song of the Soulless
Blood of the Broken
Rise of the Revenants

ALLWORLD ONLINE
Vertigo
AO: Pride & Prejudice
AO: The Wonderful Wizard of Oz

**TWILIGHT OF SHADOWS**
THE LAST VAMPIRE QUEEN
Heir of Blood and Moonlight
Guardian of Blood and Shadow

NOCTURNA FALLS
Twilight Awakening

**THE ENDING WORLD**
THE ENDING SERIES
(writing as Lindsey Fairleigh)
The Ending Beginnings: Omnibus Edition
After The Ending
Into The Fire
Out Of The Ashes
Before The Dawn
World Before

THE ENDING LEGACY
World After
The Raven Queen
The Ghost King

**For more information on Lindsey and her books:**
lindseysparks.com

**Signed books and exclusive merch:**
lindseysparksbookshop.com

**Join Lindsey's mailing list to stay up to date on releases**
AND to get access to her Subscriber Library, including
bonus stories, prequels, and more!

https://lindseysparks.com/mailing-list

For the reader who sees "too much spice" and thinks:

Oh no... don't threaten me with a good time...

# A Note from the Author

In case I wasn't clear with *Heir of Blood and Moonlight*, I just want to remind you...

This book contains quite a few explicit scenes depicting intimate encounters between the FMC, Sophie, and her consorts. While the book is undeniably spicy, the sexual content is not the sole focus of the story, which also heavily features elements of action, suspense, fantasy, and mythology. The intimate scenes serve to develop the relationships between the characters and are interwoven with the larger story and mythos of the world.

**TRIGGER WARNING:**

This book contains explicit sexual content (including all the fun words), profanity, violence, blood and gore, death and the emotional aftermath of losing someone, past trauma (including implied sexual assault), teen pregnancy and adoption, captivity and imprisonment, and alcohol consumption.

# 1

MY HEART SPLIT IN two as I stood in Javier's quarters—joy for my Prime Consort's return warring with the crushing guilt of leaving Gavin behind in that dark cell. I hadn't spent much time in Javier's personal quarters when I was a little girl. I had stepped foot in the suite maybe twice, always with Amaya, who Javier had been chosen to serve. The next High Queen of the House of the Moon had always been slated to be his queen.

But that queen wasn't supposed to be me.

My gaze swept over the sitting room, taking in everything from the furniture to the man standing stoically in loose loungewear in the doorway to the bedroom. Dark, classic pieces befitting a Gothic mansion filled the space, enhanced by silver sigils pulsing gently in the shadows.

Every heartbeat of mine felt like a betrayal. Gavin was trapped in a dungeon cell. I'd abandoned him, yet here I stood, safe and alone with another man. Guilt coiled inside me like a snake within the cage of my ribs. Yet beneath it lurked something unexpected—anticipation. My body hummed with awareness of Javier's presence even as I mourned Gavin's sacrifice. What kind of person did that make me?

A pretty damn terrible one, that's what.

Javier had nearly as many bookcases as Ash, but only half held books. The rest displayed objects straight out of an occult museum. I passed a silver athame and felt it hum through my bones, vibrating against something deep inside me.

I crossed to the fireplace. Behind me, Javier shut the door. I fidgeted with my flowy T-shirt hem while staring into the flames that did nothing for the chill in my core. Gavin's face haunted me—that resigned determination, quiet acceptance, and something else I couldn't name without shattering into a million pieces right here on the floor.

"You look well," Javier said, his voice like gravel covered in silk. He stayed by the door.

For a heartbeat, the reality of him standing there—alive, whole, after believing him lost for so long—hit me with physical force. My vision blurred with unexpected tears, my body swaying slightly before I caught myself. Twenty years of grief collapsed in an instant, leaving me disoriented in its absence.

I choked on a laugh. *Well*? I was anything but.

Twenty years gone. Twenty years that had turned me from a frightened child to this woman I barely recognized. I'd mourned him while he suffered in captivity. I had lived while he had spent two decades dying. I had lost every single thing that mattered... But then, so had he.

So, in a sense, I supposed we were both well.

"Gavin figured out what you did with the tincture," I said. "He reversed it so I could go longer between, uh, *communions*." My cheeks burned. "But it was hard before that. I was starving...for a long time. And when Gavin found me and awakened my magic, I needed a lot." Not just immortal blood. I had needed everything Gavin could give me. More, considering I'd bound three consorts in barely two days.

Gavin's name stuck in my throat like a fishbone. He had sacrificed nearly everything—for me, for our people—and I couldn't even properly grieve because he wasn't dead, just suffering somewhere beyond my reach. Our bond was stretched thin but unbroken, vibrating with pain I couldn't soothe.

"I'm sorry, Luna," Javier said from right behind me.

I spun around, my hands clutching my chest, my heart pounding. I didn't correct him on my name. Didn't tell him I was Sophie now. To him, I would always be Luna.

"Sorry," he repeated, that familiar smile flashing briefly. His eyes traced my features. "You look so much like your mother."

I stared at the floor, at his bare feet inches from mine. My mother's ghost seemed to stand between us. Would she judge me for wanting Javier while mourning Gavin? For binding multiple consorts in a matter of days? For standing here ready to *commune* with the man who practically raised me?

"Did you ever *commune* with—" I swallowed hard, my hands twisting my shirt hem. "With her? With my mom?" I met his eyes for a split second before dropping my gaze, my cheeks burning.

"No," he said. "Never." He gripped my hands, stilling them. "It is rare, but there are cases where a queen and one of her consorts have a platonic relationship."

My eyes snapped to his. "Is that what you want?" My heart turned leaden and sank. Based on the hollow feeling spreading through me, a platonic relationship wasn't what I wanted with Javier. Not even close.

Fresh guilt followed. Gavin had saved my life, awakened my powers, made me feel things I never knew possible... And now he suffered alone because of me. Because I had needed Javier, my Prime Consort. Yet here I stood, before the same man whose freedom had cost Gavin's, desperate for him not to reject me. Yearning for his hands on me. His teeth in me.

"You didn't choose me to be your Prime Consort," Javier said. "That was meant to be Gavin's role, but I stole it from him. Stole you from him. Not once, but twice."

His words cut through me. Javier was my past; Gavin was supposed to be my future. Yet fate had twisted everything inside out.

"You saved me," I countered softly. "I would have died here, with my mom and Amaya and...everyone."

"Even so," Javier said. "I took something never meant for me. I forced you into a bond you didn't understand and couldn't have chosen." He paused. "I don't expect you to treat me the same as those you did choose."

"But...I love you," I whispered, tears gathering on my lashes.

The truth felt both simple and impossibly complex. I'd always loved him, but that love had transformed. He'd been everything: father, teacher, guardian, friend. Now he was something else I couldn't define but felt unwinding inside me with each breath.

"Love me like a father?" he asked. "Like a brother? Like a friend?"

My chin trembled. "Like *you*." I turned away, pulling free and retreating to the far side of the fireplace. "But I understand if you prefer a platonic relationship," I said, hugging myself. Why did it feel like I was losing him all over again when I'd only just found him?

Gavin's last kiss haunted my lips. Every touch from Javier felt like a blessing and a betrayal simultaneously. Was this what it meant to be a queen? Holding contradictions without shattering, loving so many so deeply, feeling joy and grief at once?

"I didn't say that." Javier stood behind me again. His hands settled on my shoulders, thumbs tracing my neck. He brushed my damp hair aside, and I felt the whisper of his lips over my carotid, the faint brush of teeth.

My pulse thrummed, my blood calling to him. I tilted my head, silently offering my neck. Even as heat rushed through me, my heart ached for Gavin.

The queen in me knew this was necessary. Each bond strengthened me. Gavin himself had urged me to complete these connections, and his sacrifice would be meaningless if I didn't use this opportunity to embrace my power. But the part of me that was still Sophie Matthews from Seattle whispered this was wrong, that happiness was undeserved while he remained a prisoner.

Javier stepped forward, his body pressing flush against my back, one hand settling on my abdomen. A low growl reverberated through his chest as he grazed his teeth over my skin once more. I covered his hand with mine, threading our fingers together. His other hand curved around my neck, cradling my jaw. When his teeth cut through my skin, the initial sharp bite of pain transformed into blissful euphoria between one heartbeat and the next.

Guilt dissolved, burned away by the fire in my blood. This wasn't betraying Gavin. It was honoring his sacrifice. I would become strong enough to save him. The queen in me embraced this truth while the woman mourned.

I gripped Javier's hand tighter, pressing back until I felt his growing hardness. His fingers flexed around mine, his erection pressing into my lower back. He'd said platonic was possible, not that he wanted it.

And neither did I.

I dragged his hand lower, toward the place throbbing with need—for him. Close enough for him to understand what I wanted, but not all the way. His choice, not mine. I wouldn't force his hand while bloodlust clouded his judgment.

His fingertips dug into my pubic bone, close enough to make my clit pulse but nowhere near enough to ease the ache between my thighs. He tore his mouth from my neck, nuzzling my damp hair while holding me tight. The bite wound tingled as he initiated healing with a smear of his own immortal blood.

"Sophie," he said, breath ragged. "It's been a very long time since I—"

He'd fed while I showered, but I hadn't sensed lust through our weakened bond. He really hadn't taken more than blood since returning? What about with the other queens? The thought flashed through my mind. Had he shared more with them than blood? The thought tied my stomach in knots.

"I can't guarantee I'll be gentle," he warned.

My thighs squeezed together at the suggestion. "That's fine," I rasped and turned in his hold.

His features were tense, his pupils blown wide in his rich brown eyes, his lips stained red with my blood.

"Gentle isn't really my thing," I said, my gaze shifting from his eyes to his lips and back.

Half-truth. Each connection pulled different needs from me—Gavin, Bastian, Ash. With Javier, I sensed he needed control, reclaiming power after years without it. And maybe I needed to surrender control after days of impossible decisions.

His jaw clenched, his hand fisting my shirt. "What is your thing?" he asked roughly.

"Right now?" I pressed closer. "You." I licked my lips. "Are you recovered enough for me to..." My focus dropped to his neck.

My salivary glands tingled in anticipation. But after everything—his imprisonment, torture, and feeding over a dozen queens for so long—was he ready for a full *communion*? I reached through our bond but hit a wall, blocking me from his thoughts and feelings.

His throat bobbed as he nodded.

"Do you want me to?" I asked. "I would understand if—"

"Yes," he said, the word clawing up his throat. "Do it." Almost a plea.

Heart pounding in time with the throb between my legs, I traced his pulse point. His fist pressed me closer, his hardness digging into my belly. I leaned in, tasting him with my tongue, imagining his blood's flavor. I couldn't remember his taste. It had been so long.

I bit down, teeth digging deeper until skin broke and his immortal blood entered my mouth.

My taste buds exploded—sweet raspberries dipped in bitter dark chocolate. I groaned, pulling more of him into me. He wrapped his arms around me, lifting my feet off the floor. As his blood flowed into me, I felt our shared history, the magic binding us deeper than blood.

This was memory made liquid. Childhood laughter. Reading on the floor together. Band-Aids on skinned knees. A shoulder to cry on. Endless sacrifice and worry and fear. And love.

And now desire. An all-consuming need to give himself to me in a completely new way.

Through the haze of passion, Gavin's face appeared in my mind—not accusatory, but resigned. Understanding. His final words echoed in my mind: *I will return to you.* A promise I'd hold on to, a vow I'd make damn sure came true.

For now, though, this moment belonged to Javier and me. Healing old wounds. Forging new bonds.

I gripped his shoulders tight as he carried me across the room, pushing open a door with his back to bring me into his bedroom. I released my bite as he laid me on the bed, lifting my hips so he could drag my leggings and underwear down my legs in one smooth motion. His hands glided up my thighs, pushing my knees apart.

I'd have thought I would be past blushing after everything I'd done with the others, but seeing Javier look at me like I was a feast and he was starving made heat rush to my face. Then his mouth was on me. I arched into him, and everything else vanished. Just sensation. Just this.

I dug my fingers into his hair, pulling him closer. He lapped at my entrance, then shifted higher to my clit. He tongued the exposed head while digging in his teeth just enough to break skin.

"Holy fuck," I gasped as pain mixed with pleasure in a way that made me see stars. He sucked hard, pulling more blood to my nether regions, and the pleasure narrowed to a pinprick, then exploded outward, rocking through my body in waves. I'd never climaxed so fast.

Fresh tingles told me he'd coated the shallow wound in his blood even as he teased my clit, sending delicious aftershocks jolting through me.

He pushed up my shirt as he climbed onto the bed, gripping me around my ribcage to lift and toss me further back on the mattress. I raised my arms, letting him drag off my shirt and sweater as one. He gripped my bra and yanked, tearing it in two. Kneeling between my legs, he stared down at me, his super-heated gaze roving up and down my body as he yanked his shirt off, then pushed down his drawstring pants, revealing his lack of underwear and releasing his proud erection.

I drank him in. Broad chest covered in glowing sigils and dark hair. Taut abdomen. The thick length jutting out from between his legs.

Javier kicked off his pants and took hold of my hips, lifting my ass off the bed. He dragged my soaked slit along his hard length, using me as his personal lubricant, then angled the head of his cock at my entrance and thrust forward, plunging in deep. My fingers dug into the comforter. I threw my head back, soaking in the harsh sensation of suddenly being so full.

He bowed his head, his breaths coming faster as his fingertips dug into my hips, and held me impaled on his cock. He was still for so long that I feared something was wrong.

"Javier?" I asked softly, reaching up to touch the side of his face. "Are you all right?"

He raised his head, and I sucked in a breath when I saw the tears staining his cheeks. Sex with me had never before made a man cry.

But this wasn't just sex. This was reconciliation. Reunion. This was a man who had lost everything to find his way back to the one person he had sacrificed everything to save. Twenty years of suffering finding release in a single moment.

I captured a tear with my thumb and searched his intense gaze. "Javi?"

He turned his face into my hand and grazed his teeth over my palm. "It's a bit overwhelming," he said roughly.

Guilt tightened my throat—not for Gavin this time, but for Javier. All those years I'd lived my life while he suffered in darkness. All that time I'd believed him dead, never searching, never questioning.

"Come here," I said, tugging on his shoulder.

He leaned forward, covering my body with his, the motion pulling him out of me partway, only to push back in as he stretched out between my legs.

I shuddered, taking a shaky breath. "If you need to go slow, then go slow," I said, grazing my nails up and down either side of his neck. "If you need to fuck me hard, then fuck me hard." I searched his eyes, seeing the shadows threatening to drown out his desire. "I'm here for you. Whatever you need."

I couldn't erase his past. Couldn't undo his suffering or mine. But I could offer him this—a present where he wasn't alone, a future where he belonged.

I lifted my head and lightly pressed my lips against his. Our first kiss. And despite his cock buried inside me, it was sweet and innocent. Somehow more intimate than what we were already doing.

I broke away, resting my head back on the bed, watching his expression. He licked his lips, then bent his neck, claiming my mouth. This time, there was nothing innocent in the kiss. I opened to him, letting him in, our tongues seeking.

His hips shifted, drawing back before thrusting forward again. I groaned at the renewed invasion. Each thrust came harder, faster, rougher until his body slammed into me with bruising intensity, pushing me toward a second climax as magic welled in my chest.

Making a sound between a groan and a growl, Javier broke our kiss and dragged his lips down over my jaw to my neck. I arched my head back, offering him a better angle. Even the thought of him biting me had my insides fluttering. He sliced his teeth over his thumb and slid it into my mouth, lighting me up with his decadent blood. At that exact moment, he dug his teeth into my neck.

My eyes rolled back as my internal muscles seized. I clenched my thighs around him as silver moonlight exploded out of me, showering us in my magic. Bliss radiated from my core, deepened by the ache from the rough joining, and I dug my nails into his back, shuddering beneath him.

In that moment, I existed beyond thought. Beyond guilt. Beyond the tangle of emotions suffocating me. Just this—bodies connected, blood bonded, power exchanged. I wasn't torn between consorts or divided by loyalties. Just whole. Complete.

Yet even as ecstasy consumed me, a vow formed: I would become strong enough to save them all. I would harness this power and use it to reclaim what was stolen. Gavin would not be abandoned. The imprisoned queens would not be forgotten.

Javier pulled his thumb from my mouth and broke away from my neck as he slammed into me one last time, covering my mouth with his. His kiss tasted of his blood mixed with mine—intoxicating, right, like we had always been meant to mix together.

And maybe we had been. As our blood mingled on our tongues, I felt the wall between us crumbling, our bond strengthening, his emotions washing through me—relief, joy, devotion, protection, and beneath it all, a fierce love that had sustained him through decades of darkness.

I welcomed it all.

# 2

F INALLY, MY LIGHT FADED, and Javier relaxed on top of me, dipping his head until his lips met mine again. He kissed me once, twice more, tenderly, then pulled back, searching my face. "I hurt you." Not a question.

I winced as the pleasure of release faded, leaving behind a dull pain between my legs. And in my heart. "It's fine," I told him.

But it wasn't just physical discomfort that made me wince. In the quiet aftermath, Gavin's face materialized in my mind—not as I'd last seen him through the bars of that cell door, but from that night in his bathroom when he'd tended to me. The memory cut like a blade between my ribs, twisting deeper with each breath.

Javier growled, low and controlled, and pulled out of me, pushing back onto his knees. "Fuck," he hissed.

I pushed up onto my elbows to see what was bothering him. His waning erection was coated in a combination of arousal and blood.

His eyes met mine, heated. He bit his lip, drawing blood, then brought his hand up to his mouth, dragging his lips over his first two fingers to coat them in his blood. His focus dropped to my sex, now throbbing with a much less pleasant ache than before, and he gently grazed his fingers over my swollen lips. I sucked in a sharp breath as he pushed his fingers inside me.

The pain felt almost like penance. Perhaps I deserved this discomfort while Gavin endured far worse. The thought made me hate myself even as I recognized its irrationality. Gavin had made his choice. He would want me to be here, to heal, to grow stronger, to become the High Queen our people needed. Yet the guilt lingered like a shadow I couldn't outrun.

I closed my eyes, breathing through the ache and the healing tingle, and nodded. "You're probably wondering what happened to me to make me depraved enough to enjoy the pain."

"If only my thoughts were so wholesome," Javier said. A moment later, a sharp jolt of sensation shot through me as he pressed the pad of his thumb against my overstimulated clit.

My eyelids snapped open. I stared down the length of my body, watching his thumb circle that exposed bundle of nerves. The healing tingle inside me mixed with the electric sensation from each stroke of his thumb. He withdrew his fingers and put them in his mouth, and when he pulled them out again, he dragged his razor-sharp teeth along the length of them, cutting into his skin. He pushed those bloody fingers inside me, quadrupling the healing tingle.

Pleasure washed through me again, and with it came grief. Each *communion* felt like its own language. With Gavin, it had been fierce yet tender. This with Javier was ancient, primal, built on pain I couldn't fully comprehend.

I lifted my hips off the bed, the stroke of his thumb transforming from way-too-much to just-enough to I-need-more-right-the-fuck-now. "Don't stop," I panted. "Oh gods, Javi. Don't stop. I'm going to—"

He curled the fingers inside me just so, finding that secret place I hadn't known existed until my consorts entered my life and showed me what they could do to me. The ache faded until there was only pulsing warmth and delicious promise. My bones turned liquid, and my legs clamped shut, my vision going white as pleasure flooded me.

For one moment, I forgot everything. Who I was. What I'd lost. What I still stood to lose. But reality rushed back in like a slap, bringing with it all I'd momentarily escaped.

Javier palmed my pulsing sex and stretched out alongside me.

Feeling boneless, I flopped back onto the bed and turned my face toward him, studying the brightened crescent sigil curving from his forehead down to his jaw, standing out in stark contrast against his golden-brown skin. I moved on to the smaller sigils on his neck and shoulders, then to those on his chest. One I hadn't noticed before, larger than the others and burning brighter, covered the skin over his heart under a light dusting of dark hair. It was similar to the bonding sigils I had left on Gavin and the others, but slightly different, with ancient flourishes curling like vines around the central moon phases' markings.

"This is mine?" I asked, tracing the sigil with the tip of my index finger.

In the loft, after my first *communion* with Gavin, I'd watched my sigil manifest around his neck—an intricate design with the phases of the moon forming a collar centered on where I had bitten him. The memory of his fingers brushing over it afterward, that quiet moment of recognition between us, felt both distant and achingly near. Where was he now, in that dark dungeon? Was my mark on him glowing still, a small comfort in endless darkness?

Javier covered my hand with his, pressing my palm against the sigil on his chest. The silver light flared, seeping out beyond the edges of our hands. "It's the traditional location of a queen's first *communion* with her Prime Consort. I initiated it once it became clear we wouldn't be able to return to our people—" He searched my eyes. "Do you remember when you took blood from me here?"

My brow furrowed, and I shook my head. "But that doesn't mean much. Those first few years after are kind of a jumble in my head."

The confession felt shameful. How could I not remember something so significant? Yet I could recall with perfect clarity the way Gavin's blood had tasted that first night in that club—like dark chocolate infused with chilis and promise and sin. I remembered the way his lips had curved when he'd first called me "my queen," the way his eyes had burned silver when he looked at me. Memories I'd known for days held more clarity than those I should have carried for decades.

Javier's lips twitched. "You were so ferocious," he recalled. "The moment my blood touched your tongue, you all but attacked me, and I wondered what the hell I had gotten myself into."

My cheeks flushed, and I hid my face against his shoulder. "*Oh god, that's embarrassing.*"

He gripped my chin and tilted my face up toward his, brushing his lips over mine. "That was when I knew you were different, special, destined to be the next High Queen," he said. "The light shining from you rivaled your mother's. Even if Amaya had lived..." Shadows filled his eyes. "You would have been High Queen. I think your mother always knew it, too. It's why she chose Gavin for your Prime Consort rather than me. Born to a queen, with all that potential. It was his destiny to be the Prime Consort to the next High Queen."

"Apparently not," I said, turning my head to stare up at the intricately carved ceiling.

Something twisted inside me. Had I altered some cosmic plan by binding to Javier first? Or had this always been the design, my mother's intentions overwritten by necessity? And if Gavin had always been meant for me, why had he found me only after Javier was gone?

As my thoughts lingered on Gavin and what he was enduring, tears gathered, hot against my temples as they spilled from the corners of my eyes. "What will they do to him?" I asked, my voice unsteady, knowing Javier would sense the direction of my thoughts and understand my question.

"They won't kill him," Javier said. When he didn't add more, I looked at him to find his focus on the wall behind me, his stare thousands of miles away.

The implication hit like a fist to the gut. He would face everything but death. Javier knew what Gavin would experience in the Sun Keep because he himself had lived through it.

The knowledge hardened my guilt into determination. Gavin would suffer while the shifters held him, which meant we had to free him sooner rather than later.

I brought my hand up to Javier's face, my touch dragging his attention back to me. "I thought you were dead," I told him. "I used everything you taught me. I disappeared. I became human. But then Gavin showed up a few days ago and blew up the life I built, and I realized you were still alive..." I sighed. "I'm sorry it took me so long to find you. I'm so sorry, Javi."

"There was no difference between a year and twenty in that place," he said, a new distance in his voice. "At least, not until the young blood showed up."

I choked on a laugh—now *really* wasn't the time—but the idea that Javier thought of Thane as young in any sense only highlighted his own age. Javier had been respected here at the Moon Sanctuary—before the massacre—but that was about all I knew of his past.

"How old are you?" I asked him for about the millionth time. When I was little, he would deflect with vague answers. Would he do the same now?

"I grew up with your mother," he said.

My eyes widened. My mother, Diana, had been High Queen of the House of the Moon for over four centuries and had lived in her mother's shadow long before that. I knew almost nothing about her history, her age, or why she'd waited so long to have children.

For a moment, I saw Javier differently—not as guardian or consort, but as someone with centuries of life before I existed. Someone who'd walked with my mother, witnessed empires rise and fall, lived through more than I could comprehend. The weight of his years should have terrified me. Instead, it comforted me.

"We were close," Javier said, his gaze distant. "Diana's mother wanted me for Diana's harem, but Diana refused." He breathed out a laugh. "Much to my relief. She was my best friend, and I loved her, but not like a consort should love his queen. I never craved her." His gaze dropped to my mouth. "Not like I crave you."

He leaned in, pressing a slow, lingering kiss to my lips. His teeth grazed my jawline until his lips brushed my ear. "My Luna... I could live a thousand years buried inside you and it wouldn't be long enough."

My blood heated at his words. As much as I wanted to climb atop him and explore this attraction, my thoughts snagged on Gavin and what he was enduring right now. Our *communion* earlier had been a necessity to reestablish the bond, but anything more than that felt gluttonous.

"He is the reason I am here now, with you," Javier said, sensing my thoughts and pulling away. "Whenever you decide it's time to go after him, know I am with you."

Relief washed through me, sharp and unexpected. I hadn't realized how afraid I'd been—that Javier would resent Gavin, that he would see no urgency in rescuing the man who'd taken up his role, even for just a few days. That he would make me choose.

I smiled shakily, fighting tears. "Soon."

The word was both a promise and a failure. *Soon*, but not *now*. Not immediately. Each moment we delayed was another moment Gavin suffered. Yet rushing in unprepared would end in disaster.

The strategy we'd used to rescue Thane and Javier wouldn't work twice. The shifters knew about the escape tunnel to the mine shafts by now.

I needed to master my magic so I could be more than a glorified compass. With other queens around, I finally had a way to learn. I needed to build my power, complete my harem. And I had to do it all before Gavin's blood faded from my system, weakening us both.

His blood. I could almost taste it—rich, complex, spreading through my veins like lava. The way his eyes had darkened as he watched me taste him that first time, a mixture of awe and desire I'd never seen before.

I stared at the ceiling, focusing on the bond stretching halfway across the world to Gavin. Through it, I sent not just thoughts but feelings—gratitude for his sacrifice, determination to free him, my promise that he wouldn't be abandoned.

"Soon," I repeated, my voice ringing with power, the word crossing that vast distance between us. A promise that I was coming for him.

I felt a faint pulse of warmth through our bond—acknowledgment, or simply his awareness of me at the edges of his consciousness.

It had to be enough. Until we met again.

Soon.

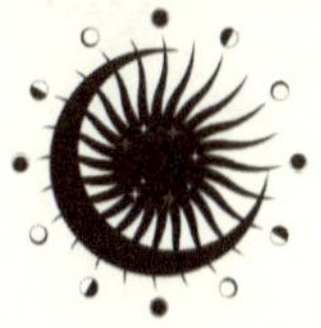

# 3

J AVIER STOOD AT THE broad picture window behind the desk in the High Queen's study, his stare roving over the grounds below, while Bastian browsed the bookshelves, his head cocked to the side so he could better read the words on the books' spines. Whenever he reached a book with a bare spine, he would carefully pull the volume free and almost reverently open the cover to leaf through the aged pages.

It heartened me to know his love of books was a genuine part of his personality, even if the rest of his grad student persona had been a lie. The bookworm part of him was real. His expert bookcase shuffle proved it.

I paced along the opposite wall of books, fidgeting with my clothing and hair. Was the low, loose bun too casual? Did the jeans, blouse, and long sweater suggest I wasn't taking my position seriously? Should I have dressed up? Or, at least, dressed more professionally? Should I have made more of an effort to look the part of High Queen? Was I even the High Queen yet, or were there rituals and ceremonies that had to happen first?

Although, I supposed the whole point of these interviews was to find the person who could either answer those questions, or at the very least, help me find the answers. The first of the three rescued queens would be arriving any minute. They had barely had a full night and day to recover, but proceeding with the hunt for a teacher had been Javier's idea, and he knew better than anyone what the queens had been through as prisoners and what they would be up for now that they were free. If he didn't think this was too soon, then neither did I.

I eyed Bastian. Maybe it was a mistake to have him here. Shifters had inflicted unending trauma upon these women. Would his presence rub their noses in their horrific experiences? Except, having him here in the room with us had also been Javier's idea. He claimed that if the queens couldn't handle being around Bastian, then they weren't fit to be my teacher. Bastian was one of my consorts, after all, so his presence in my life was nonnegotiable.

I was heading toward the back of the study when the door creaked open. I spun around, my hands clasped together in front of me, and I watched as Ash escorted a diminutive older woman into the room. The frail hand he held securely hooked around his arm was clearly more for her stability than for chivalry.

She had warm, brown skin that appeared paper thin, amber eyes, and I had no doubt her gray-streaked dark amber curls would be stunning once she recovered from the prolonged malnourishment and regained her queenly vigor. Despite her petite size, her presence was enormous, her self-assurance indomitable.

Based on Javier's descriptions of the rescued queens, this had to be Isador, the eldest of the bunch. She appeared to be in her nineties, though Javier claimed she was far older. Her lifespan had apparently been lengthened by her bonds to her immortal consorts, at least one of whom had to still be living for her to be alive after everything she had been through.

I glanced at Javier, who had turned away from the window at Isador's arrival, his expression unreadable. He had predicted she would volunteer to come and speak with me first, and he had been right.

I cleared my throat and stepped forward, forcing my hands apart. "Thank you, Ash." I nodded to my hulking consort, then turned my attention to the woman who appeared dwarfed beside him. "Welcome, Isador," I said and gestured to the pair of settees arranged around a sturdy oak coffee table in the middle of the room. "Please, sit."

I approached the nearest settee and lowered myself to the cushioned seat. The formality felt stiff and robotic, but I wasn't sure how else to be. I'd never expected to be High Queen—that role had been intended for my sister, whatever Javier said—and I had only period dramas of European royals on which to model my behavior.

Tea things were arranged on a tray in the center of the table, along with a plate of scones and a three-tiered tower of sweet and savory small bites. As Isador approached, I perched on the edge of my seat and busied myself with pouring a cup of tea for each of us and adding sugar to mine to avoid her weighty stare.

Again, this was something that seemed appropriate based on all the movies I had seen. I didn't actually want the tea. In fact, with how jittery my nerves made me feel, I doubted I would be able to lift the cup to my lips without spilling hot tea all over myself. It was a miracle I could pour any into the cups at all.

Ash remained steadfast at Isador's side as she crossed the room, only releasing her elbow when she eased down onto the opposite settee. I pressed my lips together to avoid frowning, and I set the teapot back down on the tray, nudging her cup closer to her side of the table. I had wanted to visit the recovering queens in their rooms, but Javier had been adamant about having them come to me here. Something about propriety and respect, but forcing Isador to come to me when she could barely stand on her own seemed wrong.

I suddenly felt like an idiot for requesting these interviews now. She would see through me. They all would. I was a librarian, not the ruler of an immortal race.

I abandoned my teacup on the table and wiped my sweating palms against my jeans. I glanced at Javier as he approached, coming to stand behind my settee, like he sensed that I was floundering and needed his help. It amazed me that he had been in far worse shape than Isador only a day earlier, but now appeared in the prime of health. The perks of immortality and an endless supply of mortal blood, I supposed.

"You look well, Isador," Javier said.

The queen barked a laugh. "I look ancient," she said, her amber eyes glittering as she peered up at him. Despite her appearance, there was nothing frail about her gravelly, resonant voice. "You, on the other hand..." Her lips twisted into a secretive smirk, and her focus dropped to me. "And you must be Luna—I mean, Sophie," she said, bowing her head. "Thank you for rescuing me." She twisted partway on her seat to look at Bastian, who was leaning one shoulder against the bookshelves behind her. "And thank you for choosing to unlock my cell first."

Bastian's lips curved into a tight-lipped smile, and he dipped his chin.

Isador returned her attention to me. "I've heard much about you, my lady." She glanced up at Javier, then settled back on me. "But I'm most impressed that you were able to survive without your Prime Consort for so long while so young." She tilted her head to the side, her eyes narrowing. "Did you find another immortal to sustain you after he was captured?" She snuck another glance over her shoulder at Bastian, suggesting she believed that had been his role.

"No," I said, then cleared my throat when the word came out weaker than I had intended. "It was just me." And Javier's blood tincture, but I wasn't about to go into all that right now. "I've been living as a human for nearly twenty years," I told her. "I thought all of our people were dead." I shrugged. "I didn't know how to be what I am, so I became something else."

Isador studied me with those hawkish amber eyes. "You were a prisoner in your own right."

Gripping my knees, I shook my head, unwilling to compare my experience with hers. What she had been through was unimaginable. "I made a life for myself," I said. "In the human world."

Her lips curved minutely, and there was pity in her eyes. "But you are not a human, child."

"I don't know how to be anything else," I confessed, my gaze averting to my hands, my fingertips digging into my knees.

Javier's steady hand settled on my shoulder, his grip reassuring. "Which is why you're here," he said. "Sophie's ignorance is my fault. I taught her how to identify an immortal and defend herself against them, but I neglected every other part of a queen's training in favor of an education in the ways of the human world." His grip on my shoulder tightened momentarily, like a silent apology, and I covered his hand with my own. "I thought we would have time for all that later," he added. "When she came into her power."

I craned my neck to peer up at him and flashed him a small smile. "It all worked out in the end," I said, the words souring on my tongue as I thought of Gavin locked up in the shifter prison. I swallowed the guilt and sorrow and faced Isador once more.

"I need a teacher," I told the other queen, returning my attention to her. "Javier taught me what I needed to know to survive in the human world, but I'm clueless about almost everything relating to *our* world." I took a steadying breath. "I asked you to come here today because I wish to speak with each of you to see if you would be interested in the role."

Isador studied me, long and hard. "I thought as much," she finally said, scooting forward and reaching for her cup of tea. "I will teach you what you need to know." Her gaze flicked up to Javier as she sipped. "It's better this way, with you knowing next to nothing." She set down the cup and looked at me. "Rather than being riddled with bad habits, you are a blank slate. You will learn the proper way of doing things slow and steady, with a solid foundation of knowledge first."

I licked my lips and picked at my thumbnail. "I actually need more of a crash course on how to use my powers," I said, wincing when Isador's lips pursed with disapproval. "We have to go back to the Sun Keep. We have to rescue the rest of the queens and the guardian who remained behind."

Keen understanding gleamed in Isador's amber eyes. "He is one of yours," she said, not a question.

I nodded. "Gavin was to be my Prime Consort...before."

Isador's eyes widened, her brows rising. "Gavin? Alma's boy?" she asked Javier, and I wondered if Alma was Gavin's mother, the queen he had referenced only in passing. "I didn't recognize him, but then, it was very dark, and I haven't seen him since he was quite young." Her stare grew distant. "I should have known. I haven't felt power like that from an undead since..." Again, she focused on Javier. "Well, since they brought *you* down to us."

I turned my head, eyeing Javier curiously. Had his mother been a queen as well?

Javier sliced his chin to the right, negating my silent question. He couldn't hear my thoughts exactly, but our bond allowed him to sense the general direction of my mind, just as I could sense his. At the moment, he wanted me to accept Isador's offer to teach me.

My brow furrowed. We hadn't yet met with the others. Perhaps one of them would be more open to fast-tracking my training. Once we had rescued Gavin and the other queens, then we could come back to Isador.

"Your consort will be there, waiting for you, whether you rescue him in a day, a year, or in ten," Isador said, drawing my attention back to her. "The only difference is how well you will be prepared to face his captors." She sipped her tea, then set it on the table. "But I can see you're unwilling to accept the truth just yet." She smiled kindly, belying the steel glinting in her eyes. "I won't waste any more of your time," she said, groaning as she regained her feet. "Please, do discuss your training with the others."

Ash moved from his post by the door, hurrying to meet Isador before her shuffling steps carried her to the edge of the settee. He took her hand, curling her fingers around his thick forearm once more.

"There's only half a brain between the two of them, just so you know," Isador tossed over her shoulder. "Helene lost her mind when her consorts were slaughtered, and Doris never had much of one to begin with."

Ash pulled open the study door and guided Isador into the High Queen's sitting room.

"Let me know when you're ready to start," she called back, like it was a foregone conclusion that, in the end, I would come back to her, asking for her help. "My lady." The final two words floated into the room like an afterthought after Isador and Ash were out of sight.

Thane leaned into the study from his post just outside and pulled the door shut.

I blew out a breath and turned partway on my seat to stare up at Javier. "She is…" I shook my head, at a loss for words. "A force," I finally settled on.

Javier released a dry, humorless laugh. "She had to be to retain her sanity down there."

I narrowed my eyes, wondering not for the first time why the shifters had been holding queens as prisoners in the first place. "Why not simply kill them and be done with it?" I murmured, not really expecting an answer.

"To break the curse," Bastian said. "Veris believes that after enough time, one of the queens will break and agree to appeal to Selene to lift the curse."

I shook my head, looking from Bastian to Javier and back. "But I thought the goddess only listened to the High Queen."

"Which is why Veris still hunts stray queens," Bastian said, his jaw clenching and unclenching. "He wants to capture them all to guarantee that, when the time comes, he can make his broken queen the High Queen."

Again, I shook my head. "But the only way he could guarantee that would be to make her the *only* queen." I blanched, my mouth going dry as I understood. "He'll kill them. When one breaks and agrees to help him, he'll kill the others."

"Isador was the backbone of the group," Javier said. "She kept the others strong, focused. Without her steady presence, it becomes far more likely one of the queens will give in."

I swallowed my suddenly tacky saliva. "And then all the others will die," I said, my voice sounding remote, even inside my own head. "Unless—" I turned, gripping the back of the settee. "What if I do something—a show of power or something—that makes it obvious that *I* am the High Queen?"

"Sophie, no," Bastian said, the vehemence in his voice catching me off guard. "*No.*"

"The only reason Veris isn't launching an assault on the Moon Sanctuary this instant is because he doesn't know your true identity," Javier explained, the cold edge to his words somehow even more frightening than the heat in Bastian's. "Untrained as you are, you're helpless against him."

"But I'm here, surrounded by all these wards," I countered.

"Wards that didn't protect your mother or your sister the last time they came," Javier said, ending each word like he was biting off the final sound. "You cannot reveal yourself until your power as High Queen is at full strength."

I balled my hands into fists. "Which won't happen until we have Gavin back," I snapped. "Without *him*, I will *never* be at full strength."

"Uh," Bastian started, drawing out the sound. "That might not actually be true."

My attention snapped to Bastian, who now stood behind the other settee. "What do you mean?"

"You don't need Gavin to be at full power," Bastian said. "At least, not *all* of him. You need his blood."

I scoffed. "Which is in his body."

"Maybe not all of it," Bastian said and glanced at the door. "You should talk to the vampires down in the infirmary. I overheard Gavin speaking to one, and it sounded like they were working on a new tincture—one made from his blood." Bastian shrugged one shoulder and glanced at Javier. "I think he was inspired by what you came up with.

My brows bunched together. "But, why—" I shook my head. "Why would he have thought I might need a blood tincture made from his blood?"

Bastian shrugged again, both shoulders this time. "Backup plan? He seems like a thorough planner."

"Gavin must have foreseen the possibility that someone would need to remain behind to sustain the imprisoned queens, should there be inadequate time to free them all," Javier said, his voice a low rumble. "He knew you would never be at full strength without your Prime Consort, and he would never ask a weaker subordinate to make a sacrifice he was capable of making himself. I doubt he expected to remain behind, but he entered that dungeon prepared to do so, if necessary. For our people." Javier's hand settled on my shoulder once more, his fingers splaying over my collarbone and the pad of his thumb gliding up and down the back of my neck along my spine. "And for you."

My chin trembled. I didn't deserve Gavin. He was too noble, and I was just *me*. Just a glorified librarian with a tragic and troubled past. My birthright didn't mesh with who I had become, and I felt woefully in-adequate. How would I ever fulfill the expectations of all the immortals around me, both ally and foe? How could I ever become the High Queen the House of the Moon needed? The savior my people had been hoping and waiting for? The leader they deserved?

The door to the sitting room opened again, and I hastily wiped under my eyes as Ash escorted another emaciated queen into the study. This had to be Helene, based on the limp blonde hair and dull blue eyes.

I forced a smile that I hoped looked welcoming and gestured to the settee across the table from me. "Please, sit," I said, though I had little hope that Helene would be a good fit for the role of my teacher. I sensed a vacancy within her. An absence of will. Of self. I thought of what Isador had said about Helene losing her consorts and wondered if that was the source.

After a few minutes of one-sided conversation, my suspicions about Helene being a poor fit for the role were confirmed, and I bid the other queen farewell. The interview with Doris went much the same, and once the door to the sitting room was shut and Javier, Bastian, and I were alone in the study, I sighed and slumped back on the settee.

"Isador, it is," I said, sounding resigned.

# 4

J AVIER ROUNDED THE SETTEE and sat down opposite me, leaning forward and planting his forearms on his thighs. "She'll make an excellent teacher." He reached out, pushing the tray of tea and finger foods closer to me. "You should eat. Keep up your strength for the next order of business."

I stared at him, Isador and my training forgotten as heat crept up my neck until my face flamed.

As if on cue, the door to the sitting room opened, and Ash walked in, accompanied by Thane. a.k.a. *the next order of business.*

Javier was adamant that I bind another consort as soon as possible to dampen the effects of losing Gavin. Except Gavin wasn't *lost.* We knew exactly where he was; we just couldn't get to him.

Ash shut the door, and he and Thane took up positions standing guard on either side of the doorway.

I licked my lips, my pulse racing, and looked at Javier. Bastian stood behind him, smirking. "If there really is a tincture made from Gavin's blood," I said, desperation forcing me to find the logic in the altered situation, "then we don't need to rush things, right?"

It wasn't that I didn't want to bond with Thane, but the memory of my *communion* with just three immortals *at the same time* made me flush with a combination of embarrassment and insecurity. They had worshipped me, and I had loved it. But I didn't feel like I deserved it.

They were each so perfect in their own way. How could I ever be enough for them? There was just one of me, and once Thane was added to the harem as my fifth consort, I would be divided further. The traditional size of a vampire queen's harem included seven immortal consorts. Seven hearts and minds and bodies for me to prioritize. Seven people to keep in mind with every decision I made. Seven immortals with their own unique desires for me to satisfy. It seemed like an impossible task. A balancing act that was doomed to fail.

"Soph," Bastian said, sitting beside me. "Stop." He gripped my knees, angling me toward him, and gathered my hands in his. "Stop selling yourself short. You are more than enough."

"But why?" I asked, my voice small and too high. "Because I *survived*?" Tears welled as my deep-seated inadequacy swelled. "Because I'm the High Queen *by default*?"

Bastian chuckled, low and deep. "There's nothing default about you," he said. "Everything you've been through has made you *more*. You survived shit that would have crushed most people because you're strong. Because you have the will to persevere. You're not High Queen of the

House of the Moon by default, Soph, but by right. By blood and struggle and, yeah, survival."

The devotion in his gaze made my heart swell, and tears snuck over the brims of my eyelids.

The corner of Bastian's mouth tensed, and the hint of a dimple appeared in his cheek. "And I can promise you that when it comes to *communions*, none of your consorts will ever be disappointed, because you give so fucking freely, and you take like a goddess who knows she deserves the world."

An inferno ignited in my blood, and my face felt like it was on fire.

Bastian pulled one hand free and gently wiped away my tears. "Now eat," he said, glancing at the tiered tray of food, then smirking at me, his eyes dancing. "So we can get you naked."

I laughed and teasingly pushed him away. "You're incorrigible."

He leaned in and pressed a kiss to my cheek. "I'm *yours*," he corrected, then pulled away. He released my other hand and stood, starting for the door.

"Where are you going?" I asked, watching him walk away. With the way his jeans hugged his ass, it was an excellent view.

"To grab a snack," he tossed over his shoulder, then made a show of flexing his muscled arms. He flashed me a dimple. "Gotta keep up my own strength."

Ash huffed out a silent laugh as he pulled the door open. Bastian leaned in, speaking quietly to both vampires, and a few seconds later, all three stepped out of the room, and Javier and I were alone.

"You chose well with that one," Javier said, eyeing the door like he could still see Bastian through the solid wood. He could likely still hear him, undead vampire hearing being what it was.

"Even though he's a shifter?" I reached for the tiered tray and plucked a small sandwich off the bottom level. Cucumber and cream cheese, from the looks of it. Kind of weird, but yummy.

"*Because* he is a shifter," Javier said, and my brows rose in surprise. "Empathy is one of their kind's greatest strengths, and he is exceptionally in tune with that part of himself. He fits you so well because he instinctively understands the root sources of your fears and desires."

I took a bite and frowned as I chewed, never having considered my connection with Bastian on so deep a level.

"It's almost like Selene put him in your path because she could see you needed him," Javier mused, his stare going unfocused, like he was seeing around hidden corners. "And that he needed you."

I swallowed and asked, "How so?"

Javier smiled to himself. "You give him a purpose," he said. "Something greater than himself to fight for—a reason to fight *against* his father." Javier's eyes narrowed in thought. "I think he was always meant for you." He refocused on me, the intensity in his gaze startling. "I think, perhaps, we all were."

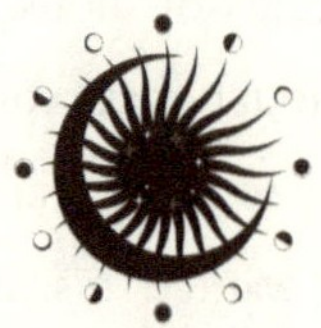

# 5

I CHEWED ON MY thumbnail as I approached Ash and Thane's suite. I had a million things to do. I needed to check on Micah and see how my very mortal, very human son was recovering after the shifter attack—and after the magical healing that had saved his life even as I upended his world. I needed to ask the healers about a possible tincture from Gavin's blood. I needed to visit Isador and ask her to teach me everything about being not just a queen, but the High Queen of the House of the Moon.

My to-do list was ever growing while time seemed to be slipping through my fingers like dry sand. Gavin was suffering, Micah was in danger, and binding Thane was the only thing that would increase my power now. That, at least, would bring me an intangible step closer to rescuing Gavin. I already had four men in my bed, though not yet all at once. What was one more?

Laughing under my breath, I jerked my hand away from my mouth and shook it out in an ineffective attempt to dispel some of my nerves. This was ridiculous. I was being ridiculous. Ash was already mine, and I had fed on Thane recently enough that I could still feel him. My sense of Thane wasn't as strong as my sense of Ash, but I could still pick up on his hopeful expectations. He wanted this. Wanted *me*.

Besides, this was about more than just me. More than just what I needed. By coming to Ash and Thane's suite and binding Thane to me, I would be linking the three of us in a way that had never been possible for the two of them before. So much of what I had experienced since Gavin discovered me was about obligation, but this—this was about choice. My choice to do something good, something beautiful. By welcoming them both into my harem, I could act as the glue between them, forever binding them together.

The door to their suite opened before I even reached it to knock. Ash stood in the doorway, shirtless, his jeans riding low to bare the glowing silver markings covering the pale skin of his hulking torso and arms. The V lines disappearing into the waistband of his pants drew my eye like a glaring neon sign, and it was impossible not to picture the equipment I knew he was packing. Nerves and excitement fluttered in my belly, battling for dominance.

Ash reached for me, his hand settling on my arm. "Sophie."

I dragged my gaze up to his face, my cheeks heating, and I cleared my throat.

Ash's brows bunched, forming a deep crease. "If you need more time..." He must have picked up on my nerves. How could he not? I was practically buzzing with anxiety.

I shook my head, swallowing the urge to take up his offer and postpone. We'd made a deal. He let me bind him, and in exchange, I promised to bind Thane as well. And beyond that, I *wanted* to do this. Not just for them, but for me and for Gavin and for Micah. The more consorts I had feeding my body and fueling my magic, the stronger I would be. The more capable I would be at protecting those I loved. I wasn't willing to let Gavin linger in that dank dungeon for a second longer than was necessary.

The idea of all those queens feeding on him...

Of what else that might lead to...

I squeezed my eyes shut and turned my face away from Ash, pushing the ugly thoughts to the back of my mind. I refused to let jealousy worm its way into my heart, not when Gavin was only doing what he had to do to ensure both he and the queens survived.

Gentle fingers gripped my chin, turning my face back toward Ash. "Sophie..." His voice was filled with echoes of my turmoil. He was possibly my most sensitive and intuitive consort. My gentle giant.

He bowed his head and leaned in until his cheek pressed against mine, the coarse whiskers from his beard brushing against my skin. "Let us distract you," he whispered, his breath caressing my ear and shifting the small hairs that had escaped from my low bun, sending pleasant tingles cascading over my flesh. "It doesn't need to be anything more than that."

I inhaled deeply, breathing him in. This position placed his neck mere inches from my mouth, and I licked my lips. My salivary glands kicked into high gear as I imagined the cinnamon and sugar taste of his blood. A distraction. Yeah, that sounded really good right about now. And if it turned into more, into bonding Thane, then so be it.

Ash's lips ghosted down to the sensitive skin beneath my ear, and he dragged his sharp teeth suggestively over my flesh. His large hands slid from my neck to my shoulders, gliding down my arms until they settled in the curve of my waist. I leaned into his solid heat, my fingertips automatically tracing the waistline of his jeans. I found the grooves between muscles that dipped lower, leading to glorious hidden places, and followed them with greedy fingertips.

Ash tightened his grip on my waist, lifting me until my feet left the floor as his lips found mine. I automatically wrapped my legs around his hips, my arms winding around his neck. His tongue caressed mine, and I pulled his lip between my teeth, biting gently, promising more.

A low growl rumbled in his chest as he backpedaled, carrying me into the sitting room of his shared suite. He kicked the door shut and pressed my back against the hard, wooden surface, his body flush against the front of me, nearly as unmovable as the door at my back. He rocked his hips, his massive erection rubbing against me in all the right places.

New hands glided along my forearms, and I broke the kiss, finally opening my eyes. I rested my head back against the door, giving Ash access to my neck. My eyes locked with Thane's, who was standing so close behind Ash that the front of his body was molded against the back of Ash, pinning my legs. The dark skin of Thane's bare torso stood out in stark contrast to Ash's pale complexion.

I sucked in a shuddering breath as Ash grazed his sharp teeth down the length of my neck, teasing, promising. Thane's hands glided up my arms and down my body, settling on my hips. His fingers dug in as he massaged my ass, increasing the friction between my center and Ash's concealed erection.

My breaths came faster, pleasure coiling in my core. I was already close to release, and nobody was even naked yet. The tantalizing effect of my bond with Ash at work, heightening desire, pumped his blood full of the dopamine that fueled my magic. Thane brushed his lips over my forearm, the faint scratch of his teeth a silent question. Should he do it? Could he feed on me? My climax sparked at the suggestion of a bite, just out of reach.

"Dear goddess, yes," I panted, near tears with anticipation.

Ash bit down on my neck at the same moment as Thane dug his teeth into my arm. I gasped. Between one heartbeat and the next, the dual shocks of pain transformed into delicious pleasure, arcing straight to the throbbing heat between my legs. I floated on a cloud of bliss for long seconds, their bites holding me on the plateau of ecstasy.

They pulled on my blood in perfect synchronicity, igniting delicious spasms that rocked my body. My eyelids rolled back, my eyelashes fluttering and my mouth opening in a silent "O".

Suddenly, Thane drew back from my arm, and Ash whirled me around. Another hard body replaced the door at my back even as Ash continued to suck from my neck, his draw on my blood gentle but enough to hold me captive in the throes of the climax. Hands moved over my body, though I couldn't tell who they belonged to. Did it matter? Everywhere they touched drew sparks of pleasure, like little bolts of lightning arcing from my core.

My head lolled to the side, resting on Thane's sturdy shoulder. His lips brushed against my cheekbone, my jawline, my chin, then claimed mine. His kiss tasted of my blood, but I didn't mind.

Ash lapped at the bite on my neck, the tingling sensation telling me he was sealing the wound with his own immortal blood. The tremors of release subsided, allowing semi-coherent thought to return to my mind, and I kissed Thane back.

Thane's lips curved into a lazy smile. "You taste even better than I remember," he murmured, dragging his mouth along my jawline until his lips brushed my ear. His hands clutched my ribcage possessively, the tips of his fingers teasing the undersides of my breasts. "I want to taste the rest of you."

A full-body shiver moved from the place where his lips brushed my ear down to my toes. "Oh dear goddess, yes," I moaned, arching my back to rub my center against the bulge in Ash's pants, making my clit throb with aftershocks of my release.

Deep, rough laughter rumbled through me from the front and back, and I clung to Ash anew as Thane stepped away, leaving my back cold. Ash carried me into their bedroom and sat me on the bed, then stepped to the side, making quick work of removing my shirt while Thane worked on unfastening and pulling off my jeans. My bra and underwear came off next, and Ash stretched out beside me as I laid back on the bed, propping myself up on my elbows.

He grazed the thick fingertips of one hand slowly up and down the centerline of my body, from neck to pubis, never quite reaching the place that ached for his touch. Goosebumps sprouted in the wake of his fingers.

Thane stepped back, letting his gaze rove over my nude form while he unbuttoned and pushed down his own jeans, dragging his underwear off with his pants. I clenched my thighs together at the sight of his thick erection. A quick glance at the lower half of Ash's body told me his pants were still on. Was he planning on sitting on the sidelines while Thane and I *communed*?

There was no way I was letting that happen.

I reached for his groin and palmed his bulging erection through his jeans. He hissed in a breath. "These better be coming off," I said, my voice husky. My mouth watered at even that teasing feel of him through the coarse fabric. I wanted to run my tongue all over that beautiful, monstrous cock of his.

Hands gliding up the insides of my thighs drew my attention back to Thane, who now knelt on the floor between my knees. When he reached the apex between my legs, he pulled my outer lips apart and trailed the pad of his thumb over my entrance and higher, spreading my wetness along the length of my pussy. He slid his thumb around my clit, avoiding direct contact as he leaned in.

The first touch of his tongue on my exposed clit made me jump, only increasing the pressure on that sensitive bundle of nerves. Thane chuckled, then dipped lower to my dripping center and fucked me with his tongue, his hands kneading and lifting my ass, allowing him to reach deeper into me.

I let my elbows slip out from beneath me and flopped back onto the bed, palming my breasts. "Pants off," I told Ash. "Now."

The corner of his mouth tensed, lifting with the hint of a smirk. As soon as he unzipped his jeans and his cock sprang free, I reached for him, licking my lips to make my intentions clear. There was no way I would be able to fit all of him in my mouth, but I could still lick every inch of that beautiful shaft.

I groaned, my back arching as Thane captured my clit between his lips, sucking it into his mouth as he flicked his tongue over the tip. My fingers clenched around Ash, and I insistently pulled him closer, not even waiting for him to push his pants down beyond the tops of his thighs.

Ash obediently shuffled to me on his knees, and I drew my tongue along the length of his shaft from base to head, peering up to watch his abdominal muscles tense and the tendons in his thick neck bulge in response. He buried his fingers in my hair, holding my head up as I laved his cock with attention.

Thane's sucking became steadier and more insistent, and he teased my entrance with the tips of his fingers, hinting at more. My breaths came faster, that familiar, promising pressure tightening in my belly. He slid a long finger in. Another. Then three, curling them expertly.

I opened my mouth wide, straining to take the head of Ash's cock between my lips, and stared down the length of my body. Thane's heated gaze locked with mine, his pupils dilated to drown his copper irises in sinful night. Moments from that first prophetic dream flashed through my mind, and I vividly recalled Thane's dark head buried between my legs.

This was meant to be. He was destined to be a part of my harem, and now that I recognized the inevitability of our bond, I wanted it. Now. I needed the world, the gods—the whole damn universe—to know that Thane was *mine*.

But I couldn't reach any part of him to bite down, to take his blood into me and complete the circuit, sparking a full *communion* and initiating the bond. I pulled my mouth off Ash's head with a *pop*, my fingers scrambling for purchase on Thane's muscled shoulder.

"I need you," I panted. My lips felt as swollen as my desire. "I need you inside me, Thane. *Now*."

With a look that was pure possession, Thane raised his head and rose to his feet. He gripped my hips and jerked me closer to the edge of the bed, lifting my ass off the mattress completely. He lined his straining erection up with my entrance and slammed into me, making my breasts sway toward my shoulders.

The pleasure of being suddenly so blissfully full momentarily whited out my vision, and I gasped, clutching at his arms. "More," I demanded, my need to claim him all-consuming. "Come here." I dug my nails into his flesh insistently. If I didn't get his blood in me soon, I was going to scream.

With a grunt, Thane pushed me further back on the bed, pulling free of me, and lithely climbed onto the mattress. He stretched out atop me, his lips covering mine as he shoved into me once more. I opened my mouth to him, wrapping my legs around his to encourage his hard thrusts. I ran my hands down his muscular back to his flexed ass and back up, practically clawing him as I gripped his shoulders and broke our kiss, angling my head to the side as my lips sought out his neck.

My teeth grazed over the bulge of his carotid artery. His motion faltered, his whole body shuddering in anticipation. Urged on by his obvious eagerness, I bit down, digging my teeth into his flesh until his skin broke and his immortal blood gushed into my mouth. Molasses and spice flowed over my tongue, tasting like the most delicious ginger cookies.

With the first swallow, heat welled in my chest, the exchange of blood and my desperate need to make him mine, initiating an instinctive response within me. My power swelled, pulsing with promise, as the blissful pressure in my core wound ever tighter.

Ash sprawled on his side beside me and wedged his hand between our bodies, moving down my belly, seeking that sodden heat between my legs. His fingers slid along either side of my clit, quadrupling my pleasure.

The power coiling within my chest snapped, exploding out of me and bathing the bedroom in magical moonlight, and a violent climax ripped through me. I gasped, tearing my mouth away from Thane's neck, overwhelmed by the sensations racking my body.

Thane rose up, gripping my hips and lifting my ass off the bed as he continued to pound into me. His rhythm faltered, my magical climax dragging him over the edge of his own release, and he slammed into me one last time, his entire body going rigid.

As the waves of the physical and spiritual release waned, my eyelids fluttered open, revealing the brand new bonding sigil wrapped around Thane's neck. Ash bent over me, bowing his head toward the place where Thane's body joined with mine. I watched, transfixed, as Ash alternated between tonguing my clit, causing aftershocks of pleasure to rock my body, and licking my and Thane's shared arousal from Thane's shaft, still half buried inside me.

The sight pushed desire buttons I hadn't even been aware of, and lust raged anew. I buried my fingers in Ash's loose hair and watched with rapt attention. I wanted to see more. I wanted to see him take Thane's cock into his mouth while his own monstrous erection filled me to bursting. I wanted to ride his big dick while he sucked off his man. Fuck, even the thought of it sent a mini orgasm quaking through me.

Impatient and needy, I pushed Ash away and sat up, scooting back so Thane's waning erection finally pulled free. I pushed Ash onto his back and bowed over his body, but instead of going for his bulging cock, I sank my teeth into his inner thigh. I sucked his blood into my mouth but only swallowed some. Shifting slightly, I dribbled the rest out over his shaft, rubbing it around with my hand. I would need that healing lubrication if fucking Ash was to bring me pleasure rather than pain.

His vibrant blue eyes darkened with lust as I straddled his hips. I reached for Thane, pulling him closer to us. "I want to watch," I said, looking pointedly from Thane's cock to Ash's mouth as I slid my throbbing, swollen slit back and forth over the head of Ash's cock to coat my outer lips in his blood.

Ash's jaw clenched, his nostrils flaring, and his hands gripped my hips as he pushed his way into me. Oh, he liked that idea. A lot. Based on

Thane's returning erection, he was equally excited about sharing this part of their relationship with me.

As Thane crawled closer and Ash worked his shaft deeper into me, I reached for Thane's cock, angling the head toward Ash's mouth. I licked my lips like I was the one preparing to take Thane into my mouth.

Finally, Ash was sheathed fully within me, and I gripped his wrists, moving his hands from my hips to Thane's. I rocked atop Ash, savoring the unique sensation of being filled full to bursting. My greedy gaze locked on Thane's cock as Ash opened his mouth to take him in.

I kept my motions slow, savoring the immense pressure, the slight tingling from immortal blood easing the tiny tears made by that massive cock, and reached between my legs to tease my clit.

Thane pumping into Ash's mouth was quite possibly the hottest thing I had ever seen in my entire life. These two virile immortals, both prime specimens of masculinity, one dark, one light. I moaned, my rocking motion atop Ash becoming more demanding, my finger moving over my clit harder and faster. I had to force myself to let up or risk coming too soon.

I gripped one breast, tugging and twisting my nipple, and pulled my bottom lip in between my teeth. Ash watched me out of the corner of his eye, sensing my impending climax, and redoubled his efforts on Thane's cock.

Thane's whole body tensed, his muscles bulging, and he gripped Ash's head, fucking the other man's mouth with hard thrusts of his hips. He was close. I could feel it through our new bond. I rubbed my clit faster, harder, edging myself closer. The instant he thrust forward, stuffing his cock so deep into Ash's mouth that the other vampire gagged, I slammed down on Ash's cock and rubbed my clit as hard and fast as I could.

The orgasm crashed through me, my inner muscles clenching around Ash. My sudden spike in pleasure leaked through our bond, dragging Ash into blissful oblivion right along with Thane and me.

Though intense, it was a pure, simple release not fueled by an active exchange of blood, and the spasming waves of pleasure quickly faded. I slumped forward, Ash still sheathed within me, and curled up atop his burly body. Thane snuggled in beside us, skimming a hand up and down my back, and I luxuriated in the intimacy that existed between these two men—this partnership they were now welcoming me into. Though some of my *communions* with the others may have been more intense or more extreme, none had ended with anything akin to a group snuggle session.

Thane kissed my shoulder, then Ash's. "That was..." He laughed under his breath and shook his head. "I don't even know what that was." He leaned closer, claiming my lips in a lingering kiss. "Thank you," he said, the words heartfelt. "I'm honored to be one of your chosen."

I laid my cheek on Ash's shoulder and smiled lazily at Thane. Ash nuzzled my hair, one burly arm curling around my back while the fingers of the other grazed over Thane's biceps. I couldn't remember the last time I had felt so cherished. So precious. So safe. Not since before, when I was a child and didn't know anything about the true horrors of my world.

"You two are amazing," I said, my eyelids drooping as the exhaustion of the past few days weighed on me and as the soothing motion of Thane's fingers lulled me ever closer to sleep.

I was the one who should be honored. I had never been part of anything so loving and comfortable. So stable and deep. So real, as much about the emotional connection as the physical.

I was already halfway in love with them both, individually and together, and I could feel space being made for them in my heart. They belonged to each other, but now they also belonged to me.

I smiled to myself as I closed my eyes, sinking into this stolen moment of tranquility. Maybe the rest of my day would be stressful, filled with urgency and desperation and fear, but right now, at least, I felt at peace.

I tossed and turned, slipping into and out of horrific dreams filled with oceans of blood, fields of fire, and demonic monsters swarming across the earth like locusts.

Hands gripped me and voices whispered through my mind—my immortals attempting to wake me—but even they couldn't drag me out of the nightmarish montage. I was a prisoner to the dreams, the visions. I could do nothing but sink further into the hellscape as a chorus of screams filled my ears, echoing in my bones.

# 6

I GROANED, ROLLING ONTO my side. The sheet beneath me was damp with sweat and stuck to my skin, audibly peeling away from my back. How I was so sweaty was beyond me when I felt like ice water had replaced the blood in my veins.

"She's waking up," someone said. Javier.

His voice was like a ghost haunting me from the past. It took my sluggish mind long seconds to recall that he was once again a part of my present. That, unlike all the other people I had lost, here was one I had actually found again.

"Soph?" Bastian said, and the mattress dipped behind me. I assumed the heated body curling around my backside belonged to him. Goddess, he felt hot enough that I wouldn't have been surprised to see the cold sweat leaving my skin in a cloud of steam.

The pervasive cold sank further in, like it was diving deeper into me in an attempt to evade his heat. Shivering, I drew in my next breath through chattering teeth.

The mattress dipped again, this time in front of me, and I assumed another of my immortals had joined me on the bed.

"Open your eyes, child," a woman said, her voice tickling the edges of my memory, though I couldn't match it with a face or a name. Of one thing I was absolutely certain, she was *not* one of my immortals.

Curious, I peeled my eyelids open.

I absolutely did not recognize the face of the woman who sat beside me on the bed, hunched down to put herself closer to my level, but there was something familiar about her keen gaze. She was stunningly beautiful, with rich brown skin, copper eyes that seemed alight with an inner glow, and long, wild, dark auburn curls. My brow furrowed as I studied her features, imagining them wasted and wrinkled, her plump skin paper thin, her luxurious hair faded to fine silver strands.

My eyes narrowed, then widened, my brows rising. "Isador?" The wizened queen no longer appeared weak and ancient, but in the prime of her life. "How—"

A mysterious smile curved her rosy lips, and her eyes glittered knowingly. Immortal blood had revived her. Likely from one of her consorts.

With her silent confirmation, it was impossible not to imagine Isador communing with an immortal—or seven. "Oh," I said, licking my lips. I cleared my throat.

Isador's smile widened. She straightened up a moment later, her focus slipping away from me and shifting to various points around the room. It landed on something or someone beyond my feet.

I followed her line of sight, finding Javier standing beside the bed, his hands fisted at his sides and his face an unreadable mask.

"She's stable now that she has emerged from the vision's grasp," Isador said.

Javier's gaze locked with mine, and he clenched and unclenched his jaw.

"Let me just—" Isador reached out, gently tracing a sigil in the middle of my forehead with the tip of her index finger. Pressing her palm flush against the invisible sigil, she closed her eyes. Her lashes fluttered as scenes from the nightmarish vision flashed through my mind's eye. Was she seeing what I saw? Was she experiencing the vision that had all but imprisoned me?

Gasping, Isador jerked her hand away, her eyes wide with horror. She paled as the blood drained from her face, and she swallowed roughly. She had seen my vision, and it was just as awful to her as it had been to me. Her reaction confirmed it.

"What does it mean?" I asked, my voice small. I was afraid to know.

"It's an omen," Isador said, then pressed her lips together and shook her head, like the vision hinted at something too horrific to even speak aloud. "Sent by the goddess herself."

"Please." I reached for her hand, but she pulled away, hastily scooting to the edge of the bed. "Please," I repeated, pushing myself up onto one elbow as she stood. "Tell me."

Isador's gaze skittered around the room. She was clearly rattled. Finally, her attention returned to me, and she licked her lips. "A storm is coming, something dark and truly vile. That the gods showed you this vision means you have a chance to stop it—and also that *they* cannot."

"How? How do I stop it?" I asked, my brow furrowing. "What *is* it?"

"The blood and fire were symbolic, but the demons—" Again, Isador shook her head. "I can't be certain without doing some research and consulting the ancient queens, but I believe it means the Shadow King is once again attempting to pierce the barrier between worlds, and if he does…" She trailed off, her stare filling with an ominous warning. "You must train, child. Learn all you can. Become as strong as you can be—and do it quickly."

"But you said—"

"I know what I said," Isador snapped.

I sucked in a breath, startled by her harsh tone.

"But we're facing the end of days, and we no longer have the luxury of educating you the right way," she said. "You will train, day and night. You will *commune* with your consorts and learn as much as you can to increase your power until you're the strongest High Queen who has ever lived, or the shadow will consume the earth, and we will all perish."

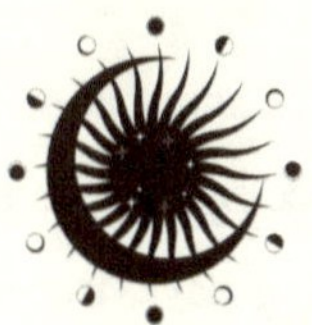

# 7

I swallowed—or I attempted to swallow—but my throat remained dry, my saliva having turned tacky and glue-like.

Isador looked at Javier. "Move her into the bath to warm up." She swept across the room, heading for the bedroom door. Though she wore tailored slacks and a soft sweater, I could easily picture her in a regal gown. "I must prepare for her first lesson."

I sat up the rest of the way as I watched Isador leave, Bastian rising with me and curling a protective arm around my waist. The more experienced queen disappeared into the sitting room, and moments later, I heard the door to the hallway open and shut. I peered around the bedroom, taking in the tense postures and grave expressions of my immortals.

Ash stood on the opposite side of the bed from Javier, Thane at the foot, all three vampires as still as statues. Bastian shifted closer on the mattress, like he could shield me from the horrors of my vision with his body alone. His heat seared into my icy flesh, but no matter how hard he tried, he couldn't protect me from what was already inside my head.

Shivering, I hugged my middle, only now realizing I was in Ash and Thane's bedroom, covered with a blanket but still naked from our *communion*. "Who, exactly, is the Shadow King?"

Javier blinked, seeming to revive before my eyes. "Come," he said, extending one hand toward me. "I'll tell you about the Shadow King while you warm up."

I placed my hand in his and scooted toward the edge of the bed, Bastian pushing gently against my back to help me along. I felt weak, like I'd just finished some strenuous physical task, not like I had just awakened from a nap.

"Prepare some food and bring it to the High Queen's study," Javier told Bastian. "We'll meet you there when she's finished here." He looked at Ash, then at Thane. "Check on the restoration progress in the royal wing. Our queen's training will be arduous, and she'll need her own space to recover—a space that allows her to communicate with the past queens and other spirits. I want the High Queen's bedchamber ready for her by the time we arrive."

Ash and Thane started for the door.

"Oh, and bring the boy up, as well," Javier said, prompting the other two guardians to pause on either side of the doorway's threshold. "She'll want him nearby."

"Micah?" I asked, perking up at the mention of my son. He was more like a *young man* than a *boy*, but compared to these immortals, I supposed he was still a relative child. Just as I was to Isador. Regardless, I was desperate to see him. I had been planning on heading down to check on him after binding Thane, but clearly that hadn't worked out as I had intended.

Javier nodded, again clenching and unclenching his jaw, and I wondered how much Bastian had told my Prime Consort about Micah's origins and my time on the street with Wes and the other boys. Enough, clearly, based on the rage simmering in his eyes.

I glanced at the other two vampires. Had Bastian filled them in as well? My stomach turned at the thought. When nobody else knew about my unsettling time on the street, it had been easier to pretend it never happened. Now, unexpected shame bubbled up inside me.

My eyes swept over all my consorts. They would sense my disquiet. Would they guess the source? Goddess, I absolutely did not want to talk about this with them, and I was terrified of how they would react. Would knowing my past change the way they saw me? Would they pity me for what had been done to me? Or be disgusted by the things I had done to survive?

"I believe Micah is sufficiently healed and can be moved into his own space," Javier said, drawing my attention back to him. "We can settle him in one of the other suites in the east wing with you, Luna. Or if you prefer, we can place him in the consort's quarters attached to your suite. His room wouldn't be as spacious there, but he would be closer to you."

I shook my head vehemently, thinking of all the *communions* bound to happen in every corner of the High Queen's—my—suite. I absolutely did not want there to be any chance that Micah might walk in on that. "He can have his own suite," I said. "I'm sure he'll appreciate the extra space."

Javier dipped his chin in a single nod and pulled me to my feet, Bastian's heat falling away. My knees felt weak, the vision and lingering chill having sapped my strength. How much power had the vision consumed?

Javier's crescent sigil still shone brightly, so I didn't think I was in dire need of a *communion*. Fun as they were, it would be nice to get a bit of a break between romps.

Javier's stare shifted past me, sending the other three immortals on their way, and he curved a sheltering arm around my shoulders. His body was wire tight, his tension thrumming into me.

I studied the side of his face. "How bad is this whole Shadow King situation?" I asked, dread settling in my gut.

He guided me toward the bathroom door. "I'll let you form your own opinion about that."

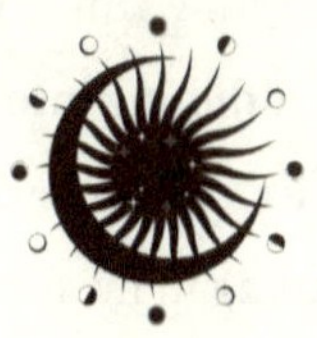

# 8

J AVIER PUSHED OPEN THE door to the bathroom, and humid steam billowed out into the bedroom. They must have been filling and refilling the bath with hot water for quite some time to turn the bathroom into a sauna like this. How long had the vision held me captive? I recalled my consorts' voices whispering through the nightmarish scenes. How long had they been trying to wake me?

Javier helped me ease down into the soaking tub tucked along one wall of the bathroom, and I hissed in discomfort as I sat, the hot water feeling scalding to my icy skin.

"Why am I so cold?" I asked through chattering teeth. I forced myself to lean back against the edge of the tub, submerging myself up to my armpits.

Javier sat on the floor beside the tub, leaning against the tiled wall and drawing up his legs. He rested his forearms on his upturned knees and threaded his fingers together. "Your mother told me once that she believed it was Selene's touch that chilled her." He rested his head back against the wall. "When her connection to the goddess was at its strongest, her body temperature would drop. She would monitor her temperature throughout the day to predict when a particularly intense or significant vision might strike. It became something of an obsession for her, but I suppose it was a way for her to feel like she had some control over the powers granted to her by the goddess."

His stare grew distant, like he was no longer seeing this bathroom but another time and place entirely. "A few days before the attack, she stopped. I remember teasing her about it—asking her where her thermometer was—and she just laughed and made some quip. But she looked so sad." He shook his head slowly. "I've often wondered if she had a vision about that day. If she knew what would happen."

"But wouldn't she have said something?" I asked. So many of our people had died that day. All her consorts and so many others. Amaya, her own daughter and heiress. Not to mention all the vampire queens captured and imprisoned. "Wouldn't she have warned everyone and tried to stop it from happening?" Wouldn't she have tried to save Amaya?

Javier blew out a breath. "I honestly don't know. I've often wondered if the vision convinced her there was some reason to remain silent. To let it happen."

"But why?" I scoffed. "What possible reason—"

Javier's attention cut to me, his stare sharp, his focus no longer on the past, but very much on the present. On me. "This," he said quietly, his stare boring into me. "*You.*"

*You will save us, my shining girl. You will save us all. It is your destiny.*

My mother's last words to me whispered through my mind. I remembered little from before the attack, but that night, those terrifying moments were crystalized in my mind. Did my mom die so I could, what, flee and live in hiding, never really understanding who or what I was? So I could lose everything a second time when Javier was captured? A third time when Wes died, and I made the heartbreaking choice to give up Micah?

Did she die so I could live the shittiest life possible?

I turned my face away from Javier so he couldn't see my trembling chin or the tears escaping over the brims of my eyelids. The weight of this suspicion threatened to suffocate me. The prospect that I was responsible for the attack on my people—my family—however passively, was crushing. I curled my hands into fists under the water, resentment toward my mom turning my few memories of her into fragile, fractured scenes.

"It wasn't your fault," Javier said, leaning forward to grip the edge of the tub. "And it wasn't Diana's."

I gritted my teeth together, his statement drawing my ire if not my gaze.

Javier reached across the water and gripped my chin, turning my face back toward him. "If you wish to blame someone, blame the goddess. Blame Selene," he said, a feral light shining in his eyes. "Your mother loved you and Amaya dearly. Nothing short of a command from the goddess herself could have convinced her to sacrifice her own daughters like that."

"Daughter," I corrected him. "*I* survived."

A bitter chuckle rumbled in Javier's chest. "I didn't realize death was the only sacrifice one could make." His eyes narrowed and his grip on my jaw tightened before he jerked his hand away and stretched out his fingers, like he was willing his hand to behave. As much as I wanted to escape his heated stare, I couldn't look away. "Was Amaya's fate not merciful compared to yours? Her suffering was intense but over in an instant. Yours stretched on for decades."

I felt mortified that he was so easily able to voice some of my most shameful thoughts. How many times had I envied Amaya for her easy escape? How often had I wished for a swift end to my misery, even as I slowly faded away, clinging to what remained of my life?

"How much did Bas tell you?" I asked, feeling betrayed. I had shared my troubled past with him in confidence, not so he could spread it around like Mardi Gras beads to every Tom, Dick, and Harry who flashed me the goods.

"I believe he told us all of it," Javier admitted. "Or, at least, all that he knew."

"Us?" I squawked.

Something that looked an awful lot like sympathy softened Javier's gaze. "Isador sent us out of the room for a time while you were locked in the vision. He filled us in then. He felt we all deserved to know what you had gone through in the past, so we could better understand and serve you in the future."

My cheeks burned hotter than the water as I thought of them all knowing about my time with the guys. I had been their plaything—by necessity, if not by desire—until Wes stepped in and put an end to the sharing. That was what really bothered me—that Javier and the others now knew about the choice I had made, how I had debased myself to survive. But I had been little more than a child, and I had been alone, and suddenly these boys were there and wanted to take care of me.

So long as I took care of them in return.

Looking back, it was almost like my queen instincts had kicked in, and I had gathered the only harem I could, however useless human men were to my actual needs. Was it possible—had *I* instigated the arrangement? Had I wanted them to take and take and *take* until my innocence lay shredded on the ground? Had I wanted to be punished? Had I desired penance for surviving when so many others had not?

My gut twisted into knots, turning my stomach. I pushed away the rancid memories, the insidious thoughts. Except, when Wes had offered me a way out, I had felt like I was being rescued. Like suddenly there was a light where there had only been darkness before. I hadn't wanted it. I hadn't wanted *them*—none except for Wes.

I swallowed, tasting bile. "Bas shouldn't have told you about that."

"I disagree," Javier said, matter-of-factly. "I've told you before, but I'll tell you again—you chose well when you bound the shifter to you. He can anticipate your needs better than you can yourself. He knew you would need us to understand your past, and also that you would be hesitant to tell us of all you had been through. So, he did it for you."

Crossing my arms over my chest, I rolled my eyes and huffed out a breath. Javier was *kind of* right. Knowing he and the others already knew about the dark times, that I wouldn't have to tell them, lifted some of the weight off my shoulders.

"Tell me about the Shadow King," I said, purposely changing the subject. It was done. They knew. I didn't want to think about it anymore.

I watched Javier linger at the tub's edge a few seconds longer, sensing hints of his indecision, but then he sighed and leaned back against the wall.

"A very long time ago," he began, "before the Houses of the Moon or the Sun or the Stars had been established and the only people who inhabited the earth were humans, there was a great war between the realms of darkness and of light. The Shadow King ripped a hole in the barrier between the realms, and his army poured through. Everything they touched withered and died, consumed by their boundless darkness."

My irritation faded as I became engrossed in the story, and my arms relaxed.

"Gods fell, transformed into ghastly shadow versions of themselves, and served the Shadow King. The light gradually faded, and the war neared its end. Selene, Helios, and Eos were all that remained to defend the light, but they were not enough. So they planted seeds of their power within select humans. They nurtured their chosen and watched their powers grow until the balance in the war shifted, and the light pushed back against the darkness. In time, Selene, Helios, and Eos were able to drive the Shadow King back into his dark realm and seal the rift between worlds."

The story felt familiar, and a vivid scene flashed through my memory: my mom sitting with me on my bed, Amaya snuggled in on her other side. Had she told us this story?

"Selene, Helios, and Eos retreated to the heavens, leaving their chosen to rule over themselves," Javier went on. "Thus, the House of the Moon, the House of the Sun, and the House of the Stars were created as a way to contain and control the incredible powers the gods had granted to us. And for a while, there was peace in the realm of the light."

I let out a bitter laugh. "So they just shot us up with magical steroids and abandoned us?" I said. "No wonder war broke out between the immortal races."

"Indeed," Javier said, his tone telling me he shared my sardonic view of the divine. "And now, with all the Houses at their weakest as this war between Sun and Moon drags out, we face the threat of another invasion from the realm of darkness. I can't help but wonder if the gods will even care, or if they have truly abandoned us."

I licked my lips, a shiver cascading down my spine. Only this time it had nothing to do with being cold.

"Except, Selene hasn't abandoned me," I said, thinking back to the vision. If my mom had been right about the source of the magical chill, it had come from the goddess.

Javier's stare locked on me. "No, I don't believe she has." The corners of his mouth tensed, hinting at a wry smile. "Which means there may be some hope for the light, yet."

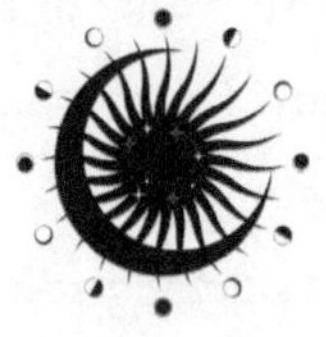

# 9

I walked alongside Javier through the winding corridors of the Moon Sanctuary, our footsteps echoing in the hushed silence. Though he was right there by my side, close enough to touch, he felt like he was a thousand miles away.

I studied him out of the corner of my eye. His jaw was tight, his gaze fixed straight ahead. Through our bond, I felt a maelstrom of emotions swirling within him—anger, sorrow, guilt, and a fierce, burning protectiveness that brought tears to my eyes.

During the two decades we had been apart, I had clung to the hope that he was still alive. I supposed that, despite my powers being subdued by his blood tincture, some intuitive part of me had still sensed the bond we shared. We had been connected all along, and our hearts could never truly be separated.

Just like with Gavin. If I closed my eyes and thought of him, the sense of connection between us deepened. I could almost see his cell walls, smell the dank air, the filth of unwashed bodies. I could almost feel the ache in his limbs. The hunger. They hadn't yet let him feed from the queens, despite letting each of the queens take some of his blood. I couldn't explain how I knew that; I just knew.

Did the connection go both ways? Was he equally aware of me and my surroundings? I glanced sidelong at Javier. Had he been aware of what I was going through while we were apart all those years? Was he more familiar with what I went through right after he was captured than he let on? I had assumed he only knew as much as Bastian and that he had only learned of my past when Bas shared it with the class. But what if Javier had always known? What if he knew *more* than Bastian? What if our bond had afforded him a front-row seat to the most humiliating moments of my life?

We came to a stop outside the door to a suite. Micah's, I assumed. Not my old suite or Amaya's, thank the gods. I wasn't sure I could handle ever stepping foot in either of those spaces again.

I faced Javier, questions caught in my throat. I wanted to know what was going through his head, what thoughts were making him feel so unsettled, and yet I feared the truth.

His eyes met mine and the violence in his gaze was answer enough. In that moment, I saw the deadly predator that lurked beneath his polished exterior.

I reached for him, grazing my fingertips along his clenched jaw. "Can we just pretend it never happened?" I asked, smiling weakly. That had been *my* go-to coping mechanism for a very long time. Why stop now? "The past is the past. All we can do is move forward."

Javier raised his hands and rested them on my shoulders, his thumbs caressing the column of my neck. His expression softened as his gaze roved over my features, finally settling on my eyes. "I am astounded by your strength." He bowed his head, leaning in until his breath caressed my lips when he spoke. His eyes locked with mine. "But I am weak, and you must allow me my revenge."

With a final, lingering look, he turned and strode away, leaving me standing alone in front of Micah's door, my heart racing and mind reeling.

"What the fuck?" I breathed, replaying his words in my head. *I am weak, and you must allow me my revenge.* "What the actual fuck?"

I stood frozen outside Micah's door, Javier's parting words echoing in my mind. The dark promise of vengeance, the barely leashed violence in his tone, had shaken me to my core. A part of me longed to call him back, to beg him not to do anything rash.

But another part, the broken girl who still lived inside me, wanted those men to suffer as I had suffered. To feel a fraction of the pain and degradation they had inflicted upon me. To take as much from them as they had taken from me.

I squeezed my eyes shut, taking a deep, steadying breath. No. I couldn't let myself go down that path. Revenge would solve nothing, only breed more darkness and despair. I had to be better than that, stronger than my own worst impulses.

I jumped when the door to Micah's suite cracked open.

"Sophie?" Micah's face appeared in the gap, and he grinned broadly, opening the door wide. "I thought I heard you."

I pasted a smile onto my face because what else was I supposed to do when I was pretty sure Javier had just promised to beat up my abusers?

Oh, who was I kidding? This was Javier. He wasn't just going to beat them up.

Micah stepped back, making room for me to enter. "You've got to see this place. The closet is bigger than my dorm room!"

Javier was going to kill them. But they killed Wes, so it was only fair, right? All my time in the human world told me his vigilante justice was *not* okay—but he wasn't human. *I* wasn't human. Wes hadn't been there when the guys first took me in, but when he did join the group, when he realized how truly twisted the situation was, he had put a stop to it. He had saved me. From them. From me.

"Soph?" Micah stepped into the doorway and touched my arm, frowning. "Are you okay? You look—not good."

I coughed out a laugh. "Thanks."

He gripped my elbow and guided me into his sitting room. The tantalizing scent of freshly baked bread, tomato sauce, and basil finally floating over to me, and my mouth watered even as my stomach churned.

"You're shaking. Are you hungry?" He led me to the cozy-looking couch near the fireplace, where an array of pizzas awaited us on the coffee table. "They just brought all this food, and I think it's more for you than for me, so you should eat. Right? You do eat food, don't you? Not just..." He pulled back his lips like he was baring vampire fangs and made a hissing Dracula sound. "You know...?

Another, weaker laugh bubbled up from my chest. "Yes, I eat food, you nerd. You've seen me pig out like a million times before. And *yes*, I'm starving." I sank onto the couch, tucking my foot under my leg, and he followed, sitting beside me. "I just—" I shook my head, unwilling to dump any of the emotional baggage I carried around from the dark times onto Micah.

It was too closely tied to Wes and my pregnancy and Micah's entire existence, and I would never—*never*—make him feel guilty or in any way responsible for any of the awfulness that happened before he was even born. It sucked more than words could ever express, but it also led me to Wes, which led to Micah...

Gods, what a mess.

I sighed. "I just have a lot on my mind."

Concern etched into Micah's features. "Do you want to talk about it?" He frowned. "Unless it has to do with that thing we agreed to never talk about again, in which case..." His frown transformed into a comical grimace. "No, thank you."

As he spoke, moonlight slanted through the window behind him, briefly illuminating his profile, and I caught my breath. For just a moment—so fleeting I might have imagined it—his skin seemed to shimmer with a subtle silvery light, not unlike the luminescence that pulsed beneath my own skin when my power surged. I blinked, and it was gone, leaving me to wonder if exhaustion was making me see things.

I opened my mouth, then closed it again. "It's nothing," I said, forcing a brittle laugh. I gestured to the food on the table. "May I?"

"Oh, shit. Yeah." Micah reached for the stack of two plates on his end of the coffee table and handed one to me.

Static electricity sparked between us, and I jerked away. "Sorry!" I hissed.

"Ow," he said, his faux wounded expression striking me like a physical blow. It was exactly the way Wes used to tease me whenever I accidentally hurt him—that same whine, the same pouty lip, the same crinkle at the corner of his eyes.

For a moment, superimposed over this capable young man, I saw the nervous thirteen-year-old I'd watched at his parents' house. I'd stood across the street with a dog I'd taken on as a dog-walking client purely because of the proximity of her home to Micah's. My heart had hammered as I watched him ride his bike down the steep driveway. He'd been lanky and uncoordinated, caught between childhood and adolescence, and both his bike and his helmet had seemed too big for him. I'd prayed to any divine force who would listen to watch over him. To protect him.

Now here he was, so grown up—a perfect blend of Wes's sharp intelligence and my stubborn resilience. The contrast between that uncertain boy and this confident young man stole my breath. He needed that divine protection now, more than ever.

Micah watched me as I piled a few slices of pizza onto my plate—one sausage and mushrooms, one Canadian bacon and pineapple, one caprese drizzled with balsamic. His concerned stare was impossible to ignore.

I lifted a slice to my mouth but paused before taking a bite, glancing at Micah sidelong. "I'm fine, really," I claimed. I even kind of believed it.

Micah scoffed and eyed my pizza dubiously. "Says the lady about to eat pizza with pineapple on it."

I flashed him a cheesy grin, then took a large bite of said pizza. "Mmm...fruity pizza," I moaned around the mouthful.

Micah narrowed his eyes. "Gross." He turned his attention to the pizzas laid out before us, selecting a few slices of his own—none with pineapple.

"How're your shoulders?" I asked. If I hadn't seen the shifter dig its claws into him myself, I never would have believed he had been so gravely injured just a few days earlier.

Micah shrugged, chewing fast and swallowing. "Good as new. Magic potions are sweet. Way better than drugs." He took another bite, speaking around the food. "Could give big pharma a run for their money."

"For real," I said between bites.

The normalcy of eating pizza with Micah grounded me. For a moment, I could pretend we were back on campus, sharing a bite during a tutoring session. Micah's presence was a balm, his easy acceptance of all the craziness of this situation inspiring me to get a grip on my flailing emotions. If he could handle having his world turned upside down and being thrust into the middle of a war between immortal Houses he hadn't even known existed a few days ago, I could handle Javier's thirst for vengeance. And the pressure to master my powers. All while I found a way to rescue Gavin and the queens. And protect my son. And avert the apocalypse and drive back the Shadow King.

I chewed mechanically, no longer tasting the sweet and savory flavors of the Hawaiian pizza.

Micah left his last slice of pizza untouched on his lap and stared at the unlit fireplace. "The last few days have been pretty intense."

I snorted softly and swallowed the bite in my mouth, feeling like an asshole when my first thoughts of how intense the last few days had been were about me and not him. Maybe it wasn't that he was handling this all so well, but just that he was better than me at hiding his inner freak-out.

"How are you doing?" I looked around the sitting room, like it represented the insanity of the immortal world. "It's a lot to take in."

"I, well—" Micah set his plate on the coffee table and faced me, angling his knees toward me, his expression pensive. "I've been thinking..." He paused, licking his lips nervously. "What if you turned me? Made me an undead vampire sooner rather than later? Like, *now* soon."

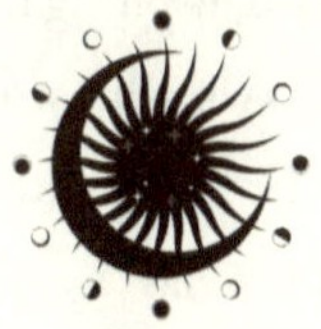

# 10

MY STOMACH TURNED LEADEN, and I froze, my half-eaten slice of pizza forgotten in my hand. "Micah, I don't think—"

He held up a hand to stall my objection. "Just hear me out," he said, leaning forward intently. "After what happened with that shifter, when I got hurt—"

I flinched at the memory of his blood-soaked sweatshirt, the deep gashes in his shoulders. The fear that had gripped me, thinking I might lose him too, had been overwhelming.

Micah let out a breathy laugh and shook out his hands. "I don't really have a choice here, Soph. If I go back home, I'm going with a target on my back and I'm putting my family in danger, so I can't do that. I get it. I'll stay here. But here, I'm like—I don't know." He shook his head, clearly searching for the right words to make me understand. "You know the proverbial bull in a china shop?"

I nodded woodenly.

"It's like the opposite of that," he said. "I'm like a china cup in a bull shop, which doesn't make any sense, but you get the idea." He laughed hollowly. "I may not be the target here, but my chances of being collateral damage have increased exponentially."

He ran a hand through his dark curls, the gesture so eerily reminiscent of Wes that an ache lanced through my chest.

My head started to shake, slowly and seemingly all on its own.

"If I was a vampire," Micah continued, talking faster to forestall my refusal. "I'd be stronger, faster, harder to kill. I could defend myself better, Soph. I could defend *you* better."

"No." The word came out harsher than I had intended, and Micah blinked, taken aback by my vehemence. I set my plate down a little too hard on the coffee table, my appetite vanishing. "Micah, I can't—" I closed my eyes and took a deep breath. "You're too young—"

"I'm older than you were when you had me," he retorted, a note of frustration in his voice. "If you were old enough to decide to have a kid—"

I spluttered, "I didn't *decide* to have a kid!"

"—and bring a whole new life into the world, I should at least be old enough to choose what to do with my *own* damn life."

"It's too dangerous!" I snapped, the frayed edges of my self-control unraveling. "The First Rite is risky, even for a fully trained queen, and—newsflash—I'm not that. I have no idea what I'm doing 90 percent of the time, and everyone expects me to just figure it out."

I stood abruptly, stepping around the coffee table to pace in front of the fireplace. "Gavin's a prisoner of the shifters, Javier wants to smite everyone who's ever hurt me, and I've had to move back into the house where my entire family was slaughtered...which my dead boyfriend is now haunting. And let's not forget the teensy-weensy detail of the fucking apocalypse hanging over our heads."

"Wait, what?" Micah blurted, standing.

I laughed bitterly, a hint of mania to the sound. "The literal king of demons is trying to break through to our world and enslave or kill us all, and apparently, I'm the only one who the goddess will communicate with to stop him. Me! The untrained queen who can only access her magic by accident!"

"Stop, Sophie." Micah planted himself in front of me and gripped my shoulders to hold me in place. "Just stop for a sec. Take a breath, okay?"

Tears burned my eyes, hot and bitter, and I dragged in a ragged inhale. "I'm drowning, Micah. I'm scared all the time, scared of failing, of losing everyone I care about. I can't—I can't lose you too. Especially if I'm to blame, because I fucked up the transformation and killed you!"

Micah wrapped his arms around me, pulling me into a sturdy hug. I collapsed against him, sobs racking my whole body. I should have been the one comforting him in what had to be a completely insane situation to him, but here I was, falling to pieces, leaving him to be the grown-up in the room.

"I'm sorry," he murmured, squeezing me tight. "I didn't mean to push. I just... I hate feeling helpless."

Something between a laugh and a sob burst out of me. "Me too."

Micah started shaking, and for a moment, I thought he was breaking down right along with me. But then I caught a choked giggle, and I froze.

"Are you *laughing*?" I asked, incredulous. I pulled back enough to see his face, his features contorted as he attempted to contain his hysterics.

"I'm sorry!" he gasped, hunching his shoulders and curling into himself like that might hold in the inappropriate laughter. "It's just so insane. It's all *so* insane."

The corners of my mouth tensed, teasing a smile, and I wiped the tears from my cheeks. The absurdity of Micah's hysterics was like a bucket of cold water, snapping me out of my own emotional tailspin. I stepped back, amusement curving my lips as I waited for his laugh attack to expend itself.

"I'm so sorry!" He drew in a deep breath, only a few rogue laughter convulsions shaking his shoulders. Straightening, he wiped under his eyes. "I'm sorry, Soph," he repeated, meeting my eyes.

"You okay?" I asked. "That looked intense."

He squeezed his sides with his hands and blew out a breath. "My abs hurt. And my face." A laughter aftershock shook him. "Have you tried hysterical laughter? Because I feel ten times better."

I snorted and shook my head. "Maybe I'll give it a try later."

Micah squinted at me. "So, what's this about the apocalypse?"

I winced, closing my eyes. "I shouldn't have dumped that on you," I said, shaking my head. "We don't even really know what's going on. It was just one vision." I shuddered. One truly awful vision.

Micah stepped forward and gripped my arms. "I believe in you, Soph," he said quietly. "I know you'll figure this out. All of it. And you're not alone. You have Bas and, like, an entire army of vampires." He gave me a gentle shake. "You got this!"

I laughed weakly. "Thanks for the pep talk."

He shook his head, smiling softly, and pulled me in for another hug. "I just wish—"

At a muffled commotion out in the hallway, we both looked toward the door. Now that I wasn't in the middle of a breakdown, I could sense my consorts out there. I could feel their agitation.

Bastian's voice rose above the others, tense and clipped. "We can't just barge in there!"

"She's upset," Javier argued. "We need—"

"She needs some gods-damned space!" Bastian snapped.

I pulled away from Micah, irritation spiking as the argument continued. "I'm sorry," I said, "but I need to deal with..." I waved a hand toward the door, beyond which the argument was escalating. "*That.*"

Micah's eyes sparkled with amusement. "Go on," he nodded toward the door.

I squeezed his hand, then turned and stalked toward the door, anger burning away the last of my tears.

It was time to knock some sense into my overprotective consorts.

# 11

I OPENED THE DOOR to find Bastian's back to me while he faced off with Javier. Thane and Ash hung back, flanking the other vampire. They reminded me of cats locked in a standoff. The tension was thick enough to choke on.

All three sets of vampire eyes snapped to me, but Bastian didn't turn. Probably because he had three deadly predators standing in front of him, ready to strike.

"My room," I said frostily, glancing down the hallway toward the door to the High Queen's chambers. "Now."

Ash and Thane backed off immediately, turning and heading that way.

I locked stares with Javier and raised my eyebrows. His eyes narrowed, and he drew in a breath like he might say something, but instead, he turned and stalked after my other consorts.

"Bas," I said, placing my hand on his tense shoulder.

He turned his head, looking at me over his shoulder.

"Thanks for trying, but you can stand down." I smiled up at him, hoping he could sense how much I appreciated him, even through my irritation at the others.

Relaxing visibly, Bastian moved aside. I stepped into the hallway, pulling the door shut behind me, and started toward the High Queen's chambers with Bastian as my shadow.

I stormed into the sitting room to find Javier in the middle of the room, his arms folded over his broad chest, while Ash and Thane stood close together near the door to the study.

Hands balled into fists at my sides, I hovered in the doorway, Bastian at my back, and stared down my vampire consorts. The irritation simmering under my skin reached a boiling point, and I couldn't hold back any longer.

"What *the hell* was that?" I demanded cooly, my gaze sweeping over each of them before settling on Javier. "I'm not a child to be coddled, and I sure as hell don't need any of you to protect me from my *own damn son.*"

Just as Javier opened his mouth to respond, the door behind him swung open. A group of vampires and humans emerged from the study, their arms laden with sheets and cleaning supplies. They froze when they saw us, their eyes widening as they took in the tense scene.

Heat crept up my neck, and I suddenly felt incredibly awkward having this confrontation in front of the house staff. I mean, I was supposed to be the High Queen of the House of the Moon, not some petulant child arguing with her—much older and more experienced—consorts.

One of the humans, an older woman with kind eyes who seemed to be in charge, bowed her head. "Apologies, my lady. We were just finishing up in the bedchamber. We'll be out of your way in a moment."

I forced a smile, nodding an acknowledgment. "Thank you."

As they hurried past us, I couldn't help but wonder, yet again, where all these people lived. The mansion was large, but there was no way it could house everyone I had seen bustling about. I made a mental note to add learning about the layout and logistics of running the Moon Sanctuary to my ever-growing list of queenly duties. I didn't even know who oversaw running the household. Had that been Gavin's job? Or was there a head housekeeper?

Once the staff had disappeared down the hallway, I turned back to Javier, my earlier frustration returning full force. He met my stare, his jaw set stubbornly.

"Well?" I asked, raising my eyebrows.

"With all due respect, Luna, you are my queen." Javier glanced at Ash and Thane. "*Our* queen. Our lives are tied to yours, which makes your safety and well-being our top priority."

I scoffed, shaking my head. "Bullshit." I held up a hand before Javier could respond. "I wasn't in any danger, and you knew it." I huffed out a breath. "I need room to breathe, Javier. I need to be able to have a single damn emotion without you running to shield me from my feelings. I *need* to be able to have a conversation with *my son* without my consorts hovering over me. I'm not made of glass. I won't break. I think I've proved that by now."

Ash and Thane shifted uncomfortably, clearly sensing that this was more about Javier and me working through some shit and less about them wanting to protect their queen. I felt kind of bad that they'd been caught in the middle of our growing pains. I'd have been much less annoyed if they had all just waited patiently in the hallway, respecting the boundary of the door. But Javier just had to push.

My shoulders slumped, much of the fight going out of me. I was still hungry, thanks to my interrupted meal, and I couldn't remember the last time I'd had a solid night's sleep. I was starting to think I might just spend the rest of my life teetering on the edge of exhaustion. I shuffled into the sitting room, making a beeline for Javier.

His stony expression softened as I drew near.

"I know I can trust you to protect me," I said, stopping in front of him, just out of arm's reach. It took everything in me not to sink into him, but we needed to clear the air before it suffocated us both. "But I'd like to think I can trust you to respect me as well."

Outrage flashed in Javier's eyes. "You think I don't respect you?"

I shrugged and stared down at our shoes, his boots looking so polished and professional compared to my slip-ons. Maybe this wasn't entirely on him. Respect had to be earned, after all, and what had I done to earn his? Run, hide, and be constantly afraid? Make shitty decisions in the name of survival? I had never really existed in the immortal world without him. Even before the uprising, he had been a constant fixture in my life.

I had been back for a few days, and look at the mess I had made of things. I didn't know what I was doing. I could barely use my magic, and when I did, it was unintentional and with poor control. I'd already lost one of my consorts, and I nearly got Micah killed. Gods, I was a failure in every possible way.

My breaths came faster, the desperation from earlier rising anew. I gritted my teeth, refusing to fall to pieces right now.

"Leave us," Javier said, his voice quiet and commanding.

I sensed varying degrees of uncertainty through my bonds with the others, but I couldn't bring myself to look at any of them. Not when I was barely holding myself together.

Nobody moved. Not me. Not Javier. And not Thane, Ash, or Bastian.

"Go," I whispered, then drew in a tremulous breath as my other consorts left the sitting room. I was more of a confrontation avoider, but this little chat between Javier and me would happen eventually. It had to. It was like an infection, festering the longer it went unaddressed. Sooner was better than later.

I chewed on the inside of my cheek, working up the nerve to raise my eyes to Javier's face. To meet his gaze.

"I need to know you won't hurt those guys," I said, sounding tired. I needed to know I could count on Javier to do what I said when it really mattered. Actions speak louder, and all that. I wanted to avoid feeling like I had to use my *will* on him every time I asked him to do—or *not* do—something.

Javier's boots shifted closer, and he gripped my jaw, tilting my face upward. "Look at me, Luna," he said. Raw emotion made his voice ragged, dragging my stare up to lock with his. The depth of the rage and sorrow shining in his eyes made my breath catch.

I blinked, setting a string of tears free.

A growl ripped through his chest, and he leaned in, his lips crashing against mine. His grip shifted from my jaw to my neck, and he angled me against the back of a couch. The kiss ended as abruptly as it started, leaving us both breathing hard.

I strained against his hold on my neck, reaching for his lips. Craving more of his kiss. His touch. His everything.

"You should save your energy for the *communion,*" he said. Like *he* wasn't enough. "I can call them back if—"

I pushed against his hand until my words came out hoarse. "No," I said. "Just you. Now."

# 12

A DARK CHUCKLE SHOOK Javier's chest, and he leaned in, barely brushing his lips over mine. "No blood," he breathed.

"Fine." I smiled against his lips as he deepened the kiss, but his hand remained on my neck, allowing him absolute control over the moment.

Javier's other hand settled on my hip, his fingers kneading. Without warning, he turned me around, our kiss breaking when his mouth drew out of reach. His hand snaked under my shirt, then dipped into the front of my leggings. I sighed as his fingers slid between my lips, pinching my clit. He teased me with long, slow, deliberate strokes of his hand.

I tilted my head to the side, arching my neck in invitation.

"No blood," he rasped, tightening his hold on my throat. His breath was hot against my flesh, and he grazed his teeth over my earlobe but didn't break the skin. "Every moan and sigh that slips from that pretty mouth is all mine, and when this tight little pussy clenches around my cock, it won't be bloodlust or the bond that makes you come," he promised. "It will be me fucking you until you scream."

Pleasure shivered through my core as his words quadrupled the effects of his masterful touch. Each slide of his fingers brought me closer. Closer. Closer.

"Oh gods," I gasped, pleasure coiling tight. "I'm going to come."

He withdrew his hand from between my thighs and pressed his palm flat against my lower abdomen, leaving me teetering on the edge of release.

I whimpered, my hips rocking, seeking. Nothing to rub against. Nothing to push me into blissful oblivion.

"Not yet," Javier whispered against my cheek. "Not until you want it so bad that it hurts." His hand slid from my belly to my hip, tugging down the waistband of my leggings to expose my ass. He teased between my legs from behind, trailing his fingertips through my wet heat but purposely avoiding my clit.

"Fuck, Luna." He sank two fingers into my core, and I groaned at the delicious invasion. "This is mine," he said and curled his fingers, teasing the spot inside me that made my knees weak. "I'm yours to command, but this—this sweet little pussy begging me to fuck it is all mine, isn't it?"

I squeezed my eyes shut and laid my head back on his shoulder. If he kept doing what he was doing, he wouldn't need to touch my clit to make me come.

Like he sensed my thoughts, Javier pulled his fingers out and smacked my ass. My body jerked, my eyelids snapping open at the sharp sting. He massaged my ass cheek, rubbing away the pain and teasing my entrance with his fingertips.

"Tell me this is mine," he said, his hold on my neck tightening with his demand.

"It's yours," I gasped.

His hand between my legs withdrew again, and I heard the clink of his belt buckle. A moment later, the blunt head of his cock nudged my entrance. "Tell me you're mine," he demanded, sliding his shaft through my swollen lips.

"I—" My voice caught when his head grazed my clit, and my legs trembled. "I'm yours, Javi," I choked out, arching my back. Opening myself to him. "Please. Please let me come."

He pulled back until he was once again teasing my entrance.

"Javier!" Desperation triggered my *will*, and my next words thrummed with power. "Let me come, please!"

Javier let out a dark chuckle. "I'm your Prime Consort," he said, his words smooth as silk, rough with promise. "That won't work on me."

I wailed, raw need tearing through me. "Please, Javi."

"Not yet," he said and thrust into me. His hand slid over my hip, his fingertips digging into my pubis, tugging on the skin around my clit but not touching it directly. "Fuck," he hissed, pulling out and slowly pushing back into me. He brushed his lips along the line of my shoulder. "Your pussy is clenching me so tight, begging me to fuck it hard."

"Please," I whined. "Yes. Gods, yes."

Another dark chuckle shook Javier's chest, and his next thrust was harder. His next harder still, until the slap of his body against mine and the sloppy, wet sounds of him fucking me filled the room alongside our heavy breaths and throaty grunts.

The pressure within me built and built. I squeezed my eyes shut, reaching. My breathing turned ragged. So close, the orgasm right there, a blinding star just out of reach.

Javier pulled out of me suddenly, and I sobbed my displeasure. His hand on my neck shifted higher, gripping my jaw and turning my face toward his. The fingers digging into my pubic bone inched lower, sliding between my lips and pressing down on either side of my clit. He pushed back into me with excruciating restraint, like he could sense just how close I was to shattering.

Javier's gaze roved over my face, the press of his fingers on either side of my clit taunting me with each slow, deliberate stroke. If he just pinched his fingers together or thrust into me harder...

But he knew exactly what he was doing to me.

I had never felt so seen. So understood. This vampire—this man—was so in tune with my body that he could hold me captive in this blissful agony forever.

"Do you see?" Javier grazed his lips along my cheekbone. "Do you see what the bond does to me? It's not the same for you as it is for the rest of us. You have a shallow awareness of each of us, but we only have you. *I* only have you, Luna. I can feel how close you are to coming, just as I can sense your every discomfort, your quiet agony, as if it were my own. It's not so easy to give you space when you're always inside me."

Javier thrust into me harder, deeper, emphasizing the depth of his side of the bond. My eyelids fluttered shut, breath hitching. Javier buried himself inside me, then stilled.

"Do you understand what you're asking of me?" he rasped against my cheek.

I nodded, tears leaking from the corners of my eyes. The agony of *almost* was breaking me. In that moment, I would have told Javier anything he wanted to hear.

"Good," he breathed. And then he circled my clit with his fingertip, pressing hard enough to let me know this was it.

I choked on a strangled scream as my insides liquefied. My knees buckled, but Javier caught me. He held me tight against him, one hand curved around my throat, the other between my legs. The press of his fingers against my pulsing clit amplified the pleasure as the waves radiated out from my core. I trembled, my limbs boneless.

Javier waited until the pleasure ebbed and my body relaxed to pull out of me. I regained my footing, and his hold loosened enough that I could turn around to face him, my hands settling on his chest, his on my hips.

I glanced down at his erection jutting up between us. My brow furrowed, and I raised my eyes to meet his.

"I can wait for the *communion*," he said, his features tense, his gaze guarded. "I don't want to make you sore, and healing your aches with my blood could trigger your bloodlust. The others may not be able to resist coming to you then, and you need to speak with Isador before the *communion* so you know how to channel the amplified power into a request for another vision from Selene."

"Oh." I frowned, hating the idea of leaving him unsatisfied after what I'd just experienced. His body practically vibrated with tension, and I sensed his raging desire through our bond. No way I was leaving him like this.

I lowered myself to my knees before him, dragging my hands down his torso. His jaw clenched and unclenched.

"You don't have to—" He sucked in a breath when I gripped his shaft. His cock twitched in my hold. "Luna," he breathed, reverent. His fingers threaded into my hair, his hands trembling.

I licked my lips and locked eyes with him, watching his reaction as I leaned in. As I parted my lips. As I pressed the gentlest kiss to the head of his cock.

His fingers clenched in my hair, and he stopped breathing altogether.

I gripped the base of his shaft and opened wide, flattening my tongue to glide along the underside of his cock as I took him into my mouth. The salty taste of his arousal hinted at the flavor notes of his blood, making my darker hunger stir.

Expression rapt, Javier drew in a shaky breath, his stare glued to my lips, to his cock disappearing inch by inch into my mouth.

"Mmmmm," I hummed, savoring the taste of him and basking in his reaction.

The history between us added layers to every touch. My love for Bastian was fluttery and fresh, and I was still in the falling phase with Gavin, Ash, and Thane. But my love for Javier was deep and weathered, seasoned by all the pain and heartache we had experienced together.

I poured all that love into the way I touched him. The way I gazed up at him. The way I sucked him.

Javier's breath hitched, and his hold on my hair tightened, becoming painful. "Luna, I—" His features tensed, his body going rigid.

I shifted my hand from his shaft to his ass and pushed forward, taking him the rest of the way into my mouth. The head of his cock pressed against the back of my throat, triggering my gag reflex. My throat convulsed, squeezing him. Heightening his pleasure as he shot out his release. I drank him down, feeling an influx of the same magic that was in his blood. Again, my bloodlust stirred but reluctantly resettled, leaving me in control.

I pulled back, choking as I suppressed a cough.

Javier dropped to his knees in front of me, his hands cradling my jaw. He gazed at me with such wonder and love that my heart warmed. He leaned in, kissing my swollen lips tenderly.

"I failed you," he said hoarsely. "You depended on me, and I abandoned you."

"You were captured!" I protested, shaking my head.

He turned his face away and shut his eyes, a tortured mask warping his features. "I sensed your every agony," he whispered, shame reaching across the bond from him. "Your hopeless desperation." Tears leaked from between his lashes and trailed down the chiseled planes of his face. "These past few years, I felt you giving up. Accepting your fate. Accepting death."

I hadn't known the connection was so much more intense on his end. I hadn't realized just how much of the dark times I had shared with him. And then he'd had what I could only describe as a trauma response when he felt my distress earlier. Gods, he likely had the immortal equivalent of PTSD, and I had yelled at him for it.

I shook my head, raising my hands to his face and turning him back to me. His pained gaze met mine, breaking my heart. "You did nothing wrong, Javi," I said, vehement. "*Nothing*. I'm the one who should be sorry." Again, I shook my head. "I didn't understand, but I do now. I won't ask you to leave me alone. I'll make sure everyone knows that you're always to be admitted, wherever I am, whoever I'm with. I love you. I love you so much, Javi, and I won't ever hurt you like that again."

Javier leaned his forehead against mine. "I love you, too, my Luna."

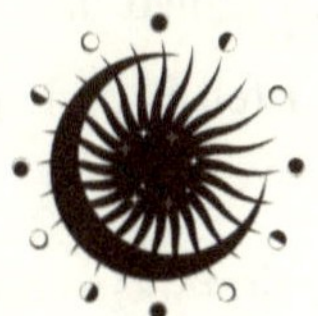

# 13

"Y OU DIDN'T EAT ENOUGH earlier," Javier said as he fastened his pants, his overprotectiveness comforting rather than frustrating now that we'd had a chance to hash things out, so to speak. "I'll bring you something."

I drew my bottom lip between my teeth, reluctant to be apart from him, even briefly, after his recent revelations about how the bond felt from his end. "I'm fine," I insisted, though my body disagreed, my stomach growling in betrayal.

Javier's lips curved into that gentle smile that had always made me feel safe. He leaned in and kissed me, unnaturally still as he did so. The sensual tenderness made my head swim. "Allow me to do this for you, my Luna," he murmured against my lips. "Please."

That blend of command and supplication, so uniquely Javier, made arguing impossible. I nodded.

He smoothed my hair back, his thumb tracing my pulse point on my neck, then stepped away with predatory grace and slipped from the room.

I sensed my other consorts out in the hallway, each allowing me space while staying close enough for me to feel the full force of our bonds. My awareness of them was comforting. And overwhelming.

When was the last time I'd truly been alone? Between binding myself to immortals and fighting destiny, quiet moments had become incredibly rare, when just a few days ago, they had been my status quo.

My attention wandered to the door leading to the High Queen's study and the bedchamber beyond. My mother's sanctum. Mine now. The thought made me feel like a little girl playing dress up in her mommy's clothes.

But the pull toward those rooms was impossible to ignore. I hadn't been in there since...well, honestly, I couldn't remember ever having been in my mother's bedroom, though I had a vague mental image of what it was like. Had Amaya and I been welcomed there? Or had we snuck in? My few clear memories of my mother were from the night of the massacre, when she had fled with me into Amaya's room.

I crossed the sitting room and the study beyond, faltering as I approached the bedroom door. Silver and moonstone inlays traced lunar phases across the carved wood, centered on a majestic eclipse. Even in the dim light, the moonstone pulsed with an ethereal glow.

My hand trembled on the handle, and I took a deep breath, steadying my nerves. I pushed the door open, half-expecting to find my mother at her vanity.

Instead, memories of my mom slammed into me. *Her*, kneeling at the moon altar before the arched window, her voice resonant with ancient power as she prayed to Selene. Huddling together on her huge four-poster bed when I fled into her room during a thunderstorm, her arms wrapped tight around me. Midnight garden walks, silvery moon flowers greeting the stars. The whisper of her footsteps as she crossed my bedroom to kiss my forehead each night when she thought I was already asleep. And yes, sneaking into my mother's study with Amaya and attempting to peek through the keyhole to find out exactly what a queen did when she *communed* with her consorts—and Javier finding us and shooing us away.

I pressed a hand to my chest, tears streaming down my cheeks, and attempted to keep it together. I could feel the concern from my consorts two rooms away, responding to my reaction to the sudden tsunami of memories. Needing a moment, I entered the bedroom fully and eased the door shut.

The room looked different from what I remembered, but it felt the same. New linens draped the four-poster bed. Bare surfaces stripped of my mom's personal items—the seashells, her silver hand mirror, our photos—waited for treasures I didn't have after decades of running.

My mom's presence lingered, embedded in the walls, the floor, the ceiling, the air. The room remembered her, and through her, it felt like it knew me.

I crossed to the moon altar, where my mom had appealed to our patron goddess. My fingers trailed over the worn wooden surface, tracing around the amethyst athame. The empty polished silver bowl at the center of the narrow table reflected a woman caught between worlds—too changed to be Sophie Matthews, not quite Luna Sofia, High Queen of the House of the Moon.

A small silver box shaped like a crescent moon sat in the corner of the altar table, tarnished to near black. Everything else in the bedroom was freshly dusted and polished—except for this. Almost like it had been overlooked. *Almost* like it hadn't been visible to anyone but me. Something about the tiny box pulled at me, a whisper I couldn't quite hear that somehow echoed in my bones.

I picked up the box, and when I lifted the lid, my breath caught.

A silver ring lay on the faded black velvet lining within, its band a dainty strip connecting to a triple moon. Within the full moon at the symbol's center, a moonstone shifted between silver and blue as if alive.

My fingers hovered over the ring, hesitant yet drawn to it. When I touched the cool metal, energy surged up my fingers and into my arm, and I sucked in a breath. A flash of blindingly bright light pulsed from the stone, and an image of my mother appeared, like the negative of a photograph. I saw her warding this crescent moon box and placing it on the altar for someone to find.

*"My shining girl,"* she whispered, her words reaching me across decades.

Not for *someone* to find. For *me* to find.

The vision faded, leaving me gasping, fresh tears streaming from my eyes. My certainty that she knew I would return was absolute. She had known I would need this connection to her.

I slipped the ring on, not surprised when it fit my finger perfectly. The band settled against my skin like it belonged there, the moonstone pulsing once before quieting to merely reflect the late afternoon light from the stormy sky through the window.

I stared down at the ring, but my focus shifted past it to the polished surface of the bowl, where my skewed reflection bore a closer resemblance to my mom than to me. "What were you thinking?" I whispered.

"Did you know? Did you see what would happen? Did you let it happen?"

A soft knock preceded the door creaking open. I spun around as Javier entered with a tray of food—pizza—his dark eyes taking in the sight of me at the window, his expression guarded. "It's leftovers from earlier," he said quietly, setting the tray on the foot of the bed. "It's been so long since I prepared food for anyone. I'm not sure I remember how."

I smiled and shook my head. "This is perfect." The domesticity felt surreal. My consort bringing me food in my mother's bedchamber. My mother's sanctuary becoming mine.

"I can almost feel her in here," he said, looking around the room.

"I know what you mean." I glanced down at the ring, twisting it on my finger, drawing comfort from its weight. "She left this for me," I said, holding up my hand so the moonstone caught the light. "Like she knew I'd return someday."

Javier's eyes widened, recognition flickering across his features. "Diana's ring," he said, his voice hushed. "She used it during rituals. It helped her focus her magic. I never saw her take it off—not even once."

A shiver ran through me. "I don't know if I can do this, Javi," I admitted, curling my fingers into a fist and tucking my hand against my chest. "Be what she was. What everyone needs me to be."

"We don't need you to be Diana," he said steadily. "Simply be yourself, my Luna."

I wrapped my arms around my middle, suddenly feeling small. "And if that's not enough?"

Javier's weak reflection appeared behind mine in the window, his expression grave but unwavering. "It will be more than enough. Your mother was extraordinary, but you are—you're something else entirely."

I turned to face him. "What do you mean?"

His jaw worked like he was weighing his words. "Your power manifests differently than hers did—than any queen I've encountered."

My pulse quickened. "Is that bad?"

He shook his head, but I saw the reservation in his eyes. Felt it across our bond. "I've long thought you were destined for something greater than simply maintaining the balance."

"What does *that* mean?" My voice barely above a whisper. His explanations only bred more questions.

Javier's gaze drifted to the window, to the angry sky. "I'm not sure." The admission seemed to cost him. Javier had always been the one with answers. It had always been, "*I'll tell you when you're older,*" and never, "*I don't know.*"

"Come," Javier said, capturing my hand and guiding me toward the bed and the tray of pizza. "You must eat before your training with Isador."

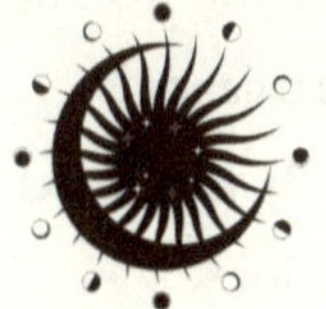

# 14

T HE COMBINED HOUSE SIGIL representing all three immortal Houses with a sun, crescent moon, and stars inlaid into the marble floor of the entryway shimmered at Isador's touch. A moment later, it vanished, revealing a narrow stone staircase spiraling down into darkness. Silver sigils in the curved descending wall flared to life, marked with various accent colors that pulsed gently, almost like the Moon Sanctuary had a heartbeat.

"These chambers were created by Selene herself," Isador said. "Only those accepted by the goddess may enter—queens and their bound consorts." She started down the winding stairs, her long bohemian skirt trailing behind her like a queen of old. "Come now, child," she commanded, her use of *child* to address me throwing me off now that she had recovered from her imprisonment and appeared no older than me.

I glanced at my consorts, standing around the newly exposed passage in the floor. Javier was on my right, his body still as he assessed the staircase for hidden dangers. Bastian stood close to my left, his amber eyes scanning the darkness. Ash and Thane waited on the far side of the opening, steady as always.

The first step down felt like crossing a threshold into some unknown realm. Power thrummed through the stone beneath my feet. My fingers trailed along the wall, feeling a surge of energy every time they crossed one of the sigils left by countless queens before me.

The staircase ended in an arched doorway that opened into a vast circular chamber that stole my breath. Above us, the domed ceiling mirrored a starlit sky, centered on a crystalline sphere glowing like a captured moon. Silver sigils marked with blood-red laid out the moon phases in a large circle on the stone floor. The walls were covered in a single, seamless black mural that depicted Selene, Helios, and Eos facing off against the Shadow King, their immortal warriors clashing with the shadow scourge.

"Welcome to the Selenarium," Isador said. "This is where you'll learn to truly harness your power as High Queen."

I stepped across the circle formed by the crimson sigils, and the crystal moon overhead pulsed brighter. The air felt thick with centuries of accumulated magic. Sensing the tension from my consorts, I glanced back toward the archway. Ash and Thane scanned the walls while Javier's attention remained locked on me. Bastian, however, seemed to be caught in an internal struggle. His eyes were squeezed shut, the tendons in his neck bulged, and his hands curled into tight fists. Energy rippled beneath his skin, making a faint golden light writhe under the black surface of the tattoos visible on his arms and neck.

"Bas?" I asked, quickly crossing to him. I raised my hands to his face, and the instant my skin touched his, a shiver of power washed over us both. His tattoos flared gold, then settled back to their usual black, and he visibly relaxed, bowing his head.

"Uh, Isador," I said, glancing toward my mentor. "What was that?"

"It would seem you had to beseech the goddess to welcome the chosen of Helios into her space. Not even your consort bond could override his primary allegiance, at least in the goddess's eyes." Isador studied Bastian from across the chamber. "Your tattoos, boy—how did you come by them?"

Bastian still seemed dazed by whatever had just happened, so I answered for him. "They just appeared," I said. "It started when he was a baby, and the markings grew as he did."

Isador's eyes narrowed as she scanned Bastian from head to toe, like she was only truly seeing him for the first time right now. "Hmph," she grunted and held out one hand, beseeching us farther into the chamber. "Come along, now. Let us begin." She retrieved a familiar vial from the pocket of her skirt.

My stomach clenched as I recognized the blood tincture—only this vial had to contain Gavin's, not Javier's. Just seeing it made my chest ache with his absence, that empty space in my newly formed harem like a phantom limb. Would I ever be complete? Or was I destined to always be missing some part or other of my heart?

"This will help you access your full strength. You've *communed* recently enough with the others," Isador explained. "Then we'll ask the goddess to bless your bonds with your consorts. If the ritual is successful, we'll see a projection of your heart sigils within the ritual space, allowing us to measure the strength of your existing bonds and ensure their long-term viability." Isador directed me to stand in the center of the chamber, directly under the crystal moon.

I licked my lips and approached, Bastian's hand in mine. "How, exactly, do I do that?"

"You use your *will* to call forth the bonds," Isador said, taking Bastian's hand from mine and exchanging it for the vial of blood tincture. "You pull the bonds out of the spirit realm and into physical reality." Isador guided Bastian to stand on the full moon sigil. "And if the goddess approves, she'll grant you the power to temporarily make the invisible visible."

A lump lodged in my throat. "I'm not good at controlling my Will," I confessed.

Isador smiled mysteriously, leaving Bastian behind and heading for Ash. "Of course you aren't." She guided Ash to stand on the waxing gibbous moon sigil. "Which is why we're down here in the Selenarium, where the goddess can help guide your power." She approached Javier next, moving him to the new moon sigil. "But you must learn this most basic diagnostic ritual." She made her way toward Thane. "It's necessary for both your safety as well as that of your consorts, and it's essential you become comfortable communicating with the goddess." She moved Thane to the waning gibbous moon sigil, effectively dispersing my consorts evenly around me.

"Now drink," she said, turning to me. "And let us begin."

I uncorked the vial with trembling fingers. The instant Gavin's blood tincture touched my tongue, completely scrubbed of his usual spiced chocolate flavor, power surged through me like electricity. The crystal moon blazed brighter, and the sigils on the floor flared.

"Now," Isador said, "feel your connection to these immortals. Sink into the bonds. Wrap them around your hands like ropes. Hold them tight. And once you have them, pull them to you."

I glanced at each of my consorts, uncertain about my ability to do what was necessary. With this. With saving Gavin. With protecting my son or ending this war or fending off the Shadow King or, well, with pretty much everything.

Releasing a resigned sigh, I closed my eyes and focused on my sense of my consorts around me. On their emotions, the shapes of their thoughts, their steady support and unwavering confidence and hopeful expectation. On their love. On their fear.

I reached out, mentally and physically, actually raising my arms. I felt the bonds coiling around my hands. I curled my fingers, gripped them tight, and pulled.

The consequences were immediate and horrifying. Thane groaned, and my eyes snapped open as his body went rigid, his muscles locking as he crashed to the ground, apparently paralyzed by whatever I had done. Through our bond, I felt his terror—not of me, but of being trapped again, helpless.

Ash dropped to his knees, his hands out in front of him, as he searched blindly, all senses stripped from him. "Thane?" he called out, panicked. "Sophie?! THANE!"

"Shit, Soph!" Bastian gasped, his form blurring as he shifted uncontrollably—first panther, then raven, then bear, his bones cracking and reforming as the shifts tore through him too quickly for the magic in his blood to keep up. Pain sliced through our bond like razor wire. His amber eyes, usually warm with devotion, clouded with feral ferocity as he lost control of his own body.

"BASTIAN!" I cried, but he couldn't hear me anymore.

The transformations accelerated, his body no longer settling into any shape. Fur sprouted and receded, feathers burst from skin only to dissolve into scales. Limbs stretched and contracted, his face elongating into muzzles, then snapping back to human features distorted with agony.

The forms began to merge—panther's claws extending from human hands, raven's wings erupting from a torso covered in gilded scales. His pupils split and multiplied, amber bleeding into gold that glowed with an ancient power that didn't belong to Bastian at all.

What emerged was a chimera of impossible parts. Through our bond, I felt his consciousness fracturing, the part of him that was Bastian drowning beneath animal instinct and something older, something that felt like sunlight and the wild heart of the forest.

The creature that had been Bastian threw back its head, now crowned with curved horns that glowed like heated metal, and roared. The sound carried harmonics that shook the stones beneath our feet. The sigils flickered, responding to a power they hadn't been designed to contain.

He lunged for me, rage in those inhuman golden eyes.

Javier moved with preternatural speed, intercepting Bastian. They crashed together, Javier's body absorbing the impact of claws that left deep furrows in his flesh. Bastian's raven wings unfurled, thrashing wildly.

"Control it, Sophie!" Isador barked. "You pulled forth their greatest fears, not their bonds. Release them!"

But how could I when every instinct screamed for me to flee? To hide. To stop the ritual and run away and abandon it all, because that would be better than this, than trying and failing and having to face the proof that I truly wasn't enough.

Bastian's monstrous form thrashed against Javier's restraint. I had no idea how Javier remained relatively unaffected by the ritual—maybe an extension of his Prime Consort immunity to my Will—but I was so incredibly grateful for it nonetheless.

Through our bond, I felt Bastian's terror—not of me, but of himself. Of being trapped in a form he couldn't control, of the ancient wildness threatening to consume him. If I let go, if I *released him* as Isador instructed, he feared he would be lost forever.

"I can't," I choked out. "I'll lose him!"

Panic surged to life within me like a miniature version of Bastian's beastly form. I would lose him, just like I'd known I would. Like I'd lost everyone I ever loved. My mom. Amaya. Javier. Wes. Micah. Gavin. I'd known this would happen. I had *known*. I hugged my middle, sobbing as I attempted to hold myself—and Bastian—together.

"I lose everyone," I whimpered.

"You won't, Soph," Wes said, his voice echoing through me as he wrapped his arms around me, cocooning me in his ghostly essence and sending tingles over me from head to toe. "You won't lose him, and you didn't lose me. I'm right here. Javier is right there. Amaya is upstairs with Micah, who is here with you. Gavin is waiting for you. You didn't lose us, Soph. We're *right here.*"

I wailed, feeling like preemptive grief would tear me apart.

"Listen to your spirit, Sophie," Isador said, pacing around the perimeter of the ritual circle. "He speaks sense."

"You're stronger than you give yourself credit for, Soph," Wes said. "You can do this."

Isador's voice cut through the chaos. "If pulling on the bond doesn't work for you, then you must find another way, Sophie. Your power flows from connection, not dominance. Use that. Use your love for him. For all of them."

Her words sparked something within me—a deep, instinctive understanding. The way each *communion* with my consorts strengthened our bonds through mutual surrender.

Taking another breath, I closed my eyes and reached for the bonds linking me to each of my consorts. Instead of pulling on those ephemeral cords, I imagined wrapping them around my body, visualizing my consorts binding me as I had bound them.

The connections felt wild and primal—like trying to hold lightning in my bare hands. Beneath the chaos, I sensed my consorts' desperation, their silent pleas echoing through our bonds. Javier wasn't unaffected after all; rather, his greatest fear was losing me, and if he released Bastian, he believed he would.

"Please," I whispered, surrendering to those bonds, to those cords now wrapped around my trembling body. I focused on Bastian's bond first, the cord connecting us bright and golden like captured sunshine. I pictured him as I'd first seen him in the library—quiet and intense with those Clark Kent glasses he'd worn in a vain attempt to blend into the human world.

The crystal moon flared blindingly bright, cutting off my words. Suddenly, I wasn't just sensing Bastian's inner torment; I was living it. His memories crashed over me like a violent tide, drowning me in his past.

I saw through his eyes as his mother's shift went wrong, her form contorting beyond natural limits. Her spine snapped and reformed, her beautiful face stretched into something unrecognizable. I witnessed her humanity being consumed heartbeat by heartbeat, recognition fading from her eyes until she no longer knew her own son. I felt Bastian's raw grief as his father, King Veris, ordered her tossed through a portal to the drowned city, Atlantis, neither human enough to live among them nor animal enough to be released into the wild. An *abomination*. Unfit to live.

In a blink, I was back in the Selenarium. I staggered under this revelation, tears streaming down my face. Bastian knelt nearby, Javier holding him upright, both men panting from exertion.

I didn't know what had happened to Bastian's mom, but I could only assume Veris's sentence had meant death for her. Much as I wanted to ask, needed to know, the unexplored bonds called to me, luring me from my heartache.

I focused on another cord—this one ice blue and shimmering with iridescence. The connection pulled me under like an arctic current, and suddenly I was Ash—mortal, human, kneeling in the shadow of a stone church beside a freshly covered grave marked with a small wooden cross. I felt the weight of the tiny carved shield and spear in my hands, meant for fierce little Freya, who would never grow old enough to hear tales of shield-maidens by the hearth fire. The plague had swept through our village like Odin's wrath, stealing Ingrid's and our child's breath in the same night while I sat helpless beside their bed, first praying to ancient gods, then to the White Christ when the old ones remained silent. The priest had permitted the small wooden offerings despite their pagan origins—a final kindness for a grieving father. At least they had gone together; my sweet Ingrid would never know a world without her baby in it.

The memory shifted, and I was able to pull myself partway out, separating myself from Ash as he watched Thane lunge through the graveyard portal mere days ago, sacrificing himself to save us from the shifter bearing a grenade. I felt the scream building in his chest, the soul-deep desperation as he lunged forward, only to be restrained by

Gavin's iron grip. He couldn't lose someone again, not after centuries of carefully guarding his heart against precisely this agony.

My breath caught as I understood. Ash didn't fear physical pain or even death—he feared loving and losing, he feared helplessness, a cycle he had endured first as a mortal and then throughout his immortal existence. Yet still he opened himself, still he loved, still he fought to protect what was his, first Freya and Ingrid, then Thane, and now me.

I met Ash's tortured gaze, a moment of perfect understanding between us that fed our bond, strengthening it. But still, I wasn't done.

I focused on another cord—this one a deep, sea green that pulsed like ocean depths. The bond thrummed, and I plunged into darkness. I was Thane, still human, working in the fields under a merciless sun when a pale hand selected me from among the other slaves. "This one," a woman's voice said, cultured and cold as winter frost. "Bring him to my chambers."

Night after night, humiliation and pain. The mistress of the plantation used my body for her pleasure while treating me as less than human. Her nails digging into my flesh, drawing blood like she was marking livestock. Her punishment when I failed to perform to her satisfaction—the lash, the hunger, the isolation. The helpless rage I swallowed until it became a poison in my veins.

The memory twisted, and I clawed away, watching Thane run after killing his mistress in self-defense rather than experiencing it firsthand. I watched as he was caught, tortured, and left standing with a rope around his neck as his attackers were slaughtered. I watched as a dainty woman picked her way through the crimson mud, hulking shadows surrounding her. "You're very pretty," she said, her voice like a song. "Do you want to live forever?"

Decades passed in a heartbeat—different queens, different masters, but the same sense of powerlessness, of being valued only for what his body could provide. Until Ash. Until someone looked at Thane and saw a person, not a possession.

Then the Sun Keep—the endless darkness, the hunger, the return of that helpless rage as he was once again reduced to a resource to be drained, a body to be used.

I gasped, my knees buckling as the weight of his trauma crashed through me. "Never again," I vowed, my voice breaking as I reached toward where Thane knelt. "*Never.*" The promise vibrated through our bond, strengthening our connection.

I focused on another cord—blood-red and scorched along the edges. This one felt ancient, weathered by decades of pain but somehow unbreakable, like a scar that refused to fade.

Suddenly I was in Javier's head, but I had a better idea of what to expect, and I was able to keep some distance between myself and his memory, observing his past instead of living it. I watched him, a young boy with skinned knees running through the halls of this very sanctuary, a dark-haired girl laughing beside him. Diana—my mom—radiant even in childhood. I sensed the fierce protectiveness he felt for her, how he loved her, a sister in every way but blood.

The memory shifted to a teenaged Diana weeping in his arms after her mother announced she would need to choose her consorts soon. "I don't want to," she whispered, her tears soaking through his shirt. "I don't want to be bound to *anyone*. I want to choose my own path." Javier's conflicted emotions—the relief that she didn't want him in that way mixed with fear for her future, his determination to stand beside her, to serve her, regardless of the cost to himself. For service to a High

Queen required complete devotion. He couldn't join another queen's harem and also serve his dearest friend.

Then Diana, older now and crowned as High Queen, her eyes heavy with knowledge as she told him, "I want you to be Prime Consort to the next High Queen, when the time comes... When I'm gone. Let this be your last act of service to me, my old friend." The shock, the honor, the confusion. "Why not Gavin?" he had asked. "He's the stronger guardian. The strongest in centuries." Diana's mysterious smile, tinged with sadness. "Because she will need your experience more than she will need his strength."

Then decades of torture in the Sun Keep, with his only anchor the tenuous connection to me. The overwhelming guilt that he had failed Diana. The bone-deep fear that I would never fulfill the destiny my mother had foreseen for me—a destiny that required sacrifices he now understood too late.

A sob tore from my throat. "She knew," I whispered, horrified by the confirmation. "She knew what would happen to all of us." The revelation gutted me, but our bond pulsed with renewed understanding, with shared grief for the woman who had brought us together.

But still, I wasn't finished. One last cord called to me, shimmering and liquid like pure quicksilver. It sucked me in, tearing me away from reality with such violent urgency that I barely had time or forethought to separate myself from Gavin as I crash landed in his memory.

Dazed, I watched a beautiful vampire queen with deep gray eyes lifting a baby—Gavin—to the moon. "My son will serve the next High Queen," she proclaimed, her voice ringing with a prophetic power that made the air itself tremble. "The goddess has shown me this truth."

I witnessed his training, his endless preparation for a role he hadn't asked for but had never questioned. His First Rite, when he became undead, and his Second Rite, when he ascended to guardian status, his amplified strength and power exceeding all predictions. The weight of expectation and disappointment crushed him as he watched other guardians find their queens and accept their bonds while he waited and trained, always training. A lifetime of purpose without fulfillment.

And then, the news he had awaited his entire existence. High Queen Diana had given birth to a girl, then another. His nervous excitement when his mother brought him to the Moon Sanctuary to meet Diana's daughters, his uncertainty when he beheld a little girl and a baby and was asked if he felt a connection to either. To a child? To a baby? He felt passing affection, as anyone would toward children, but nothing more. "Wait until they're older," his mother told him. "When they come into their power, you'll know."

And then, the devastation. Coordinated attacks against queens all over the world, including the High Queen and her daughters. Including his mother. His past, his future, gone in a single moment that left him hollow and purposeless.

He fought back that night, clearing the Moon Sanctuary of all shifters, dealing with the horrific aftermath, and in all the nights that followed, he devoted himself to hunting down stray queens. To saving as many as possible to make amends for those he couldn't protect. For the ones he had failed. For his mother. For Amaya. For me.

And then, the miracle he had stopped allowing himself to hope for—his queen was alive! His Luna. How difficult it had been for him to remain calm when he wanted to shout his joy to the heavens. How it had torn him apart to let me go while he remained behind in that cell, divided between the mission he had devoted himself to for decades and the queen he had given his life to serve.

Before I drew back into myself, I caught a glimpse of Gavin in his cell in the Sun Keep, huddled in the corner much as Javier had been when we found him. He looked up, his eyes glinting silver in the shadows, a flicker of recognition lighting his gaze.

"Sophie?" Gavin rasped, my name on his lips a prayer.

"I'm here," I whispered, reaching for him across dimensions I didn't understand. But just as my fingers brushed against his cheek, Gavin and his prison cell faded like the morning mist, leaving only the echo of his voice in my mind.

The crystal moon flared brighter, then dimmed to the darkness of a new moon. In the next heartbeat, power exploded out of my chest, making my back arch and my hair float around my head like I was under water. Sigils hovered around me, suspended by the cords binding me to my consorts.

I stared in wonder, tears chilling my cheeks as an otherworldly wind blew through the chamber. These were my consorts' sigils, the marks they had left on my heart when we bonded.

As I saw not what *I* had created, but what my consorts and I had created together, I understood: a queen's power–*my* power–wasn't just about what I could do to others, but what I would allow them to do to me. True strength lay in vulnerability, in the courage to let someone else in. In choosing when to fight and when to surrender.

"Incredible..." Isador moved around the outside of the ritual circle, closely scrutinizing each sigil. "Absolutely remarkable..."

My head pounded as the crystal moon's light intensified once more, and the glowing sigils and bond cords faded away. My body suddenly felt icy—the same chill I'd felt after the vision of the Shadow King. I swayed, suddenly dizzy.

"Sophie!" Javier caught me before I hit the ground, cradling me against his chest.

Through half-closed eyes, I saw the others huddle in close around us. Wes hovered nearby, and Isador approached, finally crossing the ritual circle created by the crimson sigils.

"No, Javier," Isador said. "No blood. She must find her way back from this on her own, or the pathways of magic won't set right within her."

Isador's expression was guarded as she studied my face. "Your bonds are fully mature, a process that usually takes many years of *communions* between queen and consorts." She bowed her head, her first true show of respect toward me. "The goddess touches you more strongly than I expected, my queen. This changes how we will proceed...when you've recovered."

Exhaustion dragged at me like chains, pulling me into darkness. As consciousness slipped away, I felt a presence, vast and ancient. Watching. Waiting.

Whispering, "*Soon...*"

# 15

I woke to a body that felt shattered despite the taste of ripe blackberries and the sunlit forest on my tongue. Bastian's blood. He must have just given it to me for me to still feel like I'd been hit by a Mack truck.

Every muscle screamed, every bone ached, while memories flashed through my mind in fragments: my untrained magic wreaking havoc in the Selenarium, Bastian's chaotic transformations, my consorts' fears unleashed, their memories revealed, my surrender required.

I peeled my eyelids open to find I was in my new bedroom—my mom's old bedroom. I tried to sit up, but the world tilted, and nausea turned my stomach.

"Careful, Soph." Bastian's voice reached me from the shadows. "You've been out for nearly a day. Isador wouldn't let us give you blood until you started to wake on your own. We've been taking turns watching over you."

I turned my head carefully and found him by the moon altar in front of the arched window, deliberately keeping his distance. Moonlight outlined his silhouette. The tattoos visible beyond the reach of his T-shirt seemed different—more substantial, with faint golden threads running beneath the black ink. His muscles were coiled tight, ready to flee.

"The others?" My voice came out rough.

"Nearby." His jaw tightened. Through our bond, I felt him wrestling with shame and fear. "I can get one of them, if you prefer. I wouldn't blame you, not after...everything."

I remembered with sickening clarity what had happened, how I flubbed the ritual and had forced my consorts' greatest fears upon them. I had stripped away Bastian's control over his shifter powers, forcing his body to change into something monstrous. The pain through our bond had been excruciating, his consciousness fracturing. *I* did that to him.

"I'm so sorry," I whispered.

Bastian laughed without humor. "*You're* sorry? I nearly tore you apart. If Javier hadn't tackled me..." His amber eyes finally found mine. "I didn't know that was inside me, Soph. I still don't know what it was, but it wasn't *me*."

I sensed the war within him—the scholar wanting to understand, the predator fearing what he would become, and something deeper that had awakened in that ritual chamber. Something that had reveled in the chaos.

As Bastian spoke, I felt the immortal blood working through my body, restoring me. The ache in my muscles subsided, replaced by an awareness of Bastian's presence and the bond thrumming between us, giving me a front-row seat to his self-loathing.

"Come here," I said, patting the edge of the bed.

He hesitated, fear flashing across his features. "I shouldn't."

"Bas," I said, gentler. "Please. I need you."

His resistance crumbled, and he crossed the room with fluid grace. The mattress dipped as he perched on the edge, maintaining careful distance. He traced the line of a tattoo snaking onto the back of his hand with his index finger. A line I was almost certain hadn't been there before.

"Talk to me," I said. "Please don't shut me out."

Staring at the wall, he was quiet for so long I thought he might not answer. His jaw worked, and his eyes held a storm of emotions.

"What happened in the ritual chamber..." His voice roughened. "That wasn't just a normal shift gone wrong. That was something else." His eyes met mine, fear laid bare. "Something that shouldn't exist."

I reached for his hand, but he pulled back, out of reach. "Don't, Soph. Please. I'm not sure I can control it if you touch me right now."

The admission hit me hard, sending fissures through my heart. "What if you don't have to control it?" I asked softly.

His head snapped up. "Soph—"

"What if what happened wasn't a mistake?" I continued, sitting up despite the lingering weakness. "What if it was a revelation?"

"A *revelation*?" Disbelief tainted his voice. "That I'm a *monster*?"

"That you're more than you thought," I corrected, extending my hand. "Show me," I whispered. When he shook his head, inching away, I pressed further. "Don't pull away, Bas, please. *Please*. I need you. All of you." I took a deep breath, rethinking my next words about a thousand times. "Show me what's inside you. Let's face it together."

Gold sparked in his eyes even as fear clouded his expression. Through our bond, I felt the wild energy responding to my invitation—not just shifter magic but something deeper. Older. Untamed.

"I don't know what will happen," Bastian admitted. "If I let it out, I don't think I can control myself like I can with my normal shifts."

"Then don't," I said simply. "I trust you. Even *that* part of you." I tugged the oversized shirt someone had dressed me in for sleep over my head, tossing it to the far side of the bed. The cool air kissed my flesh, tightening my nipples to stiff peaks, and moonlight stained my skin silver.

Bastian stared, transfixed. His breath quickened, his pupils dilating until only a thin ring of amber remained. Another flash of gold. A shiver within his pupil, threatening to split. "Sophie," he breathed, my name a warning and a prayer.

"I want this," I told him, bringing his hand to my breast. "I want you, Bas. All of you." His thumb swept across my nipple, like he just couldn't resist, and his touch sent sparks dancing along nerve endings and heat pooling low in my belly. "Let me see you too," I whispered, tugging up the hem of his T-shirt.

He remained tense as I stood on my knees to pull the shirt up over his head. His tattoos shimmered golden in the moonlight.

"You're so beautiful," I told him, tracing the lines across his chest. When my fingers trailed over black ink, gold rose to the surface, an inner glow attracted by my touch.

His control broke on a groan. He gripped me by the hips and pulled me closer, dragging me onto his lap so my legs straddled him. His mouth found mine, his teeth grazing my lower lip, drawing blood, and I gasped at the wild, unrestrained response after such hesitancy. He gripped my ass, his fingers sinking in almost painfully. Possessively. Hungrily.

I gripped his hair at the nape of his neck and pulled his head back, breaking our kiss.

A sound rumbled from his chest—not quite human, not quite animal. His amber eyes flickered gold again as he fought against his nature.

"I'm not afraid," I promised, my stare locked with his. "Stop holding back, Bas. Please."

Something shifted in his expression. His form blurred slightly, not the violent shift from before, but something controlled. His eyes changed first, amber bleeding to rich gold, with pupils narrowing to feline slits before splitting, forming what looked like infinity signs in his eyes. His bone structure sharpened, his canines lengthened into vicious fangs.

"Like this?" he asked, vulnerable despite his inhuman appearance and deeper voice.

I nodded, my throat dry with wanting. "Yes," I rasped, unconsciously rubbing myself against him. "Just like that."

His transformed hands found my waist, the whisper of claws against my skin teasing the possibility of violence as he shifted our positions on the bed, laying me on my back. Seeing his partially shifted form hovering over me sent liquid desire pulsing between my thighs.

His mouth traced down my neck, teeth grazing where my pulse hammered, then moving lower. His tongue flicked over my nipple. The unexpectedly rough texture making me arch, a cry escaping my lips.

"Gods, Soph," he growled. "The things I want to do to you..."

"Then do them," I urged, my fingers tangling in his hair, now longer and wilder. "*Please.*"

His mouth traveled lower, leaving a blazing trail across my abdomen. His hands parted my thighs with deliberate gentleness, the bite of his claws a tease rather than an attack. When he settled his shoulders between my legs, golden eyes gazing up with naked hunger, I thought I might combust.

The first touch of his tongue through the thin cotton of my underwear tore a sound from my throat I barely recognized. In this form, the texture was different—rougher and possibly ribbed, perfectly suited to drawing pleasure. His clawed hands held my thighs apart as he teased me with devastating precision, soaking my underwear with a combination of his saliva and my arousal.

"Bastian," I moaned, my hips rising to meet each stroke of his tongue. "Please, I need—"

With a dark chuckle, he hooked my underwear with a claw and tore the fabric, baring me to him. His pleased rumble sent shivers cascading over me. The first stroke of his altered tongue made me tremble. The sensations were so intense, so different from anything else I'd experienced. Rough against my soft. Ridged against my swollen.

He growled against me, the vibration sending shockwaves through me. His tongue circled my clit before he wrapped his lips around me and sucked none too gently, flicking the tip of that rougher tongue over the sensitive bundle of nerves. The combination of sensations sent me over the edge. My release crashed through me in waves, my body arching as pleasure radiated outward from my core.

Before I could recover, he moved higher, pushing his pants down and positioning himself between my thighs. The head of his cock pressed into my swollen heat, and he fucked my slit, dragging his shaft back and forth over my clit, letting me know his tongue wasn't the only thing ribbed in this form. Making me desperate to have him inside me.

"Show me, Bas," I groaned, my nails digging into his back. The texture of his skin had changed, becoming somehow both smoother and bumpier. Scales, I realized. Another layer of his mask removed. "Show me all of you."

"Like this?" He changed the angle of his hips and pushed inside me, making us both groan. The stretch was delicious, overwhelming, perfect. The ridges added an extra layer of sensation as he pulled out and pushed back in, going deeper with each thrust. "Is this enough of me?"

I touched his face, tracing the sharper angles. "Mmmm...no," I moaned. "All of you, Bas. Oh my fucking god, let me see all of you." I lifted my hips to meet his thrusts. "Let me fucking see you."

His control slipped further. Curved horns like burning metal sprouted from his curls, and wings erupted from his back, black as midnight, each feather dusted with gold around the edges. The muscles beneath my hands grew more powerful as he surrendered to what lived within him. His thrusts became deeper, more primal, forcing sounds from my throat I hadn't known I could make.

"Mine," he growled. "You're *mine*."

"Yes," I gasped, my fingers gripping the top edge of his wings, where they sprouted from his back. They flared out before curving over me like a sheltering cocoon. "Yours. Always yours."

His rhythm faltered. He lowered his head, grazing his teeth along my neck, and the teasing threat of pain catapulted me into another climax, more powerful than the first. My inner muscles clenched around him, drawing his own release with a roar.

Wave after wave of pleasure washed through me, carrying me away into an ocean of ecstasy. As I floated back to reality and my awareness returned, I found Bastian still above me, his form gradually shifting back to normal though his eyes remained gold.

"I didn't hurt you?" he asked, his voice rough with emotion.

I laughed out loud. "Ah, no. Unless you count my sanity, because apparently, I like to fuck around with monsters."

Bastian relaxed visibly, his familiar, cocky grin sliding into place. "Sophie, Sophie, Sophie," he practically purred. "You come every time a vampire sinks his fangs into you." He traced his own elongated canines along my jawline, and I shuddered out my next exhale. "We already know you like to fuck around with monsters."

I laughed again, low and throaty, running my fingers through his tousled curls. "I like the horns," I admitted, dragging my nails over the part of his scalp where they had been.

"Somebody watched *Beauty and the Beast* a lot as a kid, didn't she?" he teased, nuzzling my neck.

I snorted a laugh. "I can neither confirm nor deny that," I said, despite it being one hundred percent true.

Chuckling, Bastian stretched out beside me, blunted claws drawing sigils lightly on my abdomen. "I lied earlier," he confessed. "I think I knew it was inside me, this *beast*, especially after my mom... Like it was just waiting for the right moment to break free."

"How old were you?" I asked softly, curling toward him to lay my head on his shoulder. "When she..."

His heart beat steadily, marking time as he gathered the courage to respond. "I was seven when her shift went wrong," he finally said, words carrying the weight of decades of silence. "It didn't happen all at once. Each time she changed, she came back less *her*. More *beast*." His voice caught. "Until one day, she didn't come back at all."

I held him tighter, my silent acknowledgment of such painful truths.

"Abomination," he continued. "That's what they call it when a shifter gets stuck between forms. Veris had her exiled to Atlantis." His voice hardened. "*Exile*—a pretty way to say execution by drowning. The city's been underwater almost as long as the Houses have existed, and she didn't have sea form, so...there's no way she survived."

"Was it the curse?" I asked, fearing the answer but needing to know. "Is that what caused her to lose herself? Did my people take your mom from you?"

He was quiet long enough that I lifted my head to see his face, his pained expression.

"No," I said, sickened by the truth. "Bas, I—I'm so sorry, I—"

"It's not your fault, Soph." He pressed a kiss to my temple. "She could have stopped. Could've stayed in her human form, and she would've been fine."

My brow furrowed. A shifter *not* shifting sounded about as healthy as a vampire *not* drinking blood, and having been the latter out of necessity for far too long, I knew firsthand that she wouldn't have been *fine*. She would have been there for Bastian, but she would have lost herself in other ways.

"I've always been scared of ending up like her—of losing myself to the shift." He skimmed his claws lightly over my back, sending goosebumps cascading over my skin. "But what happened in the ritual chamber, and just now... I think that was different. Something else."

"How so?" I asked. In the Selenarium, he had seemed more wild, more at risk of losing himself, but maybe that had been my *will* pulling his fear to the surface. *Maybe* the beast that had come forth was this *something else*. Something that stepped in during the ritual, not to take him over but to protect him. Moments ago, when he had let the beast out to play, he certainly hadn't lost himself. If anything, he had seemed more himself than ever.

"Letting go felt...right," he said, echoing my thoughts. "Like finding myself."

I frowned, tracing the curved line of a tattoo, watching the gold beneath the black rise to meet my touch. "Any idea what it means?"

"Not a fucking clue."

# 16

I LAY IN BED, my heart hammering as the last fragments of a nightmare faded. Predawn light streamed through the windows, casting unfamiliar furniture in pale light. For a moment, I couldn't remember where I was or who I was supposed to be.

Sophie Matthews, librarian with a tragic past? Luna Sofia Teresi Athanasiou, High Queen of the House of the Moon? The line between those identities felt worn thin in places where my past bled into my present.

I slipped from beneath the sheets, careful not to wake Bastian. His face looked younger in sleep, the burden of fearing what we had unleashed within him absent. Part of me wanted to curl back against his warmth, to pretend we were just two people who'd found each other amid the chaos of our lives.

The aged wooden floors creaked beneath my bare feet as I crossed to the dresser to retrieve undies and a fresh oversized sleep shirt. I never slept well when naked, feeling too vulnerable, too exposed. I headed into the bathroom to pee, and as I washed my hands, I studied my reflection. The face in the ornate mirror was both foreign and familiar—eyes brighter, skin luminous from regular feeding, but with fatigue lingering beneath. I looked like my mother. The realization made my heart ache, squeezed between a vice of grief and anger.

"Is this what you wanted?" I whispered to her ghost, though I knew she couldn't hear me. Veris had made sure of that when he burned her remains and scattered her ashes. She had known. About the attack. About her death, and Amaya's. That I would flee, that Javier would be my protector, my Prime Consort. But had she known more? Had she known the extent of the suffering she was perhaps not causing directly, but allowing? "Was it worth it?"

Huffing a silent, bitter laugh, I turned my back on my reflection and crossed my arms over my chest, leaning back against the edge of the counter. "I hope you're happy," I muttered, tapping one finger against my arm.

After standing there for minutes, silently fuming at my dead mother, I released a heavy sigh. There was no way I was getting back to sleep now. I reached for the long silken robe hanging on the back of the door and tossed it on over my sleep shirt before sliding my feet into slippers. I needed air. To walk. To think alone. A rarity for me these days.

Including this morning, it turned out. Micah was already in the herb garden when I reached it, reading on the stone bench beneath an ancient rowan tree, its branches laden with clusters of bright red berries that seemed to glow in the early morning. The predawn light cast weak shadows across the ancient stone paths, making everything look slightly washed out and just a little ancient. He looked up at my approach.

"Shouldn't you be resting up for your important meeting with the elementals?" he asked, closing the leather-bound book on his lap, its pages yellowed with age.

"That's tomorrow," I said automatically.

Micah glanced at the brightening sky to the east. "It *is* tomorrow."

I froze, mentally tallying days and nights and events, and my eyes widened when I realized he was right. Ambassadors from the House of the Stars would be arriving today, and I had *no* idea what to say to them or what to do for them or how to be around them. At least Isador had taken care of Marie's *confession*, clearing the Moon Sanctuary's resident elemental after Gavin locked her up under suspicion of betrayal. When they asked me if I was holding any of their people prisoner, I could honestly say I was *not*. So that was a plus.

"You're making that face again," Micah said.

I pressed my lips together and tucked my chin. "What face?"

Micah coughed a laugh. "The someone-shoot-me face, though now you just look constipated."

I guffawed and closed the distance between us, but I hesitated before sitting. "Can I?"

"It's a free country," he said, setting the book on the bench beside him and scooting closer to the edge. "I suppose...wherever we are." He gestured to the empty space, his lips twisting into a wry smirk. "Unless you want to become a vampire."

Groaning dramatically, I settled beside him. For a moment, neither of us spoke. The early morning felt unnaturally still and quiet, though maybe that was just because the silence between us was so incredibly loud.

I sucked in a breath. Held it. Mentally debated what to say. "I've been thinking about what you said," I began, spinning the moonstone ring on my finger—this remnant of my mother, this symbol of the legacy I was still learning to bear. "About wanting the First Rite."

"You don't have to explain why you said no," Micah replied, his voice carefully neutral. His fingers tapped a restless rhythm against his knee. "I get it. I'm too young. Too human. Too—"

"Too important to risk," I interrupted softly.

His eyes, when they met mine, held a depth of understanding that startled me. He'd always been perceptive, but there was something else there now—something that recognized the weight I carried.

"It wasn't a permanent no," I continued. "Just a 'not now.'" I swallowed against the tightness in my throat. "The First Rite isn't just dangerous in the sense that I could easily screw it up and kill you, because, you know, I've never done it before." I shrugged. "I could get it right, or mostly right, or just kind of right, but the outcome—whether I get it right or wrong or somewhere in between—is irreversible. And I'd never forgive myself if I damned you to a tormented immortality because I wasn't strong enough or skilled enough to guide you through the First Rite properly."

A night bird called from the tree overhead, and I looked up.

When I glanced at Micah again, his expression was pensive. "I know you think I rushed into asking," he said, "but I've actually been thinking about it since the attack in that basement. When that shifter tackled me—" His voice caught. "I saw how quickly things can change. How vulnerable I am like this. I'm scared, Sophie," he admitted, his voice barely audible over the rustling leaves. "Not of dying, exactly. But of not living long enough to understand where I come from." His gaze drifted toward the sky, lightened to a peachy gray. "I've spent my whole life not knowing who I really was. Now that I finally do, I can't—" His voice cracked. "I can't lose you—and Wes." He waved a hand half-heartedly at the Moon Sanctuary. "All of this."

The raw honesty in his words broke something loose inside me. For decades, I'd hidden behind masks—frightened girl, agreeable teen, cautious librarian, reluctant queen—each one a shield against vulnerability. But Micah deserved better than my carefully crafted half-truths.

I reached for his tapping fingers, covering his hand with mine. "When I gave you up," I whispered, "it was the hardest thing I'd ever done. Harder than losing Wes. Harder than running from Veris's assassins or figuring out how to survive without Javier." The admission scraped my throat raw. "I did it because I thought you'd be safer without me."

He turned his hand beneath mine, his fingers curving around mine in a gesture that made me mourn all the hand-holding I'd missed during his childhood. "Maybe it was always going to end up this way, with the three of us together, here," he said. "Maybe some connections can't be severed, no matter how hard the world tries."

I smiled faintly. "You sound like Wes. The eternal optimist." I swiped away a tear that snuck past my lashes. "I just—I need you to understand that I'm not refusing the First Rite altogether. I'm waiting because *I* need to be ready."

Micah studied me with those eyes that were so like Wes's it hurt. "I know. I get it. But *I* need *you* to know that I'm ready when you are."

We sat together as the sky lightened further, the elementals' approach drawing ever nearer. But for this moment, in the quiet herb garden with Micah's hand in mine, I was simply a mother, terrified and determined to protect her child.

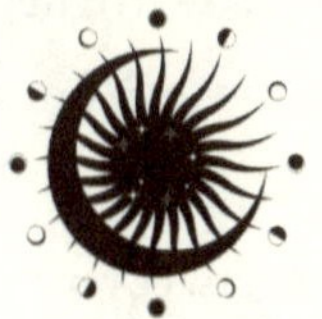

# 17

"MIGHT AS WELL LOOK the part," I muttered, slipping into a dress for the first time in ages. It was deep crimson silk, and other than the dozens of teeny tiny buttons running down the back, it wasn't all that different from the robe I'd taken to wearing when wandering the Moon Sanctuary at night, with long sleeves, a low V neckline, and a cinched waist. The skirt pooled around my feet, pretty, but impractical for anything other than fluttering around the manor like a bored Victorian lady or receiving guests. The silk whispered against my skin, making me feel far more elegant than I was.

"Stupid, dumb thing," I muttered, twisting this way and that as I attempted to fasten the buttons, trying and failing to get a decent view in the standing mirror in the corner of the bedroom.

Javier appeared in the doorway, and I gave up on the buttons, turning my back to him and peering over my shoulder. "This dress was designed by a sadist," I grumbled.

He huffed a laugh and approached. "I agree." He trailed his fingertips down my bare back, making me shiver, then started on the buttons. His eyes met mine in the mirror as he worked. "You look like her," he said quietly, his voice catching. "Like your mother."

"I'm not her," I replied, sharper than I'd intended. The weight of her ghost, her throne, her sacrifice and betrayal, pressed down on me.

"No. You are *you*, my Luna." His expression softened as he stood unnaturally still, assessing me with predatory intensity. "My queen." He fastened the top button at the nape of my neck, then gathered my long, dark auburn curls off to one side and brushed a soft kiss under my ear. "Just one final touch," he said, setting a silver circlet on my head. The lunar phases proudly displayed in gleaming moonstone on my forehead, a perfect match for the ring on my finger.

I raised one hand, touching the waxing crescent moon on the end. "I remember her wearing this." I turned to him, accepting his offered arm. "Tell me what to expect. Why are they visiting now, and what do they want from us?"

As we walked through the corridors, Javier's voice was low, meant only for me. "The House of the Stars has always been mercurial in their allegiances. They were willing to attempt to break the curse on the House of the Sun, but Diana refused, making it impossible. They remained neutral during the uprising, neither helping nor hindering the shifters' attacks on our people." Bitterness edged his words as he smoothed his thumb over the pulse point on my wrist, a gesture both possessive and reassuring. "But if the Shadow King truly threatens our world, they will need us as much as we need them."

Through our bond, I felt his controlled anger at their past neutrality, tamped down beneath centuries of political savvy. From down the hall, I sensed Bastian making his way toward us.

He rounded the corner, dressed in formal wear that somehow made him look both more dangerous and more beautiful. He stopped in his tracks, his stare appreciative. "Damn, Soph," he said, watching me like a kid in a candy shop. "I feel like one of those guys in a teen movie watching his prom date walk down the stairs." He ran a hand through his dark curls, the only part of him that remained visibly untamed. "You look..." He licked his lips, slow and deliberate, letting me know exactly what he was thinking about doing to me.

"You clean up nice," I said, stopping in front of him and offering him my lips. He kissed me thoroughly enough to ensure my lips would be rosier and swollen during the impending meeting. I didn't mind. It gave me something else to think about besides the *holy shit* panic swarming through my veins at the thought of receiving the Stars' emissaries. I hadn't been trained for this. I had no idea what I was doing.

"We'll be with you the whole time, Soph." Bastian brushed the pad of his thumb over my bottom lip. "You're not alone."

I closed my eyes, soaking up the sense of Javier at my back and Bastian in front of me. "I know," I said, smiling gently. I inhaled deeply, then blew out my breath and opened my eyes. "Let's get this over with."

The formal reception hall seemed designed to awe and intimidate, with a soaring vaulted ceiling and massive stained-glass windows along one side that transformed the late morning light into a kaleidoscope of colors. Thane and Ash waited on the dais, taking positions on either side of the throne. Their eyes roamed over me as I approached, flanked by Javier and Bastian.

Vampires and their whispers filled the hall, their presence a testament to our House's renewed strength. Imposing undead guardians stood at attention by every entrance, their silver crescent sigils glowing faintly on one side of their faces. I recognized many of them from our frantic escape from Seattle and the later infiltration of the Sun Keep. At least a dozen more undead vampires were spread throughout the room, alone or in pairs, their stillness unnerving.

Ghosts filled the remaining space, leaving only an aisle open down the center of the room leading to the dais and throne. The collective power of so many undead vampires created a palpable energy in the room, only amplified by the ghosts' presence.

Wes and Amaya stood with Micah, Isador, and her trio of consorts near the dais, though only the other queen was aware of the ghosts' presence. Micah looked incredibly uncomfortable but determined not to stick out like a sore thumb, and the three-piece suit that had clearly been tailored for him helped. His eyes met mine, offering encouragement through his obvious nervousness.

Isador looked like she should have been the one on the throne, not me. Her rejuvenated beauty commanded attention, her copper eyes seeming to glow in the filtered light. She inclined her head slightly as I passed, the gesture conveying both respect and subtle caution.

Across the aisle from her, Doris and Helene had taken up positions with their own small retinue of consorts. Youthful twin vampires with identical watchful expressions flanked Doris, while Helene clutched the arm of a more mature consort whose protective stance suggested centuries of devotion.

I offered them smiles, not trusting my voice with the nerves currently lodged in my throat. My legs felt shaky as I stopped in front of the throne and hesitated, unsure what to do. I turned to Javier and whispered, "Do I stand, or..." I looked from Javier to the throne and back.

"You sit," Javier said, his voice hushed. "You are the High Queen of the House of the Moon. You stand for no one, save for the goddess herself. Once the emissaries arrive and bow, you can stand, if you wish, or even offer to speak with them in the seating area." He glanced toward the cluster of armchairs and small tables set up off to the side of the dais. "But you don't need to. If you stand as they approach, they'll view it as an act of deference, and this must not happen."

I gulped and sat, my body humming with anxiety. I desperately wanted to sink into myself and hide, but I forced myself to sit tall, back straight, forearms on the armrests. I crossed my ankles, uncrossed them, then crossed them again.

The vampires throughout the hall shifted into a formation that spoke of centuries of court protocol, the ghosts fading out when in the way, only to fade back in elsewhere. Two particularly imposing guardians moved to flank the main doors, their hands resting casually on concealed weapons.

The doors opened, and I jumped, my heart lurching into my throat.

The man who entered first radiated power. Magic crackled around him, making the air thick with the scent of ozone. My consorts tensed in unison, their varied energies bristling. Throughout the hall, the vampires' collective awareness sharpened to penetrating focus, a ripple of silent readiness sweeping through their ranks, warrior and civilian alike.

"High Queen," the elemental said, stopping a few steps away from the dais. His bow was perfectly calculated, deep enough to show respect without appearing to grovel. "I am Prince Reiji of the House of the Stars. We come seeking alliance in these troubled times."

I started to respond, but movement behind him caught my attention. A woman emerged from his shadow—tall and lean, with short black hair and dark eyes that seemed to strip me bare, weighing and measuring me in a single sweep. Unlike Reiji's dramatic entrance, she moved with subdued potency.

"And this is Ren," Reiji added, his tone suggesting she was an afterthought. "My guard."

But the way she carried herself spoke of someone too powerful to be dismissed so casually. Her striking features held an androgynous beauty that drew the eye, the sharp angles of her face softened by full lips that seemed perpetually on the verge of a knowing smile. Her stare lingered on Wes's pendant nestled between my breasts, and I fought the urge to curl my fingers around the silver tree of life. When our eyes met, her gaze held curiosity—and secrets.

"Welcome to the Moon Sanctuary," I said, keeping my voice steady despite the way Ren's stare and Reiji's circling magic unsettled me. "We weren't expecting you until later."

"The stars suggested haste was prudent." Reiji's smile was meant to dazzle. "And who are we to argue with the heavens?"

Ren's expression flickered—just the slightest tightening around her eyes. I filed that reaction away, adding it to my growing suspicion that "guard" was the least interesting thing about her.

"Who, indeed." I stood and gestured to the formal seating area set off to the side of the dais. "Please, join me. We have much to discuss."

As we moved to sit, I watched how Ren positioned herself—not following behind Reiji, but walking alongside him, like an equal. Her movements were liquid grace, reminding me of Bastian in his panther form. When she caught me watching, her dark eyes met mine with an intensity that made my cheeks heat and my skin prickle.

Something flickered in her gaze, a brief, unexpected softness that contradicted her otherwise guarded demeanor. It vanished so quickly I might have imagined it, but the momentary connection left me strangely unsettled in a way that wasn't entirely unpleasant.

Javier's hand brushed my shoulder as he took his position beside my chair, his energy wrapping around me like a shield against Reiji's persistent magical prodding. His eyes never left our visitors, tracking their every movement even as he appeared relaxed.

Micah, Isador, and her consorts arranged themselves strategically to my right, close enough to signal their allegiance but far enough to give me autonomy. One of Isador's consorts—an undead vampire gentleman with silver hair—whispered something in her ear, causing her to cast a measured glance at Ren.

Reiji settled into his chair with practiced elegance, Ren taking up a watchful stance behind him. "We've heard fascinating rumors," Reiji said, his voice hitting that exact note of cultured interest I was still struggling to master. His smile turned sharp. "About the rather *diverse* collection of consorts you've chosen to serve you."

Through our bonds, I felt my immortals bristle at the implied insult. Near the walls, the additional vampire guardians shifted almost imperceptibly, reading the tension in my consorts' postures and adjusting their own stances in response.

"I prefer to think of them as partners," I said, keeping my tone pleasant. "Each brings unique strengths to our alliance."

"As you say." Reiji's gaze flickered between my consorts with poorly concealed interest. "Though I notice you're still short of the traditional seven. Perhaps the House of the Stars could assist with that?"

Was he suggesting *he* could fill that role? Behind me, Bastian made a sound low in his throat, and I felt Javier's cold fury through our bond.

Throughout the hall, the temperature seemed to drop as dozens of vampire eyes focused with predatory intensity on the elemental prince.

Before I could tell Reiji exactly where he could stick that suggestion, Ren made a soft sound—not quite a snort, but close enough to draw Reiji's attention. Ren moved around from behind Reiji's chair and sat, their eyes meeting in what seemed like a silent argument.

"What my *colleague* means," Ren said, her voice low and rich, "is that we seek true, lasting alliance, not merely political maneuvering." Her dark eyes met mine. "The shadow grows stronger. We all feel it."

The direct acknowledgment of the threat sent a chill down my spine. My vision of the Shadow King's invasion flashed through my mind—blood and fire and endless darkness consuming everything I loved. Through our connection, I felt my consorts' attention sharpen.

"Tell me what you know," I said, dropping the diplomatic facade. Screw politics—if they had information about the shadow, I needed to hear it.

Reiji's smile faltered slightly, but Ren's expression remained steady as she held my gaze.

"The shadow seeks gaps in the barrier between realms," Ren said, her voice dropping lower. "Places where the barrier has grown thin."

Reiji's magic pulsed with irritation, but Ren seemed utterly immune to his attempts to silence her. "The House of the Stars has preserved certain records," Reiji interjected smoothly, trying to regain control of the conversation. "Prophecies that speak of a High Queen who will either save or destroy us all. Though they're frustratingly vague about which outcome is more likely."

My mouth went dry. "Prophecies can be misinterpreted," I said, remembering how my own visions were, at best, confusing, and at worst, utterly indecipherable. "Or misunderstood entirely."

"True." Ren's voice carried a weight that drew all eyes to her. "But the gathering darkness is harder to misinterpret. It hungers." Her gaze flickered to the window, where storm clouds loomed on the horizon. "And it remembers the taste of our world."

As she spoke, her formal mask slipped just slightly, and I glimpsed genuine concern beneath her calculated exterior. Her eyes held mine a moment longer than necessary, an unspoken acknowledgment passing between us—we both understood what was at stake, perhaps more clearly than those around us. I couldn't quite place why, but something about her resonated with me on a level that transcended diplomatic posturing.

The careful game of politics suddenly felt hollow compared to the threat we faced—not merely the House of the Moon or the Stars, but *the world*. "No more riddles. Tell me your prophecy, and I'll tell you mine."

Ren's lips curved slightly, but her eyes remained serious. "The Shadow King isn't just trying to break through," she said, ignoring Reiji's sharp look. "He's already begun. Each breach weakens the barriers further."

"How long?" I asked, impressing myself with the steadiness of my voice.

"Weeks," Reiji said smoothly, clearly not wanting to be left out. "Perhaps months if we're fortunate. The stars grow darker each night." His smile grew teeth. "Though I suspect you've seen this yourself, assuming Selene has blessed you with any visions." A test.

"The visions show possibilities," I said carefully. "Not certainties."

"Truly? Is that how yours work?" Ren's dark eyes met mine, and my gut told me her question was genuine. Her brows drew together. "I didn't know that."

"It's not the same for you?" I asked, leaning forward.

Ren shook her head. "We have prophecies, not visions."

I waved a hand, dismissing the difference. "What does your *prophecy* say, exactly?"

Ren and Reiji exchanged a look. "Don't let me stop you now," Reiji said, gesturing for Ren to continue.

Ren stared at him for a moment longer, then returned her focus to me. "Our prophecy is long and tedious, but one verse is crystal clear:

*"When the Shadow King stirs in his endless hunger,*

*The last High Queen must seek counsel beyond mortality's veil.*

*Into her circle must come one born of stars,*

*Completing the seven bonds that strengthen her light.*

*The departed queens shall rise at her calling,*

*Silver wisdom from beyond the grave guiding her hand.*

*What was broken by necessity shall be mended through sacrifice."*

Anger heated my blood. Not at Ren. Not even at Reiji, though it was clear he came here to become the "one born of stars" to join my harem. I was mad as hell at yet another twist of fate forcing me to do something I didn't want to do for the sake of survival. I was so damn tired of sacrificing. Hadn't I given enough? Couldn't I *at least* choose who would fill the remaining two spots in my harem? Or was this yet another thing to be taken from me?

Not trusting myself to keep a civil tongue, I stood abruptly and stalked out of the reception hall, my silk skirt fluttering around my feet, my consorts trailing behind me.

I would do what had to be done to stop the Shadow King. To protect my people. To protect my son.

But that didn't mean I had to like it.

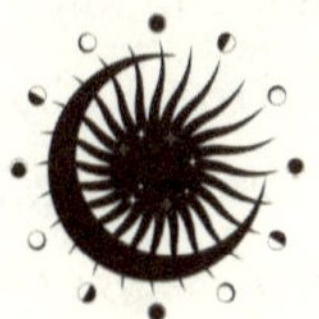

# 18

T HE MIDNIGHT AIR CRACKLED as I followed Isador up the hillside toward the ancient graveyard. My bare feet caught on dew-dampened grass—because apparently proper queens didn't need shoes for mysterious midnight rituals.

Isador had waved away my fury at the Stars emissary's none too subtle attempt to maneuver me into a bond, instead latching onto another part of the elementals' prophecy: *The last High Queen must seek counsel beyond mortality's veil...the departed queens shall rise at her calling, silver wisdom from beyond the grave guiding her hand.*

And so, our next lesson had been determined. A ritual to summon the ghosts of vampire queens past.

Moonlight spilled across weathered headstones, casting long shadows. My consorts fanned out behind me, Javier close enough that I could feel his heat. Through our bonds, I sensed their collective unease. None of them liked me leaving the wards of the manor house, especially not with a couple of relatively unfamiliar elementals roaming around the Moon Sanctuary, but none had challenged Isador when she announced we were heading out for tonight's lesson.

We reached a circular clearing at the heart of the graveyard, ringed by eight marble statues of the goddess in various forms and ages, each representing a different lunar phase. The ground beneath my feet hummed with old power, making my skin prickle.

In the new moon position stood a statue of Selene as a child, her marble form barely visible in the darkness, small hands raised in what could be either surrender or defense. Something in her posture—the tension in her shoulders or the wariness in her stance—made it seem like she was ready to run away.

The waxing crescent depicted her as a young woman, half her face obscured by a cloak, one foot positioned as though preparing to slip away and hide.

The first quarter showed her with child, her stone hands cradling a swollen belly, her face a complex blend of fear and fierce protectiveness. I felt a phantom ache in my womb, remembering those months with Micah growing inside me, terrified of what the world might do to him.

The waxing gibbous portrayed Selene in a moment of quiet power. Her marble hands were outstretched, as if conducting unseen energies that rippled through the stone itself. Silver threads of moonlight seemed woven into her hair, and her eyes held a knowing that transcended mortal concerns.

The full moon statue dominated the circle—Selene at the height of her power, nude and unashamed, arms spread wide as though embracing the vastness of her true nature. Silver veins ran through the marble, catching moonlight in a way that made her seem almost alive.

The waning gibbous depicted her making a sacrifice, offering something precious with reluctant hands. The last quarter showed her between worlds, one foot planted firmly in the physical realm while the other seemed to dissolve into rippling stone. And finally, the waning crescent portrayed her return—changed, marked by her journey, but carrying a quiet determination in eyes that had witnessed worlds beyond mortal understanding.

I stared at the progression, a strange vertigo sweeping through me.

"Consorts must remain outside the circle," Isador said, her voice cutting through the still night. She passed between two statues and beckoned me to join her with an outstretched hand. "Every High Queen who came before you is buried in this sacred ground." She paused, then added with deliberate weight, "Except, of course, your mother."

The reminder of my mom's missing body sent a familiar ache through my chest. Weighed down by that reminder, I followed as bade, coming to stand beside Isador.

At the center of the circle lay a small pool of still water, maybe three feet across. Its surface was untouched by even the gentlest breeze, a perfect mirror reflecting both the nearly full moon above and my face below.

"What exactly are we doing out here?" I asked, focusing on the task rather than on old wounds.

Isador's smile was sharp in the darkness. "Teaching you to listen." She gestured to the ground. "Sit."

I eyed the dew-soaked grass, hesitating for only a moment before lowering myself to the ground, hyper-aware of the ancient queens buried beneath us. The power in the earth pulsed, like a heartbeat just slightly out of sync with my own.

"Close your eyes," Isador instructed, slowly pacing around the pool. "Reach for the bonds you share with your consorts, but don't pull on them. Just *feel* them. Acknowledge them and set them aside. They are not our focus this night."

I did as instructed. At first, all I sensed was the damp chill seeping through my leggings, but I pushed that aside, inconsequential. Four bright threads of connection lit up my awareness. Javier's was like touching a live wire, electric and protective. Bastian's felt wild and untamed, crackling with energy that could never be fully contained. Ash's steady presence reminded me of ancient stone, weathered but unbreakable. Thane was an ocean, deep, endless, eternal.

Another cord, faint and stretching into the distance. Gavin. I couldn't sense much of him other than that he was still alive, and even that tenuous connection provided comfort, though his absence ached like a phantom limb.

"Good," Isador murmured. "Now reach deeper. Past the bonds, past your own power. Feel the earth beneath you, the memories in these stones, in your blood."

Taking a deep breath, I sank my awareness into the ground like roots seeking water. At first, there was only darkness.

But then, *something*.

Like tuning into a distant radio station, voices began to whisper at the edges of my awareness. Not just voices—emotions, memories, fragments of lives. The power thrumming through the earth wasn't just magic, but the collected essence of generations of queens.

Unlike the blinding surge that had nearly shattered me in the Selenarium, this power rose slowly like the tide, each pulse bringing new awareness rather than drowning me. The ritual chamber had forced power into me, but here, the magic recognized something within me, answering a call I hadn't consciously made.

My breath caught as the first clear image formed: a woman with silver-streaked hair standing exactly where I sat, her face lifted to a blood moon. The vision shifted to another queen weeping over a fallen consort, her grief so raw it made my chest ache. More images followed, faster now—centuries of triumphs and sacrifices spinning past.

"Focus," Isador's voice cut through the chaos. "Don't let the memories overwhelm you. You're not here to absorb their existence, but to request their guidance and to learn from their experience."

I clenched my jaw and tried to steady myself, to find some anchor point in the flood. I opened my eyes, focusing on the reflection of the moon in the pool. Throughout the clearing, the moonlight began to bend, streaming around the statues, weaving into something tangible. The clearing grew thick with power.

Through our bonds, I felt my consorts' alarm spike. Javier lunged forward, but the woven moonlight proved to be an impenetrable barrier. The others paced, seeking a way through.

"Isador? Is this what's supposed to happen?"

But when I searched for her within the statue circle, I found the clearing was no longer empty. Spirits crowded the space, dozens of women, their opalescent forms glowing in the strange, concentrated moonlight. Queens from every era of vampire history. I searched for Isador among them, finally finding her on the opposite side of the pool, staring around with widened eyes.

At all the queens who were staring at *me*.

My heart thundered against my ribs as the spirits watched me, waiting. But for what? For me?

"Isador?" I asked, my voice resonant and ethereal. "What do I do?"

But before she could respond, the reflection of the moon in the pool warped, the water beginning to swirl, the distorted image of the moon spreading through the water until it looked like liquid mercury.

"What's happening?" I whispered.

"I don't know," Isador said, her voice hushed. "This is unprecedented."

But I barely heard her. Because there, emerging from the swirling pool of liquid moonlight, was a figure so insubstantial I almost didn't recognize her. Unlike the clear manifestations of the other spirits, she appeared more like smoke given form. Veris had scattered her ashes to the wind, leaving her nothing to anchor to, yet somehow, she was here.

"Mom," I whispered, the word catching in my throat.

Her presence hit me harder than any physical blow. Memories I'd buried beneath years of survival instincts surfaced—her fingers combing through my hair while humming lullabies, the scent of herbs that lingered on her after she spent time in the garden, the way her eyes crinkled when she smiled.

The question burned in my chest: Did you know what would happen to me? Did you see the cold nights, the hunger, the hands that would touch me when I had nothing left to bargain with?

"My shining girl," she whispered, her voice carrying on the wind. "I'm so sorry."

I wanted to scream at her, to demand answers for every scar I'd earned in her absence. Instead, I reached for her with trembling fingers. "I needed you," I managed, the words raw and inadequate for the ocean of loss between us.

The moonlight pulsed brighter, and I felt something stirring beneath my feet. It rose through me like sap through a tree, filling every cell with ancient power. My skin felt translucent, the light literally shining through me.

"Mom," I repeated, reaching for her ghostly form. But when our fingers should have touched, she pulled back, her expression turning from love to urgency.

"There isn't time," she said. "The shadow comes, and you're not ready. Not yet."

"What do you mean?" I asked, fighting to stay upright as more power poured into me. "Please, tell me what to do!"

Her form flickered like a fragile flame. "Trust your instincts," she said, each word heavy with prophecy. "Trust what you are becoming. Blood remembers, even if you don't."

The moonlight wasn't just bending toward me anymore; it was part of me, as natural as my own heartbeat.

"My shining girl," my mom repeated. "The truth lives within you. Remember."

The words triggered something deep inside me, like a key turning in a lock I hadn't known existed. The power surged higher, and I cried out as silver light exploded from my skin in waves.

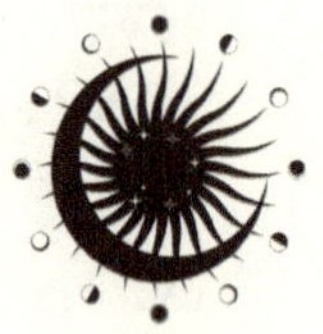

# 19

I STOOD IN AN ancient forest clearing beneath a blood-red moon. The ground beneath my bare feet felt raw, alive with memory that both was and wasn't mine. Bodies littered the earth—human and something other—while survivors ringed a central point, their skin marked with grime, open wounds, and dried blood. The air itself was saturated with power that burned my lungs.

"*The truth lives within you. Remember.*" My mother's voice whispered through me, as integral a part of me as my own heartbeat. The words settled into my bones as a smoky darkness poured from a tear in reality—not just shadow, but something that consumed light itself.

Creatures with too many limbs and eyes that burned with hunger spilled forth, led by a presence that made my soul recoil. Not fully formed, more concept than being. Hunger given form. Malice made manifest.

I wanted to run, but I found myself rooted in place. Three luminous figures faced the tide of darkness—one shining like captured moonlight, one blazing like the sun, one glowing with the gentle radiance of scattered stars. Their combined light merged, flaring so brightly it hurt to look directly at them. Yet I couldn't turn away. They moved among a gathered crowd, their chosen people. They touched the foreheads of their chosen, who fell to their knees as divine power transformed them.

The silvery figure's touch left crescent marks that shimmered beneath the skin of her chosen, covering one side of their faces. The golden one's touch ignited a primal fire, something that could shift and change within its host. The third's touch called forth the elements and bound them to her chosen's will.

My breath caught as understanding dawned. I was witnessing the birth of the three immortal races. The first vampires rose with silver light coursing through their veins. The first shifters roared as golden power reshaped their flesh. The first elementals wove the very air into protective barriers, shielding them all from the corruptive shadow.

The scene blurred, time accelerating.

The combined forces drove back the shadow, sealing the breach with magic that cost many lives. The three radiant figures grew dimmer, giving more and more of their divine essence to their chosen, each sacrificing something essential to secure victory.

"*Remember*," my mother's voice echoed again as the scene shifted.

A grand chamber materialized around me, filled with representatives from all three Houses. Peace, briefly, before the shadow crept in, bringing arguments and accusations. A shifter losing control, transforming into something monstrous that tore through vampires and elementals alike. More shifters following suit, consumed by mindless bloodlust that turned their eyes and hearts black.

A vampire and an elemental stood together, hands joined as they wove moonlight and starlight into a pattern that resonated within my blood. The curse. The reason for the war between vampires and shifters. The reason Veris had killed my family. The magic wrapped around the shifters, settling into their blood, their bones, their souls.

The curse wasn't a punishment but a protection—for the shifters as much as for everyone else. Their golden light had been tainted by the shadow, and they were losing themselves to the corruption. Muting their power also stifled the shadow's hold. But it couldn't stamp it out altogether.

A heaviness settled in my chest. So much of what I'd been taught was incomplete, history reshaped by those who survived to tell it.

"*Remember.*" The vision shifted again.

The Moon Sanctuary materialized, centuries ago but recognizable in its bones. A queen with my mother's eyes stood in the Selenarium, surrounded by seven kneeling consorts, channeling so much power that moonlight broke through her skin like light through the holes of a sieve. It was too much. It was consuming her and her consorts. But it had to be done.

Beyond the sanctuary walls, the shadow had gathered once more, toxic and corrosive, assaulting the barrier between worlds. She and her consorts gave their lives to buy time for the next High Queen—my mother—to find a way to defeat the shadow once and for all.

"*Remember.*" Another shift.

The new scene was so familiar it made my heart weep. The night of the massacre. My mom kneeling before my sister and me, her eyes filled with terrible knowledge and love so fierce it burned.

Tears streamed down my face—not just for what had been lost, but for the burden of being the one who remained. For the weight of living when so many had died. The vision offered no comfort, only shifting again while my heart shattered.

*"Remember."*

The final scene emerged from a swirling mist. Seven thrones in a circle, five occupied by shadowy figures I recognized as my consorts, two empty. Beyond them loomed a presence of such immense hunger that I recoiled instinctively. A silver cord stretched from my heart to each occupied throne, then split, branching out to shield us in a complex weave. But the empty seats created gaps in the protective sphere—gaps through which darkness seeped like poison.

"You must fill the seats. Complete the circle," my mother said, suddenly beside me. "Choose correctly, and you can end this once and for all. Choose wrong, and the barrier will fall, and the shadow will consume the world."

"What does that *mean*?" I asked desperately. "Fill the seats? With who? Choose *who*? How do I know who to choose?"

My mom pointed to one of the empty thrones, this one made of some otherworldly material that swirled with a cosmic nebula. "That seat is for an elemental. I don't know who." She pointed to the other empty throne, seemingly made of iridescent mist. "This one belongs to one who was once of this world, but no longer is."

"What—" I looked from her to the thrones and back. "What does *that* mean?"

She offered me a sad smile, an apology. "I wish I could tell you more, but that's all I know. I'm sorry."

The vision began to dissolve as my mother's form grew more transparent. I lunged forward, trying to grasp her fading essence, and though the scene continued to fade, she remained.

She raised a transparent hand to the side of my face, her touch tingling. "I'm so sorry, my shining girl. The moment you were born, I knew. You shone so brightly. You were the one we had been waiting for. The culmination of so much time and power and sacrifice. The return of what once was."

Her form faded, consumed by the moonlight that had birthed the vision.

"Mom, wait!" I cried, my voice breaking as I reached for her desperately. "I don't understand! Please—"

The moonlight intensified until it was blinding, washing away the last fragments of my mom and the vision.

"*Remember*," she whispered one final time.

Everything went white.

When my vision cleared, I knelt by the pool in the center of the circle, chest heaving, dazed by the whirlwind vision and wrung out from channeling all that power.

Isador stared at me from across the pool, her composure shattered. "The past queens have never—" she began, then stopped herself, swallowing whatever revelation had nearly escaped. "What did you see? What did they show you?"

But before I could respond, my consorts broke through the moonlight barrier as it dissipated and converged around me. Javier dropped to his knees in front of me, his hands frantic as they moved over me, checking me for harm. Thane knelt on my left, Ash on my right, both capturing a hand, weaving their fingers through mine. Bastian settled behind me, those gold-dusted black wings he had revealed the other night flaring out, then wrapping around us all even as his arms curled around my middle.

Their combined touch grounded me, pulling me back from a precipice I hadn't realized I'd been teetering on. And their blood, when it touched my tongue, revived me, reminding me I wasn't just a conduit for power. That I wasn't just a queen. But that I was a woman—their woman—and I was loved.

# 20

I COULDN'T SLEEP. My body hummed with residual magic, making rest impossible.

Not so for my consorts. Even the vampires who rarely slept were out cold after feeding me so thoroughly in the graveyard. My need had been bottomless, my thirst seemingly unquenchable. I had drained them, leaving them ready to collapse. Now, Javier's arm was draped across my waist, his fingers twitching against my skin. Bastian radiated heat against my back, and Ash and Thane bracketed us. My guys. My immortals. My consorts. They should have been enough to anchor me. To make me feel safe.

And yet...

Every time I closed my eyes, I saw them—the ancient queens. My mother. The shadow that wanted to consume us all. The way Isador had stared at me.

The look in Isador's eyes—part fear, part awe—had lodged inside me like splinters. I needed to speak with her. Needed her to explain what had happened out there. But by the time I had emerged from within the shelter of Bastian's wings, replenished, she had already gone, and with her, any chance of rest. I couldn't sleep with such a massive WTF hanging over my head.

I stared up at the carved ceiling. I had to complete my harem—bind an elemental and someone else. I'd understood that much from the vision. Oh, and if I chose the wrong people, we were all doomed. I understood that, too.

A familiar electric tingle brushed my awareness. The fine hairs along my arms stood on end, letting me know I had a ghostly visitor. I raised my head and peered around the dark bedroom.

Wes hovered by the window, his ethereal form appearing more substantial than usual in the light of the nearly full moon. Unlike the overwhelming presence of the ghosts of the ancient queens, he was familiar, comforting—a piece of my past that had followed me into this unexpected future.

I extracted myself from the tangle of immortal limbs. Javier's fingers tightened on my hip, his protective instincts surging even in sleep. "I'll be right back," I whispered, managing to wriggle out without disrupting any of them further, and pulled a T-shirt over my head. From the faintly sweet, woodsy scent, it was Bastian's.

Wes didn't turn as I approached, his attention fixed on the hillside graveyard. "Can't sleep, firefly?" he asked softly, his voice carrying that old soul quality that had first drawn me to him when we were little more than kids.

"Too loud in my head," I admitted, studying his profile. "I don't know how to make sense of what happened out there."

"You could try talking about it," Wes suggested. "Might make things a little quieter inside your head if you let them out."

I gave him a look he used to receive often, whenever he would give me a hard time about bottling everything up inside.

Wes smiled faintly, moonlight streaming through his translucent form. "You've always guarded your thoughts so carefully. Like if you let the wrong ones out, even for a moment, it'd be *the end of the world*."

I snorted softly. "Wouldn't it have been?" Talking to him like this unwound something in my chest, a knot I'd been carrying for decades. "It was safer that way," I admitted. "Back then, anyway. To be quiet. Small. Made it easier to hide."

"And now?" he asked, his ghostly fingers hovering near mine, the familiar tingle of his presence raising goosebumps along my arm.

I looked back at the bed where my consorts slept; four powerful immortals bound to me by blood and magic and something deeper I still couldn't fully name. Fate, perhaps.

"Now, I don't know how to be anything but small," I whispered, my fingers finding Wes's pendant through the fabric of Bastian's shirt. The tree of life felt warm against my skin. "I spent twenty years making myself invisible, and suddenly everyone expects me to be enormous."

"The queens," Wes said, his gaze drifting toward the window, the garden, the graveyard beyond. "They saw something in you tonight. Something that frightened even Isador."

I nodded, my fingers finding my mother's ring, twisting it around and around. Another inheritance I hadn't earned and didn't understand.

"They looked at me like—I don't even know. Like I've done something—anything—to deserve their respect. Something beyond just *being* Diana's daughter. The one *who lived*."

Wes's form shimmered, moonlight passing through him in waves that distorted his edges. "You were always more than just someone's daughter, Soph."

Movement caught my eye in the garden below. A lone figure passed between the raised beds. Even from this distance, I recognized the elemental prince, Reiji. He wore dark clothes that accentuated his tall frame, his long hair pulled back, gleaming silver in the moonlight as he bent to examine something in the nearest bed.

"Speaking of hidden natures," Wes murmured, following my gaze. "He's been watching you since he arrived. From a distance. Like a creeper."

I raised an eyebrow. "Probably trying to figure out how to slither his way into my harem."

Wes tilted his head, his ghostly form shimmering slightly. "Yes, and...I think it's more complicated than that. He's calculating but also curious."

"And the 'guard'—Ren?" I asked. Because not for one second did I believe she wasn't more than either of them claimed. "What does he say to her when they're alone?"

Wes frowned thoughtfully. "Not much. She's quiet, standoffish, almost disapproving. Which seems to bother him. It's a strange dynamic. She thinks he's wasting his time here, that the House of the Moon is dying, but he seems to believe there's something here worth fighting for."

I studied Reiji as he moved through the garden, his fingers brushing stalks and leaves with unexpected gentleness. "Maybe I judged him too harshly," I admitted, surprised by the regret in my voice. "Something about his presumption just set me off."

"First impressions are rarely the whole story," Wes observed, his voice softening. "You, of all people, should know that."

My lips curved into a reluctant smile. "I *am* supposed to bind an elemental consort. What if he *is* the one?"

"Only one way to find out," Wes said.

I watched Reiji kneel beside a patch of moonflowers, his expression shifting to something less guarded, almost reverent as he cupped one of the blooms in his palm.

I narrowed my eyes. "What if this is a scheme?" I asked, my voice barely audible. "He's down there, in perfect view of *my* window, lingering in *my* herb garden, fondling *my* moonflowers... What if he's trying to lure me out to—"

"To have his way with you?" Wes scoffed and glanced behind us at the four deadly immortals slumbering in my bed. "Soph, they would tear him apart in a heartbeat if he so much as looked at you wrong." He bumped me with his shoulder, sending cool tingles cascading down my arm. "What if you're right? What if he *is* trying to lure you down there—to talk? What if you discover he *is* the Star consort? Or just an ally?"

I glanced at Wes, suddenly feeling like the uncertain girl I'd been when we first met. "When did you get so wise?"

He laughed under his breath. "Death offers perspective," he said simply. "And I've had years to watch you build walls that keep out friends as effectively as enemies."

His words settled in my chest like stones dropped in still water, rippling outward with uncomfortable truth. I'd survived by keeping people at a distance. Even now, even with my consorts, I struggled to lower my guard completely.

I returned my gaze to Reiji, who was now sitting on a stone bench, his head tilted back to take in the night sky, looking surprisingly vulnerable. Without the political posturing and calculated charm, he seemed almost...human.

"I should talk to him," I said, surprising myself with the decision.

Wes smiled, that crooked half-smile that had always made my heart skip. "Yeah," he agreed simply. "You should."

# 21

T HE HERB GARDEN FELT different in this liminal hour—not quite night, not quite dawn. Apparently, I liked it because I kept finding myself walking the garden's stone paths in my robe in the predawn hour.

Reiji didn't look up as I approached where he knelt by a raised bed, but his movements shifted—becoming more deliberate. Up close, I could see the aristocratic planes of his face softened by the dim light, the careful precision in his shadowed eyes. A silver chain glinted at his throat, disappearing beneath his collar. The moonlight caught in his long hair, the strands pulled back loosely, highlighting silver undertones I hadn't noticed during our formal meeting.

Wes drifted beside me, his presence crackling against my skin.

"Your aura shifts when spirits are near," Reiji said quietly, his fingers arranging sprigs of something fragrant into neat bundles with practiced grace. He glanced up, his gaze sweeping past Wes's location without focusing on the ghost.

"You can sense him?" I asked, my curiosity overriding caution. "But not see him?"

Reiji shook his head, a half-smile playing at the corner of his lips. The expression softened his usually composed features, making him suddenly seem younger, less calculating. "Neither. I feel disturbances where the veil thins around you. Impressions of your ghost's presence, but not the being itself." He tilted his head, studying me with an intensity that made me more aware of my disheveled appearance in a T-shirt and robe despite the chill. "Your ghost watches over you with great devotion. Strong attachments leave deeper impressions in the fabric between worlds."

"He was important to me," I said, barely above a whisper. "He still is, even though he's gone." I touched my pendant through the T-shirt, aware of how Reiji's gaze followed the movement. "He's one of the few connections I have to who I was before all this."

"Before you became the High Queen," Reiji said quietly, his eyes holding mine. Something in them softened when I didn't look away. "Though I imagine you were always meant for this role, even when hidden away. The stars have patterns that go unnoticed until we learn to see them." He returned to his herb gathering.

"You're out here awfully late...or early, depending on your perspective," I said. "Couldn't sleep?"

Reiji's hands paused, just briefly enough that someone less observant might have missed it. A smile touched his lips that reached his eyes this time. "I was hoping we might speak. Somewhere away from politics and protocols." He gave a self-deprecating shrug. "I thought perhaps we got off on the wrong foot yesterday."

I nodded once, appreciating his candor. "Your proposal wasn't exactly subtle."

He blew out a breath and sat back on his heels. "I've been told diplomacy isn't my strong suit. I tend to be too direct. It puts people off."

I narrowed my eyes at him, testing his apparent sincerity. "Is that what you're doing out here at dawn? Being direct?"

He studied me for a long moment, then gestured to the space beside him. "I'm trying to be authentic. There's a difference." He returned to gathering herbs, his movements fluid and practiced. "Not everything is political maneuvering, though I understand why you'd think so."

I considered his words for a long moment. "What are you gathering?" I asked, sitting on the edge of the raised bed near him, tucking my hands into the pockets of my robe.

"Mostly protection herbs." He lifted a sprig to his nose, inhaling deeply before adding it to his bundle. "Rosemary for clarity, sage for purification." He glanced at me, his expression thoughtful. "Does your ghost approve of our conversation, I wonder?"

I glanced at Wes, who shrugged, his spectral features suspicious. "He's reserving judgment," I shared.

Reiji rose to his feet in one fluid motion. He stepped closer, close enough that I could catch his scent beneath the herbs—something like amber and warm spices, with a hint of something celestial, like stardust. "And you?" he asked, staring down at me.

"Still deciding," I said, my voice steadier than I felt.

He held a hand out to me. "Would you walk with me?"

Hesitating only for a moment, I placed my hand in his. As I stood, he tucked my hand into the crook of his arm, like we were setting out for a good old-fashioned stroll like a couple in a Jane Austen novel. "I believe we face a common enemy far greater than the petty rivalries between our

Houses, and I believe you may be the only one who can unite us against it."

My eyebrows rose. Finally, we were getting to the point. "And your proposal yesterday? Was that just political calculation?"

"Partially," he admitted with surprising honesty. "The prophecies speak of a star-born consort, and I am a prince of my House. It seemed beneficial for all." His expression shifted to something more vulnerable. "But there was more to it than duty. Something about you calls to me in ways I don't fully understand."

Before I could respond, a figure emerged from the shadows of the garden path, and I tensed as I recognized Ren, Reiji's supposed guard. Her dark eyes assessed the scene with clear suspicion, her stance seemingly casual but ready for action.

"Reiji," she said, her voice carrying an edge beneath its deference. "I've been looking for you."

Reiji straightened, his open expression closing like a book snapped shut. "Thank you, Ren. I was just gathering herbs for the morning ritual."

Something in their exchange felt off—a current of tension that belied their supposed roles. Ren's eyes flicked to me, then back to Reiji, her gaze guarded.

"High Queen," she acknowledged with a shallow bow that seemed purely performative.

I felt a surge of protective energy through my bonds—my consorts awakening to my absence. Javier's presence grew stronger, moving through the house with vampiric speed.

"We have company," Reiji said, already stepping away. "Your Prime Consort approaches." He handed me the herb bundle he'd so carefully prepared. "For protection," he said, his voice carrying a weight that hadn't been there moments before. "You may need it sooner than you think."

Ren's eyes narrowed at the exchange, her attention fixed on the bundle in my hands with an intensity that felt almost predatory. She placed a hand on Reiji's arm, guiding him away with subtle urgency.

As they retreated down the path, Reiji glanced back once, his expression unreadable in the growing dawn light. I looked down at the herb bundle in my hand, wrapped in a silver thread that caught the rising sunlight. The scent was complex—rosemary and sage, yes, but something else underneath. Something like starlight made tangible. Something that whispered of ancient knowledge.

Reiji slipped out of view around a bend, but Ren lingered a moment longer, her dark eyes meeting mine with an unexpected intensity. Unlike Reiji's calculated charm, her gaze held something raw and genuine—a silent assessment that went deeper than mere appraisal. Her lips parted slightly like she wanted to say something else, something unrelated to her role as guard, before she seemed to think better of it and turned away.

Reiji called her name, and the connection snapped as she stepped out of sight.

The moment left me with a strange feeling of recognition, as though we'd met before in some forgotten life. Even as she disappeared down the path, I felt the lingering weight of her attention like a physical touch against my skin.

"Luna?" Javier's voice carried from the kitchen doorway, sleep-rough but alert.

I stared down the path where Reiji and Ren had disappeared, an inexplicable chill washing over me.

"Everything all right?" Javier asked as he reached me, his hand settling at the small of my back, his thumb smoothing over my spine as his eyes tracked the direction of my gaze.

"I don't know," I whispered, the herb bundle suddenly feeling like both a gift and a warning in my hands.

# 22

THE ANCIENT LEATHER-BOUND TOME felt like a betrayal in my hands. After years of finding safety in books and building a life among their predictable pages and sturdy bindings, this one had failed me, like so many of the others stacked on the coffee table.

I could feel my consorts' eyes on me. Javier stood by the door, deadly and alert, his hawkish gaze missing nothing. Bastian leaned against a bookcase within my line of sight, periodically glancing my way as he leafed through book after book, the barely leashed power simmering beneath his skin, making his tattoos gleam with subtle golden light. Since letting the beast out the other night, that primal part of him always seemed to be right beneath the surface, waiting to come out.

Behind me, Ash and Thane kept watch, ready to shield me with their bodies or whisk me away to safety—whatever the situation required.

Their presence was a steady calm, balancing the sense of flailing tension that seemed to be unraveling around Isador. She hadn't had many answers about what happened with the queens in the graveyard, merely more questions. But at least she had a direction. And—and I meant this with my whole heart—*at least* that direction didn't involve another ritual.

Yet.

Instead, it relied on something I was much more comfortable with: research.

"Here," Isador said, pushing an open book across the coffee table toward me and turning it sideways. The pages were yellowed by age and worn around the edges. Her elegant finger pointed to a passage written in what looked disturbingly like dried blood. "This account suggests Queen Maeve was able to tap into Selene's divine power through ritual."

Her voice still carried the self-assurance afforded to her by centuries of queenly practice and experience as a high-ranking queen within the House of the Moon, though something had changed between us. Not respect, exactly. I hadn't earned that. But there was a level of genuine deference where she had only gone through the motions before. She hadn't called me "child" once since the graveyard ritual, so that was something.

"Fourteen days of fasting, starting on the new moon and ending on the full moon, daily *communions* with a full harem of seven..." She met my eyes, her copper irises gleaming. "Nothing like what you did."

"Maybe I just got lucky," I suggested halfheartedly. The words felt hollow even to me. Nothing about that night had felt like luck; it had felt like reading a book written in a language I'd never learned but could somehow understand fluently.

Isador's laugh was sharp and humorless. "Luck doesn't bend moonlight to its will, Sophie. *Luck* doesn't pull a ghost back from beyond the veil. And *luck* doesn't allow an untrained vampire queen to channel the power of the goddess herself."

She pulled another book from the stack, this one bound in something that looked suspiciously like a prime example of anthropodermic bibliopegy—a book bound in human skin, for those outside the rare book world. I'd only seen one example of the macabre practice before, and I'd been as disturbed then as I was now. I fought the urge to recoil.

"Every recorded instance of a queen channeling divine power required preparation. Ritual. Control." Isador's eyes met mine, unwavering. "Except you." Her brow furrowed. "What's wrong? Why are you making that face?"

I forced myself to swallow, fighting the urge to gag. "Where did that book come from?"

Isador looked completely baffled. She glanced toward the shelves in the back corner of the study. "Why?"

"The binding isn't animal leather," I said, my throat tightening. "It's human skin."

Isador's expression didn't change, which somehow made it worse. "Yes, and?"

The only other time I'd encountered an anthropodermic book—a medical text from the 1800s that the university kept under glass—I'd handled it with gloves and proper distance. Now, with the heightened senses awakened by my consorts' blood, I could detect subtle differences in the scent, even see the faint patterns of pores and wrinkles across the surface. And was that a *scar*?

This had been a *person*. They had lived. They had been someone's child. And now they were the muted brown binding on a book.

"And that doesn't bother you?" I asked Isador, unable to keep the edge from my voice.

She tilted her head, studying me with the curious look of someone observing an unusual creature. "This book is nearly two thousand years old, Sophie. The queen who donated her skin for its binding did so willingly after her last consort died—a final sacrifice to pass on her knowledge and experience before she lost her will to live. Binding the book in her flesh guaranteed that queens possessing the book for generations to come would not only have access to the knowledge she wrote down, but the wisdom and guidance of her spirit anchored to the book."

At her words, I peered around the study, wondering where the queen in question was at this moment. Not here with us, that much was clear. Wes was currently the only ghost braving the residual wards my mother had left on the High Queen's chambers, and he did so from the relative safety of the bedroom, which was apparently far less repellent to spirits than the study, where she had centered her final protections.

A sudden surge of power rippled through the wards—the Moon Sanctuary's ancient wards, not those additional protections placed on these rooms three decades ago—making my teeth ache as foreign magic pressed against our defenses. The windows rattled in their frames, and the acrid scent of burning magic filled my nostrils, like ozone, but fouler, with undertones of rot.

My consorts snapped to attention.

"Someone's probing the wards," Isador said, easing the ancient book shut. Her eyes fixed on the windows where the cloudy afternoon sky seemed to warp, like I was viewing it through a mirage of heatwaves.

The door burst open with such force that it slammed against the wall, and Reiji appeared on the threshold, his normally composed features taut with urgency. Before he could fully enter, Javier was there, his preternatural speed carrying him across the room. His hand shot out, pinning the elemental against the doorframe by his throat. The princely veneer stripped away instantly, revealing something fiercer beneath as Reiji met Javier's hold with unexpected dignity, making no move to struggle against the iron grip.

Through our bond, I felt centuries of hard-earned suspicion flowing from Javier—the same instincts that had kept my mom alive through countless betrayals. His voice carried that particular softness that invariably preceded violence. "Convenient timing, prince. You appear just as our defenses are compromised."

Despite his precarious position, Reiji's eyes blazed with urgent purpose, his gaze moving past Javier to find me.

"Someone is launching coordinated strikes against your wards," he said, his voice strained but steady despite the pressure against his throat. "The old wards. Selene's wards."

A second tremor rolled through the sanctuary, this one stronger than the first.

"My guard—Ren—" he managed, his face reddening from Javier's grip. "She's missing. I can't find her anywhere."

The implication hung in the air like a blade about to fall. I remembered her intense scrutiny of my herb bundle earlier, the predatory assessment in her eyes.

Outside in the corridor, I could hear shouts and running footsteps, vampires moving with urgent purpose. Someone called for weapons. Another voice shouted orders about defending the eastern perimeter.

Bastian pushed away from the bookcase, the golden light beneath his tattoos brightening as the beast within him stirred. "How do we know you're not part of this?"

"You don't," Reiji admitted, his stark honesty unexpected. His gaze shifted back to me, steady even as he struggled for breath. "But I swear on the stars themselves, I came here seeking an alliance against the darkness, not to bring it to your doorstep."

"Let him go," I said to Javier, my voice tight with urgency.

Javier released Reiji reluctantly, his body still positioned between us, coiled and ready to strike at the slightest provocation.

The study shuddered around us as another wave of power crashed against the sanctuary's defenses. Somewhere in the distance, glass shattered, and someone screamed.

Micah's face flashed in my mind—my son, wherever he was in the Moon Sanctuary right now, unaware of the incredible danger closing in around us. My heart seized with absolute terror.

"We'll get him," Ash said as he and Thane slipped out through the doorway, navigating past frantic vampires stacking furniture against windows and distributing crystalline grenades that glowed with otherworldly power.

Wes's form flickered at the edge of my awareness, his ethereal energy struggling against whatever interference disrupted the ghostly plane. His features contracted with effort, his mouth moving urgently.

"Sophie—" His voice sounded distorted, like a radio station caught between frequencies. "They're trying to—" Static consumed his warning, his form dispersing like smoke in a strong wind, leaving nothing but cold, empty air where he had stood.

My heart lurched at his disappearance. In the few weeks since discovering his ghost, I'd grown accustomed to his presence, a comforting constant amid the chaos my life had become. Losing him again, even temporarily, carved a hollow space in my chest that felt painfully familiar—that same emptiness I'd carried for years after his death.

The ground trembled beneath our feet as another wave of power crashed against the wards. Books tumbled from shelves, pages fluttering like startled birds. The ancient chandelier swayed ominously overhead, chains clanging. A patrol of vampires rushed past the open door, their faces grim with battle-readiness.

"Come," Isador said, striding toward the doorway. "To the Selenarium. Now."

Javier's hand settled at the small of my back. His fingers pressed against my spine, not guiding but supporting.

We moved through the corridors with urgent purpose, Javier and Bastian flanking me while Isador led us toward the secret staircase. Reiji followed close behind, his eyes constantly scanning our surroundings. Vampires sprinted past us, carrying weapons or supplies, some calling out status reports about parts of the sanctuary.

The hidden passage in the floor opened at Isador's touch, the marble dissolving to reveal the spiraling stone staircase leading down into darkness. Silver sigils flared to life along the curved wall, their pulsing light casting strange shadows across our faces, transforming familiar features into something otherworldly.

"Only those accepted by the goddess may enter the chamber at the bottom," Isador told Reiji, her voice carrying a note of solemn warning. "Queens and their bound consorts."

A thread of panic wove through me again. "What about Micah?" The thought of my son being barred from safety while the sanctuary crumbled around him sent ice through my veins.

"Your son will be granted passage," Isador assured me, her copper eyes softening. "He carries your blood. The goddess always recognizes her own."

Reiji's face betrayed nothing at this exchange, but something in his eyes shifted, a subtle assessment recalibrating what he knew—or what he thought he knew—about me and my son. "I'm coming with you," Reiji said, lifting his chin slightly. "At least down the stairs. If I can't cross the threshold, so be it."

"You *won't* be able to cross," Isador snapped.

A shudder rippled through the sanctuary, stronger than before. The sound of breaking stone echoed from somewhere above us.

"It doesn't matter," I said, my voice tight with urgency. "Let's go!"

We hurried down the stairs, each step taking us deeper into the sanctuary's heart. The silver sigils brightened as I passed. The air grew heavier with each step, charged with ancient power and the promise of divine secrets.

I stepped through the archway beyond the base of the stairs without hesitation, and Isador, Bastian, and Javier filed in behind me. I spun around at Reiji's sharp intake of breath. He stood frozen at the threshold, one hand raised against an invisible barrier. Silver light rippled from the archway where his palm pressed against it, like disturbed water reflecting moonlight.

I caught the flicker of disappointment—or perhaps resignation—in his eyes. "I'll stand guard from here," he vowed.

Javier's hand pressed gently at my back, his touch drawing me back to the immediate danger.

I turned away from Reiji reluctantly and took in the chamber fully. The crystalline sphere at the apex of the domed ceiling glowed crimson, like a captured blood moon. The red sigils marking the moon phases in a large circle on the stone floor pulsed in time with my heartbeat.

Urgent voices and echoing footsteps drew my attention back to the archway. Ash passed through, followed by Micah, then Thane. Micah's eyes widened at the sight of me, relief and confusion warring in his expression.

I crossed to him quickly, pulling him into a tight hug. "Are you okay?" I asked, pulling away and scanning him for any sign of injury.

He nodded, his eyes wide as he took in our surroundings. "What's happening? What is this place?"

"The Selenarium," I explained, keeping my voice steady despite the chaos around us. "The safest place in the Moon Sanctuary."

The floor shook again, stone groaning under the assault. Even here, surrounded by the strongest, oldest wards, I could feel the malevolent force pushing against the edges of our defenses.

"Sophie!" Isador said. "You must act, now!"

# 23

"**S**TAY CLOSE TO THE wall," I told Micah, pointing toward the archway. If something went wrong in the ritual, at least that would give him a chance to flee. "And whatever happens, don't cross into the ritual circle."

Isador directed each of my consorts to their positions—Javier to the new moon sigil, Bastian to the full moon, Ash to the waxing gibbous, and Thane to the waning gibbous. The remaining phases—waxing and waning crescent, and first and third quarters—remained painfully empty. I felt those absences acutely, particularly the space where Gavin should have stood. The waxing crescent. I knew it without needing to be told.

In the back of my mind, I noticed a detail I hadn't before—there were eight lunar sigils in the ritual circle, even though the standard harem size was seven. But my gut told me all eight spots were supposed to be filled.

"What exactly are we doing?" I asked, centering myself beneath the crystal moon.

Isador's expression turned grave. "Connecting to the original warding magic laid down by Selene herself." She crossed the line of the sigil circle, entering the ritual space. "The wards are failing because they've been supported by the magic of individual queens for too long. They need to be reconnected to their source—to Selene. To her magic."

The implications settled heavily in my chest. Because as I'd shown in the graveyard, I could channel Selene's divine power.

Another assault against the wards sent tremors through the chamber. The crystal moon dimmed momentarily before flaring back to life.

Isador touched my arm, pressing a vial into my hand. I knew it was Gavin's blood tincture without having to look down. "This ritual requires *communion* to initiate the connection between you and the wards," she said, glancing at Micah. "Focus on the blood. Just a little. Just to initiate the ritual." She backed toward the edge of the circle. "The original wards will resist. They've grown wild over centuries of separation from their source. You must bend them to your will."

With those cryptic instructions, she stepped out of the ritual circle, retreating to join Micah near the archway. Their expressions were nearly identical, both tense with worry—versus Reiji's rapt attention from just beyond the archway. His eyes gleamed with barely contained fascination, tracking every movement of the ritual preparation.

Turning my back to them, I closed my eyes, centering myself as power began to build beneath my feet.

"Start with your Prime Consort," Isador called from the edge of the chamber. "Work your way around the circle."

I opened my eyes and moved toward Javier, his dark stare meeting mine with decades of devotion and carefully controlled fear. Through our bond, I felt his need to protect me from whatever was coming, even as he knew he couldn't shield me from this burden.

I took his hand in mine, expecting the usual ignition of heat and need. But something had shifted since our last *communion*. Or maybe it was simply knowing that my son was in the room with us. As I brought Javier's wrist to my lips, my teeth breaking skin with practiced ease, I found the desperate craving for physical connection oddly muted. The first taste of his blood, rich and familiar, filled me with warmth but not heat.

I drank slowly, taking just enough to feel his essence flowing through me before pulling away. When I offered my wrist in return, his teeth found my pulse with careful precision. The exchange carried none of our usual desperate passion, yet the connection felt deeper.

Silver light spiraled up from the sigil beneath his feet, drowning out the crimson glow, feeding into the crystal moon above.

The ritual pulled me forward, drawing me to the empty position where Gavin should have been. "I haven't forgotten you," I murmured as I unstoppered the vial of his blood tincture. I tilted it back, swallowing his essence, then held my wrist out, letting blood drip onto the floor where he should have stood.

The waxing crescent moon sigil flared silver, a beam of magic flowing toward the crystal moon just as it had happened at Javier's position.

"It's working," Isador called. "Keep going!"

I moved to Ash next, fighting the urge to lean into him as he extended his wrist. His blood carried centuries of vigilance, grief transformed into strength. When he took mine in return, I felt the weight of his restraint, how he channeled his deepest pain into protecting others.

The waxing gibbous sigil beneath his feet shifted to silver, and once again, a moonbeam of magic shot upward. The chamber's temperature dropped further as power surged between us, feeding into the crystal moon.

Bastian was next. Golden light writhed beneath the black of his tattoos as I approached, his beast close to the surface. I took his hand in both of mine, soothing the wild creature inside him with a gentle touch. His blood tasted of fields of wildflowers and babbling brooks sparkling with sunlight. When he took mine in return, I felt his beast finally calm.

Silver light threaded with strands of gold connected the full moon sigil beneath his feet to the crystal moon above, which pulsed faster as power built, sending patterns of light dancing across the chamber walls.

I moved to Thane, the last of my consorts, to finish the ritual. Through his blood, I glimpsed pathways between worlds, knowledge hiding in the spaces between heartbeats. And when he took my blood, the sigil beneath his feet flashed silver, and the crystal moon overhead flared blindingly bright.

The patterns on the floor spiraled up in columns of light, forming a complex lattice that stretched toward the ceiling. Yet the empty spaces in our circle throbbed with absence.

I returned to the center, kneeling beneath the crystal moon as its light washed over me in waves.

But something was wrong. The power built without direction, wild and unstable. The wards surrounding the Moon Sanctuary trembled under continued assault, absorbing trickles of our ritual's energy but unable to properly weave it into the existing ward structure.

"It's not working!" I called out, my voice echoing strangely through the charged air.

Isador stepped away from the wall, her copper eyes wide with alarm. "Bend the power to your will, Sophie!"

"The circle is incomplete." Reiji's voice carried from the archway, urgent and compelling. "The prophecy speaks of a star-born consort. I could be that for you. I could help strengthen the ritual."

My consorts tensed, unified in their rejection of his offer.

"Stay back," Javier warned, his voice deadly quiet.

But Reiji pressed his hand against the barrier, his voice carrying an edge of desperation. "The wards will fail without a full circle. Let me in—let me help you."

I shook my head. Even with him, it wouldn't be a full harem, so there was no point in binding him in haste.

Another tremor shook the sanctuary, stronger than any before. Dust rained from the ceiling as cracks appeared in the ancient stonework. Outside our protective circle, Micah pressed himself against the wall, the blood drained from his face.

"Mom!" he called out, using a name he had never spoken aloud to me. The sound of it sent a jolt through me, anchoring me to the physical world when the flow of magic threatened to sweep me away. I couldn't fail. I could *not*.

I glanced toward Reiji, seeing the naked hunger in his eyes as he watched the power flow through me. Whatever his offer might truly mean, this wasn't the moment to find out.

I reached out through my bonds with my consorts, drawing their energy toward me. Their power flowed through me like rivers to an ocean, filling spaces within me I hadn't known existed. The gaps remained, three empty positions in our circle where power should have flowed but didn't, but I was able to weave the flow of magic into a patch, mimicking the missing consorts. A poor stand-in. Barely functional, but if I shaped it just so...

The crystal moon's light shifted, concentrating into a narrower beam that struck me directly. Pain lanced through my body as raw power flooded my system, more than in the graveyard with the queens. More than I'd ever channeled before. It burned through my veins like liquid fire, seeking release.

I cried out, my back arching as the power threatened to tear me apart from within. Through our bonds, I felt my consorts' alarm spike.

"Mom!" Micah shouted.

"Stay where you are!" Isador commanded. "The flames will consume you!"

I couldn't speak, couldn't reassure him as the power built beyond what I could contain. My skin felt too small for what moved through me, ancient and raw. But the reminder that Micah was there anchored me, pulling me back from the edge of dissolution.

I raised my free hand toward the ceiling, toward the wards beyond, and released the gathered power in a controlled surge. Moonlight exploded outward from my palm, racing along invisible channels to the sanctuary's boundaries. Where it touched the failing wards, they flared to life, ancient patterns reactivating with renewed strength.

The chamber went dark and quiet as the power drained away, feeding into the ward structure like water soaking into parched earth. Through some newfound sense, I felt the sanctuary's defenses knitting themselves back together, closing the breaches that had formed during the attack. The tremors stilled as the wards stabilized, pushing back against whatever had been testing them.

I swayed on my knees, utterly wiped out. My consorts broke formation, rushing to my side. Javier reached me first, his arms encircling me with careful precision as Bastian hovered behind him. Ash and Thane formed a protective perimeter around us, their attention divided between me and the chamber's entrance.

"Did it work?" I asked, my voice hoarse, as though I'd been screaming. Had I been screaming?

"Better than expected," Isador replied, approaching cautiously, Micah at her side. "The wards are stronger than they've been in centuries...in places."

"It was a patch," Reiji said from the archway, his voice tinged with irritation. "A Band-Aid. Without your full circle, the solution is temporary." His eyes met mine with renewed intensity. "You need what I offer, Sophie. Sooner than you think."

Micah broke ahead of Isador, sliding to his knees beside Javier. "Are you okay?" he asked, scanning my face. "You were burning. We couldn't even see you through the flames."

I managed a weak smile, lifting a hand to his cheek. "I'm okay. Just tired." I glanced at Isador. "Will the wards hold?"

She nodded. "For now."

# 24

A SURGE OF HOSTILE magic slammed against the wards, cold and oily, jolting me from sleep. It had been three days since the attack on the wards, and I'd slowly grown used to being constantly aware of them, like I'd sprung a brand new limb. And just like if I'd sprouted a new leg, I kept tripping and stumbling, adjusting to this new extension of me.

I'd grown familiar enough with my new sense of the wards to recognize the sensual caress of an undead vampire brushing up against them, the wild crackle of Bastian's shifter magic, the whisper of a spirit, or even Ren's starlight, which tickled like champagne bubbles.

But *this* was nothing like that. This felt like razor-sharp nails scratching against glass, making every muscle in my body tense. Ice seeped into me, the magic from the wards backfilling me as the assault focused on a single weak point in the protective weave shielding the Moon Sanctuary.

Bastian stirred beside me, his body radiating heat that contrasted with the chill spreading through my veins. His muscles tensed as his amber eyes snapped open, already glowing with flecks of gold, the beast awakening with him. "What is it?" he growled, his voice rough with sleep.

"The wards," I whispered, my fingers curling into the sheets.

I sensed Javier outside, patrolling the grounds with a handful of vampire guardians. His smoky presence hardened into something deadly as he registered my alarm, and he immediately changed course to race toward me. I sensed Ash and Thane downstairs; their steady vigilance sharpened into urgent purpose as they moved in tandem toward Micah's room to protect my son.

The wards screamed as another lance of power slammed into them. I clutched my chest, panting through the pain. It felt like I was being attacked personally.

"Soph," Bastian said, curling an arm around me. "What can I—" His focus snapped to the wall, like he could see through both the study and sitting room to the hallway beyond. "Someone's coming."

"Javier," I offered, my teeth chattering. Except he didn't feel close enough yet.

Bastian's nostrils flared. "Not him." He moved with liquid grace, sliding from the bed and standing protectively between me and the door. The golden light beneath the black ink of his tattoos writhed, and his body seemed to strain against its current form, muscles shifting beneath skin that couldn't quite contain what lived within him.

I reached for him, my fingers brushing his arm. Where I touched, his tattoos flared brighter. The wild power inside him recognized me, leaning into my touch even as his body coiled tighter with tension.

My bedroom door burst inward.

Reiji stood in the doorway, power crackling around him like dark lightning. His pleasant mask had fallen away, his eyes glowing with unnatural light as he gathered elemental magic between his palms. Something felt wrong about Reiji's power. "I am truly sorry about this, Sophie," he said, satisfaction outweighing remorse. "But some sacrifices are necessary for the greater good."

Bastian's growl reverberated through the room, the sound too deep and resonant to have come from a human throat. His form blurred around the edges, the wild beast within him forcing its way out.

Golden light burst through his tattoos, and his shoulders broadened, bones cracking as they realigned. The curved horns like molten gold emerged from his dark curls, and wings of midnight feathers edged in gold unfurled from his back, spanning the width of the room.

I stood on my knees on the mattress so I could see over Bastian's shoulder and wing.

Reiji faltered for a moment, surprise flashing across his features before his mask of control returned. "Interesting," he murmured. His lips curled into a cruel smile. "Perhaps Veris was right to fear what might awaken in you, bastard."

The first blast of elemental magic shook the entire room, dark and corrupted.

Bastian's wings swept forward, shielding us both as debris rained down from the ceiling.

The sanctuary shuddered as the external attack on the wards continued. My hearing picked up sounds of fighting throughout the building—clashing steel, popping gunfire, explosive magic, and desperate cries as my people tried to defend their home. How many enemies had Reiji smuggled in while playing ally?

"You should have heeded the warnings in the ward testing," Reiji said, his voice carrying an edge of madness. "There would be no need for this if only you'd bound me then!" The corrupted magic pouring off him carried echoes of something darker—something harboring the Shadow King's hungry presence.

Reiji hadn't acted alone in his systematic attack on our wards the other day, and he wasn't acting alone now. I knew exactly who had guided his hand.

"You've let him in," I said, silver light gathering around me as I stood on the bed in my oversized sleep shirt. Bastian's wings flared out, ready to block any magical blasts Reiji threw at us. "You're the Shadow King's bitch."

Reiji's smile wavered. For a moment, I glimpsed something beneath his madness—a desperate need for validation. "You don't know what you're talking about," he snapped, his corrupted magic crackling between his palms like lightning dipped in tar.

Running footsteps drew closer. Ren appeared in the doorway behind Reiji, her dark eyes wide with shock. Her confidence had shattered, leaving only raw pain as she stared at him.

"Reiji?" she whispered, her voice breaking. "Little brother, what have you done?"

"Brother," I mouthed, stunned by the revelation.

Reiji's power fluctuated wildly. "What I had to," he snarled, though his tone betrayed deeper wounds. "What you and mother were too afraid to do. The House of the Moon is weak. There's no reason for us to bow and scrape and beg for the approval of this—" He sneered at me. "This *bitch*. We're the strongest House. *She* should be on her knees, begging *me* to join her harem. Then, maybe you and Mother would finally see me."

"Reji, please," Ren begged, her heart breaking right in front of us, her voice carrying such profound sorrow that my chest ached. "We do see you. We *love* you."

Reiji's expression hardened as corrupted power gathered around him. "*Love*? What good is love without power? Without recognition?" His eyes blazed with an unnatural darkness that seemed to consume the light. "When I deliver *her* to the Shadow King, I won't need *love*. I'll be more powerful than you or Mother." He held his head higher. "I'll be the first High Priest of the House of the Stars."

Ren guffawed. "If you do this, there won't *be* a House of the Stars."

"You're wrong!" Reiji shouted, his eyes blazing.

Ren flinched, then stepped farther into the room. "Reiji," she whispered, "please. This isn't who you are. The corruption is speaking, not you."

Reiji's laugh held no warmth. "Who I *am*? I'm what you and Mother made me. The unwanted prince. The disappointment. The one who was never enough." His voice cracked on that last word, revealing the wounded child beneath the madness.

The sight of this powerful man breaking apart from within made my chest ache with unwanted recognition. How many times had I felt the exact same way? Never enough, always the second choice, the backup plan. I was never supposed to be High Queen. That had been meant for Amaya.

Javier crept into view behind Reiji, but I stilled him with a slice of my chin before he attacked.

"Reiji," Ren's voice softened as she moved closer to her brother, palms open in a plea. "This isn't about power or worthiness. This is about family. About trust. Please, let me help you."

For a moment, something flickered in Reiji's expression—grief, raw and profound. The wrongness in his magic wavered. But then his eyes hardened again and corrupted power crackled around him.

"Help me? Like you helped me when Mother named you heir? Like you helped me prove myself worthy of our bloodline?" The corrupted magic intensified, filling the room with the stench of ozone and rot. "I don't need your help anymore, sister. I have real power now."

Ren's anguish was a physical thing, her shoulders sinking as though bearing an invisible weight. "Some choices," she whispered, "can't be unmade."

The corrupted magic surged forward like a cancerous mass. I braced for impact, silver light instinctively rising around me, but Ren moved with unexpected speed, positioning herself between us. Her hands sliced through the air in a complex pattern, starlight dancing at her fingertips, and everything immediately around her froze—Javier lunging at Reiji, my moonlight, her brother—as if solidified in amber.

"I'm sorry, little brother," she said, her voice breaking. A constellation of light points erupted from her hands, expanding into a web of pure starlight that wrapped around Reiji.

He collapsed to his knees, his skin smoking where Ren's magical net touched him.

Ren's first spell faded, and Javier dropped unceremoniously to the floor as my blast of moonlight fizzled out.

Bastian's wings slowly retracted, his transformed features easing back into his human form, though his eyes remained golden. "Soph," he said softly, his hand reaching for mine. He steadied me as I climbed down from the bed. "You okay?"

"I'm fine," I whispered, though power still hummed beneath my skin.

Ren knelt beside her captured brother, holding her hands over his head and murmuring words I couldn't understand. A warm glow spread out from her hands and surrounded Reiji, and he went limp on the floor. Tenderly, she gathered his head onto her lap, brushing the hair from his forehead with gentle fingers. Her expression was an aching mixture of grief and relief.

"Thank you," she said quietly, peering up at me. "For not destroying him when you had the chance."

I nodded. "The Shadow King's influence," I said. "Can it be removed?"

Ren sighed. "That depends," she said, measuring each word, "on how far the corruption has spread. And how much of *him* is left to save." She looked at Javier. "He can't travel through a portal bespelled like this. Is there a holding cell we can use? Something heavily warded against my kind, where he can be contained while I work to remove the shadow's taint?"

"The dungeon," Javier offered. "We have elemental cells."

Ren nodded, her attention returning to me. "I'm sorry you got caught up in our little family drama," she said wryly. "But you need to be careful. For whatever reason, the Shadow King is targeting you specifically. Reiji was right about one thing—you need to complete your harem as soon as possible. It's the only way you'll have even a hope of a chance against him."

"Why—" I started, but floundered for words.

"Why did we lie?" Ren ventured. When I nodded, she said, "Our envoys guessed you'd welcome a courting prince more than a sword-wielding princess, and Reiji was eager to taste the throne. I let him—uncertain whether I even wanted it—and hiding in his shadow let me study you unguarded."

"I'll show you the way," Javier said, holding an arm toward the doorway.

Ren stood, raising her brother off the floor with a flick of her wrist. He hovered behind her as she followed Javier.

I blew out a breath and flopped backward onto the bed.

Ren was the elemental heir. And her brother was working for the Shadow King.

What. A. Mess.

# 25

ORNING LIGHT FILTERED THROUGH the cracked stained-glass windows of my study, casting fractured jewel-toned patterns across the chaos of scattered books and fallen shelves. The previous night's confrontation with Reiji had left its mark—scorched wood where his corrupted magic had struck bookcases, shattered glass from light fixtures, and, worst of all, hundreds of ancient texts strewn across the floor, many scarred with tears or char marks.

I knelt beside a stack of books, carefully checking each spine for damage before placing it in one of the growing piles around me. My librarian's soul wept at the disorganized mess of such rare, priceless books.

"This classification system makes no sense," I muttered, squinting at faded runes on a leather binding. "Why would you shelve a grimoire on classical elemental practice next to a history of vampire lineages?"

Micah glanced up from his laptop, where he was cataloging the salvaged books I'd already cleared for re-shelving into a makeshift spreadsheet. His fingers paused over the keyboard. "Maybe they were organized by author instead of subject?"

"Doubtful." I sighed, pushing a stray strand of hair from my face. Many of the books didn't even have named authors. "When we're done, I'm implementing Library of Congress standards. At least then we might be able to find something when we need it."

The normality of the task—organizing books, creating systems, applying order to chaos—provided a thin veneer of comfort over the turmoil beneath. My connection to Gavin had grown fainter overnight, wisps of sensation where there should have been a solid tether. Each time I reached for him through our bond, I felt only echoes of pain. That, paired with Reiji's revelations and Ren's warning—that the Shadow King wasn't just after our world, but he was after *me*, in particular—had my thoughts spinning around and around a single conclusion.

I needed Gavin here with me. I couldn't wait another day. I had to go to the Sun Keep and free him. Now.

But *how*?

Micah set his laptop aside and picked up the next book from his current stack, carefully dusting debris from its embossed cover. Since Reiji's attack, he'd thrown himself into helping me with a quiet determination. In place of the awkward freshman I'd tutored was a young man who understood far more about the immortal world than I'd ever wanted him to.

"I found something interesting," he said, nodding toward the spreadsheet. "A bunch of these books deal with curses—specifically, the shifter curse. It's like your mom researched it. A lot."

I stood on my knees and carefully placed a cracked crystal moon paperweight back on the desk. "She must have been looking for a solution." It was common knowledge that Veris had attacked the House of the Moon because my mom refused to even attempt to break the curse.

But what if that was only half the truth? If my mom knew the curse had been placed on the shifters to protect them from the shadow taint infecting their magic, then maybe she had refused *until* she could find a better alternative. What if she'd been looking for a way to cleanse the shadow taint from their magic altogether? *Or* maybe she'd been looking for a way to curse them harder.

"Look at this," Micah said, holding open a leather-bound volume filled with yellowed pages and spidery writing.

But before I could rise to take a closer look, the door to the study opened, revealing Ren. The elemental moved with fluid grace, stepping carefully over a fallen shelf. Without her brother's shadow falling over her, she seemed somehow more substantial, the guarded mask giving way to something more authentic.

"No consorts?" she asked, one brow cocked, her dark eyes meeting mine after scanning the room.

I grabbed a book and hugged it to my chest, like armor. "They're worried about another attack."

She sniffed. "Shouldn't they be with you, then?"

I smiled, mostly to myself. "They're never far from me." In fact, at that very moment, I could sense Ash making his way down the hallway, just a few doors away.

Something shifted in Ren's expression, a subtle crack in her composed exterior. Her gaze flicked to the books stacked around me, and she moved deeper into the study, her fingers trailing over a shelf of artifacts that had somehow remained upright through Reiji's assault.

"I need to tell you something about my brother," she said. "I've been working to isolate the shadow corruption in him, but..." She hesitated, uncertainty flickering across her features, and leaned her hip on the edge of the desk. "I can't find it."

I blinked, unsure I'd heard correctly. "What do you mean, you can't find it?"

"I mean, there's no trace of shadow corruption in him. Nothing." Ren's brow furrowed. "I've searched his spirit thoroughly. There's nothing there."

"But we all saw him," I said. "The darkness in his magic, the way he spoke..."

"I don't know what it means," she said, her stare haunted. "I can't explain it."

"But..." I shook my head. "We *felt* the shadow's influence."

Ren sighed. "Maybe if Reiji was working with the shadow voluntarily, he wouldn't need a mark of corruption to coerce him. If he chose the shadow. Sought it out. If it was something he did, not something that was done to him. Maybe?"

The implication settled like ice in my veins, despite her uncertainty. How much harder to face a betrayal born of choice rather than corruption?

"Ren, if that's true..." My heart broke for her all over again. "I'm so sorry."

Her stare hardened. "I'm not sharing this for sympathy," she said, a slight edge to her voice. "It's a warning. There's a good chance the Shadow King's influence has spread further into this world than we realized." She absently traced a scorch mark on the desk. "Your House is weak, Sophie, but *you* are not. I understand the frustration of feeling forced into a role you never wanted. Of having to lead and make choices that impact the lives of thousands. Of knowing that every decision that benefits one group of people will hurt another. Of feeling like everything you do, even if it's a win, is also a failure."

I swallowed, a sinking feeling gnawing in my gut.

"You no longer have the luxury of waiting," she went on. "You *must* complete your harem and claim your birthright, or the House of the Moon and the House of the Stars and the House of the Sun, along with every other living being—mortal and immortal alike—will be wiped from the face of the earth."

Micah looked from Ren to me and back, his eyes opened wide.

Ren pushed off the edge of the desk, crossed to me, and knelt before me. "I will help you in any way I can," she said. "Obviously, you can't bind Reiji after last night, but you still need a consort from the House of the Stars. I would offer myself to fulfill that role." She bowed her head. "If you would have me."

"I—" I glanced at Micah, swallowing hard. Something in my expression made him jump to his feet.

"I'm going to pee or get a sandwich or something," he blurted. "Not at the same time, obviously," he rambled. "First sandwich, then pee, or... It doesn't really matter." He made a beeline for the door.

After he was gone, I returned my attention to Ren, who watched me closely. I licked my lips and looked down at my knees. "I can't always differentiate between blood lust and normal lust," I confessed, my cheeks heating. "I'm getting better at it, but *communions* are usually pretty intense," I added in a rush. I dragged my focus back up to her face. "Just so you know what you're volunteering for."

A sly Mona Lisa smile curved Ren's lips, making my belly do a pleasant flip flop. "I have no problem with that arrangement, if you don't."

"I—" I stared at her, a pleasant, full-body buzz spreading through me. To my own surprise, I found myself nodding without hesitation. The certainty that bloomed inside me caught me off guard—this felt right in a way I couldn't explain. "I don't have a problem with it either."

Ren snagged my hand, peeling my fingers away from the book's spine, placed her palm flush against mine. I felt a wash of effervescent power cascade up my arm and through my body. "Good," she said softly. "But first, you need to retrieve your absent consort... And I think I can *also* help you with that."

My brow furrowed. "What do you mean?" I stared at her hand against mine, at the source of that pleasant, full-body buzz. "What are you doing to me?"

"Blocking your consorts from eavesdropping on our conversation," she said, drawing my attention back up to her face.

"They're already on their way," I said, sensing them approaching.

"Then I'll speak quickly," she said. "There is one thing Veris wants more than anything else."

"To break the curse," I guessed. "But that'll increase the shadow's influence on all the shifters."

She laughed, the sound dark. "What does it matter now? The Shadow King is already breaking down the door." Her expression turned deadly serious. "I can get you through the portal to the Sun Keep, but you must not bring your consorts, or Veris will use them against you. You must go alone, offer a trade—the curse for your consort—fulfill the trade, and return. I'll join you, of course. You'll need a Star consort to work the ritual in tandem, appealing to both Selene and Eos."

"I have to get the queens too," I said in a rush, glancing over my shoulder at the door. Javier was almost here, Bastian close behind him. "Gavin will never leave without them."

Ren waved a hand dismissively. "He has no need for them once the curse is broken. Meet me tonight. The graveyard. Midnight."

"They're here," I breathed.

And Ren shocked me by standing on her knees, grasping my face in her hands, and pressing her lips against mine just as the door swung open.

The kiss landed like a shooting star—brilliant and unexpected. Her lips were cool against mine, tasting of floral herbs and something both ancient and new. Not demanding like my consorts' kisses, but exploratory. A question. An answer.

I heard the sharp intake of breath from the doorway, sensing the immediate tension radiating from my consorts through our bonds. But I couldn't break away, caught in this unforeseen moment of connection.

When Ren finally pulled back, her dark eyes glittered with secrets like distant galaxies. The corner of her mouth lifted in subtle satisfaction as she cast a deliberate glance toward the doorway where Javier and Bastian stood frozen.

Neither of my consorts spoke, but the silent storm brewing in Javier's eyes and the golden gleam surfacing in Bastian's said everything. Centuries of possessive instinct warred with their respect for my autonomy.

"Midnight," Ren mouthed. She rose gracefully to her feet, smoothing her clothing with unhurried precision. The confidence in her posture as she walked toward my consorts was a masterclass in calculated nonchalance.

Javier didn't move away from the doorway, forcing her to pause before him. The silent standoff lasted only seconds, but felt infinite—Prime Consort and Star heir, ancient powers sizing each other up. Finally, he shifted just enough to let her pass, his jaw clenched tight enough that I could see the muscle twitching from across the room.

I touched my fingertips to my lips, still feeling the lingering tingle of her kiss. Heat crept into my cheeks as I met Bastian's stare.

The weight of tonight's task settled in my chest like a stone. What was I willing to risk? What might I have to sacrifice? For Gavin. For all of us.

The door clicked shut behind Ren, leaving me alone with my consorts and the dangerous hope burning in my chest.

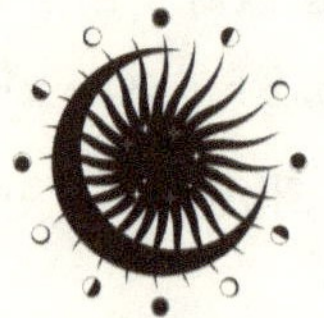

# 26

THE WATER HAD BEEN scalding, but even as steam filled the bathroom, the heat couldn't wash away the chill settling in my bones. I stood under the spray, letting droplets trace paths down my skin, each one counting down to midnight when everything would change.

My mother's ring rested heavy on my finger, a constant reminder of my duty to our people.

I dried quickly and wrapped myself in a silk robe, catching my reflection in the fogged mirror. My features were sharper, my eyes brighter, as though channeling Selene's divine power was changing me, much like unleashing Bastian's inner beast changed him.

Before I even opened the bathroom door, I knew my consorts would be waiting for me in the bedroom, drawn by the storm of emotions I couldn't hide, even if Ren's temporary spell had concealed the source.

My bonds with each of my immortals thrummed with tension—save for Gavin, which ached like a festering phantom limb.

Blowing out my breath, I pulled open the door.

My immortals stood like sentinels in my bedroom. Moonlight filtered through the arched windows, casting their faces in silver and shadow.

"What's wrong?" Javier said, his voice carrying that perfect balance of command and devotion. He approached me, his movements deliberate, controlled.

"What aren't you telling us, Soph?" Bastian moved closer, the gold in his tattoos rising to the surface, mingling with the black ink. Anxiety blazed through our connection. He ran a hand through his dark curls, amber eyes flickering with gold. "Is it Ren? The kiss...?"

I shook my head, smiling sadly.

The air in the corner rippled with silvery energy—Wes trying to manifest. He'd been flickering in and out of view for days, ever since I'd reinforced the wards. He could hold his form better outside the house, farther from the Selenarium, long enough to let me know he was fine and that the wards were the issue. Now, his ghostly form appeared in the corner of the room just long enough for me to catch his expression of concern before he dissolved again.

I couldn't do anything for him right now. So I focused instead on the four immortals whose blood and devotion had reshaped my very being. My consorts. My protectors. Each bond between us pulsed with a different signature, but all carried the same desperate need to keep me safe.

A need that would drive them to try to stop me if they knew what I planned to do.

"What are you hiding?" Javier asked, his voice low, intimate. His hands settled at my waist, the touch both possessive and steadying.

I couldn't meet his eyes, not with guilt burning through my veins. He knew me too well. Of course he would recognize the signs of me preparing to do something reckless.

Ren's words about Veris echoed in my mind—about using his obsession with breaking the curse as leverage, about offering myself as bait. About going alone because bringing my consorts would only give Veris more hostages to use against me.

"I'm just processing everything," I lied, the words tasting like ashes. "So much has happened..."

Javier's hands shifted lower, settling on my hips. When he pulled me closer, I went willingly, letting the familiar heat of his body chase away some of the chill in mine. His lips traced the curve of my neck, finding the spot where my pulse thrummed beneath my skin.

"You're lying," he murmured against my neck.

I sucked in a breath, my heartbeat erratic. But before I could respond, his fangs grazed my throat, making heat pool low in my belly despite the gravity of what lay ahead. When his teeth finally sank into my flesh, the sharp sting of pleasure-pain made me gasp, my hands flying up to grip his shoulders.

Our bond blazed brighter with each pull, memories flooding between us—him whisking me away from the massacre, teaching me to survive in the human world, helping me grow into someone who could bear the weight of a crown he'd always known I would wear.

"You are mine, Luna," he growled against my broken skin, his voice rough with possession. "My queen. My purpose. *Mine.*"

The raw emotion in his voice nearly broke my resolve. Through our bond, I felt everything he couldn't say directly—his fear of losing me, his frustration at threats he couldn't simply eliminate, his desperate love.

His free hand slipped under my robe, pausing below my belly button, like he was giving me a chance to pull away. When I didn't move, his fingers slid lower, delving between my legs with practiced ease.

I gasped, my hands clutching his shoulders as my knees threatened to give out. He stroked my clit, his touch both reverent and commanding, knowing exactly how to make my body respond.

"Javier," I whispered, his name a prayer and a plea. My fingers tangled in his hair, holding him close as the world narrowed to his mouth on my skin, his hand between my thighs, the bond that tied us together.

He pulled back slightly, his lips brushing my ear. "I will never let you go," he vowed, his voice a rough growl. "No matter what happens. No matter where you go."

My breath hitched. Did he know? Could he tell I was planning to make a deal with Veris? To steal away in the middle of the night, without them, into the lion's den? The thought of leaving him—of leaving any of them—twisted in my chest like a knife.

"I love you, my Luna," he murmured. His words sent a shiver through me, desire and sorrow tangled together.

I surrendered to the moment, letting the shadows hide the tears in my eyes. I felt the others drawing closer, each bond burning with the same desperate need to hold on to me before something tore us apart.

Javier's fingers moved faster, his rhythm relentless as he circled my clit with expert precision. His mouth returned to my throat, tongue lapping at the wound he'd made, and I felt the pleasure coiling tight in my belly. My body trembled, balancing on the edge of release, and I clung to him like he was the only solid thing in a world turning to liquid.

Pleasure crashed over me, sharp and consuming. He held me as I trembled, his arm wrapping around me like he could shield me from fate itself. But he couldn't shield me from myself.

Bastian closed in, his hand settling on my back, heat bleeding through the silk of my robe. Ash and Thane moved in sync, taking up positions that enclosed me in a protective circle.

I leaned into Javier, the silk robe slipping off one shoulder as I surrendered to this. To them. "Help me forget," I whispered. I needed this—needed them—before I did what had to be done. "Help me forget *everything*."

Bastian turned me around in Javier's arms and knelt before me, his hands sliding up my thighs beneath the silky robe. His touch sent shivers cascading over my skin. He looked up, his gaze locking onto mine with an intensity that made my breath catch.

His hands pushed the robe further aside, baring me to his hungry gaze. His lips followed, trailing kisses along my inner thighs. I gasped as his teeth grazed me—a hint of the beast he kept carefully contained. A promise of what lurked beneath his human form.

His mouth moved higher, teasing me with deliberate slowness until I wanted to scream. When his tongue finally found my clit, pleasure jolted through me like lightning. My fingers tangled in his dark curls, holding him against me as he devoured me with primal intensity.

Ash and Thane's hands claimed my breasts, teasing and pinching my nipples while Javier lapped at the bite on my neck, the telltale tingling telling me he was healing the wound with his blood. The onslaught of sensations ricocheted through me, pushing me toward another peak with devastating precision.

Bastian worked my clit until my legs trembled and my knees threatened to give out. With a growl, he gripped my thighs and hoisted my legs onto his shoulders, opening me to him so he could lick the length of my slit in long, slow strokes.

I groaned, grinding against his face, wanting more of him. More of all of them.

Javier pressed his wrist against my lips, offering me his blood. I bit down without hesitation, his taste exploding across my tongue, tangy and bittersweet, like raspberries and dark chocolate. Power surged through me, ancient and wild, igniting every nerve ending just as Bastian refocused his attention on my clit. He sucked it, hard, and I came undone.

My orgasm hit like a tidal wave, pleasure ripping through me in violent waves that made silver light pulse beneath my skin. Bastian's arms were like steel bands around my thighs, holding me against him as my body shuddered, Javier's blood sliding down my throat and the endless assault on my clit making the climax stretch on and on and *on*.

Javier finally pulled his wrist away, and Bastian released my clit, instead grazing his lips back and forth along my inner thigh. Ash moved behind me, taking Javier's place as the aftershocks of the marathon orgasm racked my body, his large hands settling on my shoulders with firm tenderness. His warm body pressed against my back, solid and reassuring. His lips found the nape of my neck, sending a shiver straight down my spine.

Ash's hands traced down my arms, fingers drawing patterns on my skin that left trails of heat in their wake. Thane pressed in on my side, dark eyes burning as he lowered his head. He cupped my face, his thumbs brushing my cheeks as his lips captured mine in a kiss that stole my breath.

The silk robe slipped further open as Ash gathered the fabric at my hips, exposing more skin to the cool air. His teeth grazed my shoulder, sending another jolt straight through my core. I moaned into Thane's mouth, surrendering to the sensations.

Together, they carried me to the bed, laying me down so the gaping silk robe pooled around me like dark water as they surrounded me. I lost myself in them—in how they surrounded me, consumed me, claimed me as theirs. Thane offered me his blood as Ash made sweet love to my pussy with his mouth, the two of them drawing out my next orgasm until my nerve endings felt singed from the overexposure to pleasure.

Finally, they released me from the chokehold of ecstasy, only for Bastian to position himself between my legs, his hungry eyes, pulsing gold, never leaving mine. The hard length of him pressed against my entrance, and I gasped as he thrust in, filling me completely. His hands gripped my hips, holding me steady as he began to move with slow, deliberate strokes that dragged against that secret spot inside me just right.

Ash and Thane settled on either side of me, their hands exploring every inch of exposed skin. Ash's lips found my breasts, his tongue teasing a nipple with gentle flicks that contrasted with the intensity of Bastian's thrusts. On my other side, Thane's fingers slid between my legs, stroking my clit with steady pressure.

Javier claimed my mouth, his kiss deep and demanding, and his fingers tangled with Thane's between my legs, and I jerked at the jolt of intensified pleasure.

Bastian's thrusts quickened, his grip on my hips dragging me onto him even as he pushed forward. Ash's mouth joined Javier's, tasting of sex and blood, and I moaned into the tangle of lips and tongues and teeth. My body tightened around Bastian as another orgasm tore through me.

I was drowning in sensation, lost in the storm they created around me. Every touch, every kiss, every taste of blood blended into a symphony of shared hunger.

Bastian withdrew with a reluctant groan. My body clenched at the sudden emptiness, but Ash was there immediately, filling me with that massive cock. I cried out as he pushed in, in, in, my vaginal walls tingling at the rush of immortal blood coating him.

His hands settled on either side of my head, his massive frame caging me as he began to move with controlled power. I reached for him, my nails digging into his shoulders as my hips rose to meet each thrust.

Bastian didn't retreat, crawling around me so his throbbing cock was within mouth's reach. I licked my lips and opened wide, taking him in until I was nearly gagging. He was so hard, his shaft slick and salty with the combination of his precum and my arousal. I moaned around the mouthful, knowing it wouldn't take much to make him explode.

"Fuuuuck, Soph," he groaned, his fingers tangling in my hair as he thrust into my mouth again and again until... His whole body stiffened, his tattoos flaring gold, and he shot his load down my throat. His come had the same effect as his blood, and my magic flared in response to the completed *communion*, moonlight radiating from my skin as pleasure rolled through me in waves.

"Sophie," Ash gasped, my clenching pussy pushing him closer to the edge. His rhythm faltered, then changed, becoming slower but deeper. He withdrew almost completely before sliding back in, the delicious friction making my eyes roll back.

"Mmm...yes," I purred.

With a deep, dark, masculine chuckle, Ash wrapped his arms around me and lifted me off the bed, hugging me against his chest.

I grinned, dragging my lips along the length of his collarbone and wrapping my arms around his neck, already anticipating where this was heading.

Thane moved in close behind me, his lips at my ear, whispering promises in a language I didn't understand as he rubbed the head of his cock back and forth along my ass crack. I felt the dribble of something warm and knew he'd spilled his own blood to use as lubricant. My insides fluttered in anticipation.

I rested my head back on Thane's shoulder, relaxing as he oh-so-slowly pushed into my ass. He whispered against my temple, praised me, kissed me. And then he was inside me, and Ash and Thane were moving together, finding a primal rhythm that seemed to sync with my heartbeat.

Bastian supported me on one side, holding my leg and dusting my shoulder with kisses.

I sensed Javier farther away on my other side, and I turned my head to find him standing beside the bed, stroking his cock, his eyes on fire as he watched us. I reached for him. "Come here," I begged, desperate for him to be closer.

He climbed onto the bed and stood on the mattress, balancing against the rocking motion from Ash and Thane's combined thrusts. I opened my mouth and stuck out my tongue, welcoming him into me. I needed him in me. Needed all of them in me.

He did not disappoint.

I was surrounded by them, held by them, filled by them. Every inch of my skin came alive under their touch, every nerve ending singing with pleasure. Ash's thrusts grew more urgent, Thane's grunts more animalistic.

I was close—so close—the pressure building to an almost unbearable intensity.

Bastian wedged his hand between my body and Ash's, sliding his fingers on either side of my clit and pinching them together. The additional sensation made me cry out, my body tightening around Ash and Thane as I dove headfirst into an ocean of mind-numbing pleasure.

Javier pulled out of my mouth, pumping his hand along his length.

The world narrowed to sensation—to the places where their bodies connected with mine, to the bonds that linked us, to the silver light building beneath my skin. I was theirs, and they were mine, and in this moment, nothing else existed.

My orgasm crashed through me with devastating force, magical moonlight exploding from my skin as pleasure ripped through every nerve ending. Waves of release shuddered through me, making my body jerk and spasm. Ash and Thane followed immediately, Javier right behind them, spurting hot come on my neck and chest. Their emotions flooded me through our bonds until I couldn't tell where their pleasure ended and mine began.

They held me as aftershocks rippled through my trembling body, their arms forming a fortress around my sweat-slick skin. My light dimmed as ancient power settled beneath my skin once more. I breathed them in, storing this moment away like a treasure I could revisit when I needed strength.

For a heartbeat, everything else faded away—the weight of prophecy, the fear of what was coming, the dread of the choice I had already made. In that moment, there was only them, their love, their devotion, their fierce need to protect me.

"I love you," I whispered, the words tiny against the storm building in my chest. "All of you." I spoke a silent apology in my mind as I climbed atop Javier, straddling him and rubbing my swollen sex against his hardening cock. If this were going to work, I would have to fully wear out my guys, which meant *more*. More sex. More *communion*. More blood. I had to take and take and take from them as I had in the graveyard.

I groaned as I slid onto Javier's cock, his fingers digging into my hips. At least, in terms of betrayals, this was one we would all enjoy.

# 27

M Y HEART WAS HEAVY as I slipped from the bed filled with my sleeping consorts. Their warmth had chased away the chill for a few hours, but now purpose settled over me like frost. I gathered my clothes silently, each movement deliberate.

I dressed quickly. Black jeans that wouldn't show blood. A dark oversized sweater that reminded me of my librarian days—soft armor I'd hidden behind while pretending to be Sophie Matthews. Sturdy boots, because practical footwear was always a good idea. My mother's ring and Wes's pendant felt heavier than usual, reminders of everything at stake. I added a sheathed hairpin dagger—engraved silver with tiny crescent moons dangling from the dagger's hilt—and used it to secure my hair into a bun on the crown of my head.

I gulped down a few vials of Gavin's blood tincture, thinking that where I was headed, I'd need as much power as I could get. If a full harem would make me a match for the Shadow King, surely being fully charged up from a gluttonous *communion* with just four consorts and topping off with a few doses of a fifth consort's blood tincture would be enough to face off with the shifter king.

I paused in the doorway for one last look at the four immortals, whose continued existence was as integral to me as my own beating heart. They were why I was doing this—them, and Gavin and Micah. These people who made the world worth saving.

I eased the door shut, picked my way around the organized stacks and chaotic piles of books in the study, and crossed the sitting room as quickly and as quietly as I could, silence being an impossibility on the aged floorboards. Beyond my chambers, the corridor stretched before me, ward sigils pulsing in my presence.

Down the hallway, Micah's door stood ajar, golden light spilling out. Through the gap, I saw him hunched over ancient texts, tracing ward patterns with his fingertip.

He sensed me before I could decide whether or not to intrude, looking up with eyes too knowing for someone so young.

"You're leaving," he said quietly, no question in his voice. "To get Gavin?"

I nodded, the words caught somewhere between my heart and my throat.

"I'm coming with you," he said, rising with that stubborn set to his jaw that I recognized from my own reflection.

I gripped Wes's tree of life pendant as I entered Micah's room, hoping Wes was around even if he wasn't able to manifest. Micah's desk overflowed with research—ancient texts, drawings of ward patterns, notes in his meticulous handwriting about the Shadow King.

"You can't," I said softly, reaching out to brush dark curls from his forehead, a gesture I'd been denied for seventeen years. "This isn't your fight."

"Bullshit," he replied, the harshness of the word startling a laugh from me. "You're my mother. That makes it my fight."

I shook my head, my throat tightening. "I need you safe," I said softly. I cupped his face between my palms, wincing at the unexpected sting from the cut on my left hand—a slender crescent-shaped bite wound my consorts had forgotten to heal. A faint smear of blood stained his cheek where my palm had touched him, more vibrant than it should have been, almost luminous in the dim light.

"I need to know that whatever happens, you're okay," I told him, wiping the blood smudge away with a sweep of my thumb.

"At least take Bastian," he said, a plea in his voice. "Or Javier, or *someone*. Dad doesn't count. Just—just don't go alone."

I smiled sadly, remembering the countless hours spent working together in the library, back when I was just Sophie Matthews, when the biggest worry in my life was whether he'd pass his midterms. "I'm not going alone. Ren's coming, and Gavin will be there."

"Sophie," he said, then amended, "Mom." The word was still new enough on his lips to carry weight, still raw with seventeen years of absence. "Please…" His voice broke slightly. "We just found each other. I'm not ready to lose you."

Instead of answering, I pressed my bleeding palm to his forehead, following an instinct deeper than conscious thought. Marking him like this, with a mother's blood, was the strongest protection ward I could provide in my absence. I knew it in my gut. In my magic. In my soul. *This* would keep him safe.

The moment my blood touched his skin, something shifted between us. Not the fierce heat of consort bonding, but a gentler warmth that spread outward from the point of contact, like sunlight melting frost. My blood didn't just smear against his skin—it sank in, absorbed completely as if his body recognized it as its own.

Moonlight bloomed between us, not the cool radiance I shared with my consorts but something warmer, tinged with gold at the edges, like the light of a harvest moon.

My vision swam as power surged through our awakening connection, and a wave of dizziness forced me to steady myself against his shoulder.

"Mom?" Micah's voice came from far away, laced with concern.

When my vision cleared, a crescent moon sigil glowed on Micah's forehead. It pulsed once, twice, then fractured into dozens of smaller patterns—stars, crescents, spiraling galaxies that spread across his skin like constellations before sinking beneath the surface, leaving only the original crescent visible for a heartbeat longer before it too faded.

His eyes widened, briefly flashing like moonlight on water. The light came from within, his irises ringed with an opalescent luminescence that hadn't been there before. The ward wasn't just sitting on his skin, shielding him; it had sunken into him, becoming part of him in ways I hadn't intended.

"What *was* that?" he whispered, touching his forehead where the sigil had been. His skin radiated heat, and I could see the ghost of the ward beneath his flesh, like veins of silver running just below the surface. "It felt warm...and kind of tingly." The uncertainty in his eyes mirrored my own.

"Just protection," I said, certain that was the truth, just not sure it was the *whole* truth. "I love you," I whispered roughly, pulling him close one last time, breathing in his scent of books and mint and something else now, faintly metallic, like blood. "Whatever happens, remember that."

Before he could respond, I left, closing the door firmly behind me. I placed my palm against the wood.

Something tugged at my awareness—a connection to Micah. A silver thread binding us, mother and child. Through it, I sensed him standing on the other side of the door, his hand mirroring mine, his heart heavy in his chest.

I turned from the door before my resolve could weaken further and walked away. Whatever I'd done couldn't be undone now.

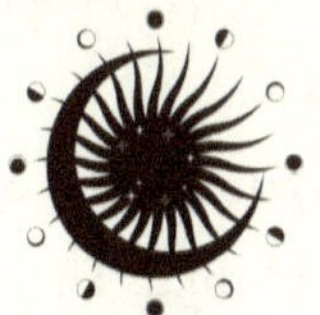

# 28

I MOVED SILENTLY THROUGH ancient corridors, monitoring my consorts through our bonds—Javier's smoke and lightning, Bastian's wild essence, Ash's steadfast stone, Thane's oceanic depths—each connection pulsing against my consciousness like a second heartbeat.

The waxing moon was low in the sky and the stars were bright when I reached the sanctuary's entrance. The grassy expanse spreading across the front part of the grounds stretched before me. Beyond it, the upward sloping ground and the hillside graveyard, with the moonlit statues of Selene in her many forms standing like silent sentinels. Ren waited beside the wrought-iron gate, her silhouette barely visible from this distance in the dim light.

I hurried out into the night, throwing furtive glances over my shoulder despite sensing that my consorts were still in the manor house. My breaths came faster as I closed in on Ren.

"You came," she said with careful neutrality. "Alone. Good."

I nodded, my stomach tangled in knots.

She didn't say anything else, no gentle assurances. No praise, though I totally deserved it. I'd worn my guys out. That took dedication. Instead of speaking, Ren produced a small vial of iridescent blue liquid.

"Drink this before you go. It will mask your energy signature from the wards."

"What about the ward code? I'd rather not melt, or—"

"I can disable it," she interrupted, glancing over her shoulder toward the house. "How much time do we have?"

I shrugged, hugging my middle. "They're sleeping, but anything could wake them, especially Javier." If he woke and sensed me out in the graveyard, I figured it would take him about twenty seconds to reach us. "Work fast."

Ren laughed softly, an edge of bitterness in the sound. "Of course," she said, her fingers tracing portal sigils in the air. Power moved around her like light through water, and a dark vortex formed at the center of the wrought-iron gate.

A spike of awareness shot through me, and I peered down at the Gothic mansion whose spires speared the sky. Javier was awake. And based on the way my awareness of my other consorts flared brighter in my mind, he was waking them, too.

"Hurry," I urged, wringing my hands. "They're coming."

Ren's movements changed, becoming faster, jerkier.

"Stop!" Javier's voice cut through the night, balanced between command and desperation. He materialized from the shadows, moving toward us with predatory grace. "Whatever you're planning, Luna, whatever you believe you must face alone..." His eyes held decades of knowing me, even when I didn't fully know myself. "I *will* be at your side."

He positioned himself between me and the gate where Ren worked, his stance unmistakable. He wasn't letting me leave. Not without him.

More footsteps pounded across the graveyard. Bastian surged forward, the only one of my consorts who moved slow enough for me to track.

"Don't do this, Soph!" he called roughly.

Ash and Thane appeared at the edges of my awareness, positioning themselves on my right and left sides.

My heart sank. So much for wearing them out.

"I need you to stay here," I said desperately, my voice ringing with the full power of my *will*. "Micah needs protection. The sanctuary needs defenders. I can't risk all of you. You will not try to stop me, and you will *stay here*."

I saw their resistance—the straining tendons and bulging muscles, the groans as they fought to get close to me—and felt their urgency through our bonds. Only Javier remained unmoved, his dark eyes narrowed as he stood his ground between me and the gate, the crescent moon sigil on his face shining steadily.

"You're not going without me," he said, his voice dropping to that dangerous register that made my heart race. "You promised. No more shutting me out. No more carrying burdens alone." His eyes softened slightly. "I have spent twenty years sensing your pain across a great distance. Did you truly believe I would not feel this coming?"

"Javier," I began, but stopped at the finality in his expression. His protective fury had crystallized into something colder, more calculated.

"I will not lose you again," he said simply, stepping aside as the portal solidified behind him in a vortex of black lightning.

"You must go now, Sophie," Ren shouted. "I can't hold this for long."

"Aren't you coming with me?" I asked, startled by her words. "I'll need you for the curse-breaking ritual."

She glanced down the hill at the mansion. "I have to reset the containment spell on Reiji. It must be done every three hours. I timed this so you would have time to negotiate with Veris before I joined you. Otherwise, his containment spell could wear off while I'm still away, and that...that would be a very bad thing."

"How long?" I asked.

"About thirty minutes."

"All right." Anxiety knotted my stomach, and I looked at those I was leaving behind—Bastian, Ash, and Thane. Through our bonds, I felt their love and concern, their anger, their willingness to follow me into danger.

"I'm sorry," I whispered, grabbing Javier's arm and leaping into the open portal.

# 29

I *HATED* PORTAL TRAVEL.

Reality twisted as the portal pulled us through space. That disorienting lurch in my stomach reminded me of passing through that first portal with Gavin, when I'd abandoned the careful, quiet life I'd built for myself. I told myself this was different. I wasn't abandoning the Moon Sanctuary or the life waiting for me there; I was trying to preserve it.

For a moment, Javier and I existed in nothingness. There was only darkness and the sensation of falling, and then we crashed onto cold stone, the return to reality knocking the breath from my lungs. I landed on my hands and knees, coughing to capture some air.

Javier curved over me instantly, his arm banding around my waist as he landed in a defensive crouch. "Breathe, Luna," he murmured against my ear, his voice pitched low.

Finally, the spasming in my lungs subsided, and I was able to take full, deep breaths. I raised my head and looked around. I'd been here before, when we rescued Javier, but then the portal chamber had been filled with a toxic smoke that made all who breathed it live out their worst nightmares. Now, there was nothing to block my view, and not a single shifter in sight.

Ancient stone walls surrounded us on all sides, inscribed with ward patterns that made my skin itch. But I wasn't melting or combusting or screaming in pain, so Ren had been as good as her word. The air carried a trace of something dank and acrid, but maybe that was due to the Sun Keep's underground nature.

My sense of Gavin was exponentially stronger, his pain echoing sharper with proximity, and I fought against the urge to run blindly toward him.

"Something isn't right," Javier said, straightening and helping me up to my feet, my legs still unsteady. "This chamber should be guarded, especially after your last incursion." His dark eyes scanned the shadows, his head tilting as he listened closely. "Why would Veris leave the front door wide open?"

"Maybe he thought the wards would be enough?" I suggested, though doubt crept through me. Ren had been confident about breaching the Sun Keep's defenses, but had it been *too* easy for her?

"Perhaps," Javier murmured, his voice carrying careful neutrality that meant real concern. His hand found mine, his fingers intertwining with practiced familiarity.

The bizarre thing about this situation was that I wasn't trying to avoid detection. I was here to deal with Veris directly, not to sneak around.

We moved forward cautiously, each step echoing against the ancient stone. The ward patterns pulsed, responding to our presence. Manganese veins ran through the stone walls, glinting pewter. I pulled Javier closer to the wall, sensing something disturbing, and traced my fingers along a grayish-silver vein of manganese.

I hissed in a breath and jerked my hand away. It was faint, but the foul taint of shadow corruption was there, like the metal's magical properties had absorbed it.

"Can you feel it?" I whispered to Javier, my fingers digging into his forearm as ice crawled down my spine. "The shadow taint?"

He shook his head. "Luna...," he warned, his body coiling tighter as footsteps echoed faintly from a corridor beyond the chamber. He placed his body between me and the broad arched doorway.

I held my breath as shifter warriors filed into the chamber, moving purposefully but not rushing. Within seconds, we were surrounded by at least twenty shifters, their eyes gleaming like wolves anticipating a kill.

"Well, well, well," a cultured voice intoned from the corridor, smooth as silk and sharp as a blade. "What an *unexpected* surprise." The guards parted as a figure stepped into the chamber, confident and lethal.

Veris. King of the shifters. Bastian's father. Killer of my people.

He was shorter than I'd expected, not quite as tall as Bastian, but his frame was immensely powerful. His impeccably tailored charcoal suit somehow enhanced rather than diminished the sense of violence that hovered around him. His copper-bronze skin seemed to glow with internal fire.

His amber eyes held me frozen—like Bastian's, but glacial, assessing me with dispassionate interest. The terrible symmetry of genetics had given father and son the same strong jaw and the same proud nose, but where Bastian's features held warmth, his father's seemed carved from stone. Beautiful but cold.

Standing before him, I felt small. A librarian who had spent twenty years hiding behind cardigans and careful smiles now faced the architect of my family's destruction. I'd spent decades running from him, and now I'd walked straight into his waiting hands.

"Luna Sofia," he said, my true name sounding like a violation on his lips. "Or do you prefer Sophie?" His smile never reached those cold eyes. "Such a mundane name for a High Queen." His gaze traveled over me with invasive thoroughness. "The photos don't do you justice. You're much more vibrant in person."

I stiffened, my stomach turning at the idea of him having pictures of me.

Javier's body coiled with barely contained violence. I placed a steadying hand on his arm, silently urging him to stand down. *This* was why I was here, after all.

"King Veris," I said, forcing my voice to hold steady despite the hatred burning through my veins. This was the monster who had burned my mom's body so thoroughly that her spirit couldn't anchor to this world. The same king who now kept Gavin prisoner while corruption seeped through the stone beneath our feet.

"You have something that belongs to me," I said, my head held high.

A smile curved his lips. "So direct. I wonder... Are you as direct in all things?" He stepped closer, deliberately provocative. "And as stupid? The last High Queen, prophesied savior, and you walk straight into my stronghold with only a single guardian?" He clicked his tongue. "Your mother would be ashamed."

At the mention of my mom, something flickered at the edge of my vision—a shimmer of smoky light that disappeared when I tried to focus on it.

"I came to make a deal, not to fight," I said, moonlight pulsing beneath my skin as divine power stirred. "Assuming you're interested in breaking the curse. If you're not..." I turned partway, sending a meaningful glance back at the portal.

Something flashed in Veris's eyes—surprise quickly masked. "Interesting." He circled us slowly, like a wolf assessing his quarry. His guards, or commanders, or whatever they were, maintained their positions with mechanical precision. "You astound me, young queen, and that is something that rarely happens."

Veris stopped directly before me, with only Javier between us. The family resemblance to Bastian faded up close, Veris's cold calculation supplanting the physical similarities.

"I must admit," Veris said, his voice dropping lower, "I'm curious about what my son sees in you. What made him betray his bloodline, his heritage?" His gaze traveled over me again, lingering in ways that made Javier's muscles bunch beneath my fingers. "Though I can appreciate the physical appeal." He rubbed his fingertips over his lips suggestively.

The crude implication made bile rise in my throat. This was a test, a deliberate provocation designed to reveal weaknesses he could exploit.

"Your son chose love over hatred," I said steadily. "He chose building something new over clinging to ancient grievances. You could learn a thing or two from him, unless you'd rather let the curse continue to erode your power and destroy your people."

Something flickered across Veris's features at the mention of the curse—a tightening around his eyes that told me I'd struck a chord. Through the cracks in his control, I glimpsed genuine concern.

He laughed, masking his reaction, the sound devoid of humor but carrying tension. "Love. Such a human concept. Useful for manipulation, but hardly worth sacrificing power for." His amber eyes hardened.

"Though I shouldn't be surprised. The boy's mother was equally sentimental before, well…"

The silver shimmer in my peripheral vision grew stronger—a ghost attempting to manifest, fighting the suppression and expulsion wards.

"Come," Veris said abruptly, turning away with casual confidence. "We have much to discuss, and I prefer more comfortable surroundings for important conversations." He walked back toward the arched doorway, his guards parting before him.

Javier's hand found mine, our fingers intertwining. "Proceed with caution, my Luna," he whispered, barely audible. "Veris has always been duplicitous."

As we followed the shifter king deeper into his stronghold, my mother's moonstone ring heated on my finger, like she was sending me a warning from beyond the grave.

Each step deeper into the Sun Keep brought me closer to Gavin but also intensified that troubling sense of wrongness. The shadow taint grew stronger in the stone around us, no longer just faint traces in manganese veins but a subtle corruption permeating the walls themselves. So subtle that I might have missed it if I hadn't been looking, if I hadn't already felt it in Reiji's magic.

I caught Javier's eye, wondering if he sensed it too, but his expression remained carefully neutral, revealing nothing to our enemies. The air felt heavier here, each breath coating my lungs with something that wasn't quite physical but wasn't purely magical either. Something in-between.

I thumbed the back of the moonstone ring, seeking a connection to a woman whose choices I only partially understood. The curse had been a shield against something worse. I knew that. What if breaking it was exactly what the Shadow King wanted?

But as Gavin's presence intensified through our bond, his pain echoing through me like a physical wound, I pushed those doubts away. The Shadow King was already breaking through. The time for caution was over. The ancient bargain of the curse had served its purpose—had bought us centuries—but that time was ending.

We continued deeper into the Sun Keep, moving through corridors and descending stairs that seemed to go on forever, the shadow taint growing stronger with each level. The stone beneath my feet felt almost alive, pulsing with corrupted power that reached hungry tendrils toward me.

My consorts' blood within me responded, fueling my moonlight, pushing back against that reaching shadow.

For a moment, I saw it clearly—what breaking the curse would mean. The shifters unshackled but fully exposed to the Shadow King's corruption. Their golden light of transformation struck through with shadow taint. How long would it take to set in? Would I notice it within Bastian right away?

The moonstone burned hotter against my skin, a silent plea from a mother who couldn't speak. A warning I couldn't fully understand.

But we had passed the point of caution. If the Shadow King was already breaking through, perhaps the only way forward was to tear down all the barriers between us and to face him directly. To confront the darkness that had been seeping into our world for centuries rather than continuing to patch the holes.

I clenched my hand into a fist, the moonstone's heat spreading up my arm. The curse had to be broken, consequences be damned. Gavin had to be freed. The queens rescued. My harem whole.

And as I followed Veris into what felt like the very heart of darkness, I wondered if I was walking in my mom's footsteps, making the same terrible choice she had made.

Was I sacrificing everything for a future I wouldn't even live to see?

# 30

V ERIS LED US DEEPER into his stronghold, each step carrying us farther from escape and closer to an endgame I supposed I had been running from in one way or another for thirty years, since fleeing from the Moon Sanctuary.

The corridor widened into a vast chamber that could only be described as a war room. A massive circular table dominated the center, carved with an intricate topographical map of the Olympic Peninsula—the location of the Sun Keep—with various places marked by small, engraved medallions of polished metal, gleaming like dark pewter with subtle silver undertones. Manganese, if I wasn't mistaken, though it was impossible to sense any shadow taint within the small pieces of the metal when surrounded by the expansive manganese deposits in the earth.

Arched windows lined one wall, but instead of glass, they displayed a view of a rough rock wall, deep gray cut through by streaks of dull, metallic manganese that caught the light like veins of tarnished silver.

Several shifters stood around the table, their military bearing marking them as commanders. Their watchful stares tracked us with predatory focus. One woman nonchalantly pulled a cover over the three-dimensional map, only making me more curious about the places marked by the medallions.

"Please, sit," Veris said, gesturing to chairs across from his ornate throne-like seat positioned in front of the manganese wall. The fake politeness made my skin crawl, a parody of diplomacy in a room designed for conquest. Had he given the order to attack the Moon Sanctuary from this room? Had he sentenced my mom and sister and countless queens to death from *right here*?

I remained standing, Javier a solid presence at my back. Through our bond, I felt him cataloging every threat, every weakness, every escape route. His knuckles grazed my spine, a gentle touch Veris and his minions might not notice, but enough to assure me I wasn't alone.

"I didn't come here to chitchat," I said, my voice sharp enough to cut.

"No," Veris agreed, his smile cold and practiced. "You came for your consort, I'm sure. That's the deal you offer, is it not? You'll *attempt* to break the curse in exchange for your servant. How predictable." He settled into his chair and flicked his fingers at a commander. "Bring the corpse."

Those three words made my heart turn leaden and sink into my gut. Frantically, I reached through my bond with Gavin, and I felt him, very much alive. Or rather, *undead*. But not *corpse* dead.

Javier lowered his head, bringing his lips close to my ear. "*Corpse* is a derogatory term for an undead vampire," he whispered, his voice barely audible, just for me.

"While we wait," Veris continued, studying me like a collector eyeing a rare specimen, "perhaps we should discuss terms. You want your consort. I want the curse broken." His amber eyes gleamed with covetous hunger. "A simple exchange, wouldn't you agree?"

"Simple, but incomplete," I replied. "You'll release the captive queens as well."

Veris leaned forward, his massive hands splayed on the throne's armrests. "Break the curse that has limited my people for millennia. In exchange, I will release your consort and the remaining queens."

A side door opened. Gavin's presence crashed through our bond—aware, just barely. Exhausted. Pissed off.

His scent hit me next—dried blood and an undercurrent of foul corruption, like the shadow taint had seeped into him during his imprisonment, but beneath it all was a mouth-watering aroma that was intrinsically *Gavin*. My chest tightened painfully, and my nails bit into my palms as I fought to maintain even a shred of queenly composure.

When they half-dragged him in, something inside me cracked. They'd chained him, iron shackles around his ankles and wrists, and a dull iron mask covering his face; mere slivers cut into the metal for his eyes, nose, and mouth. Not iron, I realized. Manganese. *This* was the source of the foulness tangled with his scent. *This* was why Javier hadn't carried the same lingering shadow taint after spending so much longer as a prisoner here. They were poisoning Gavin with corrupted bindings.

I clenched my jaw. Did they know? Were they aware of the taint corrupting their precious metal? The taint they had spread to the manganese through their own corrupted magic? Or was this just a really shitty accident?

Javier placed a hand on my shoulder, steadying me as I took in the sight of my powerful guardian—the vampire whose calculated grace had anchored me when my carefully constructed world turned upside down.

Gavin's short, black hair was matted with dried blood, his clothes torn and filthy, skin ashen where it had once glowed with vitality. The bond mark on his neck had dulled to a faint shimmer, barely visible through the dried and crusted blood staining his skin. But the mask undid me, hiding his distinctive silver eyes. Erasing his identity. Turning him into a walking blood bag for the queens.

"Gavin," I whispered, his name catching in my throat. Guilt hit me like a physical blow, tears welling instantly. While I'd been wrapped in pleasure with my other consorts, Gavin had been suffering alone in the darkness. "I'm so sorry."

"Touching reunion," Veris intruded, examining his nails with exaggerated boredom. "But we have business." He gestured to the guards flanking Gavin. "As you can see, your consort lives. For now."

"Remove his bindings," I demanded. "I won't agree to a single thing until you get those chains and that ridiculous mask off him."

Veris smirked, smug. "His bindings come off when mine do."

I stepped forward, and Javier's hand slipped off my shoulder. "He poses no threat in this state. Remove his bindings," I repeated, taking another step. Moonlight pulsed inside me, my *will* straining for release. "Before I *make you*."

"You think you can?" Veris barked a laugh. "You think you're stronger than the great High Queen Diana with a full harem fueling her power and centuries of experience using it?" His laughter expanded, filling the space. "Your mother tried to use her *will* on me." He leaned forward, menacing. Mocking. "About three seconds before I ripped her throat out."

I reared back like his words held physical weight. "I *am not* my mother."

"No," Veris said. "You're a child playing at being queen."

Rage boiled my blood, and moonlight seeped from my pores.

Veris sat up straighter, some of the amusement draining from his eyes.

"If I have to repeat myself again," I said, my voice ringing with power, "then we'll all find out how wrong—or right—you are." I glanced at his sycophants. "I'm sure they would love to know if a *child* can best you. I'm sure it would make them wonder if your own child, Bastian—" I glanced at the watching shifters. "One of my consorts," I reminded them. "—would be a stronger king."

Veris stared me down for long seconds before flicking his fingers at the guards standing over Gavin. "Do it." He bared his teeth at me in a mockery of a smile. "As an act of goodwill."

I crossed my arms, watching as Gavin's shackles were removed, first from his ankles, then from his arms. Lastly, they removed his mask. I cataloged the wear wounds on his ankles, wrists, and face, silently vowing to make sure Veris felt Gavin's pain. When this was over. When the deals had been set and met.

"If I agree to remove the curse," I said, each word measured and precise, "I want Gavin and all the queens released immediately. Before I attempt anything."

Veris laughed, the sound like breaking ice. "You're in no position to dictate terms, *little girl*." He leaned back, his posture falsely relaxed. "But I'm feeling generous. I'll release half the queens now. The rest, including your consort, remain until the curse is broken."

"I need assurances," I said, stalling. "A blood oath that you'll honor your word."

Something flashed in Veris's eyes—triumph quickly masked. "A blood oath. How appropriate." He extended his hand, palm up, a gesture as old as bargaining itself. "I accept."

My mom's ring flared hot enough to burn. I balled my hand into a fist in an attempt to suppress the pain, but I heeded the warning. The blood oath spelled danger—but why?

My lip curled, suspicion turning my stomach. "Not a blood exchange," I clarified. "I'm not offering to bond with you."

Veris's smile thinned, the calculated charm slipping. "Come now, Luna. I can call you that, can't I—*Luna*?"

I gritted my teeth.

His cheeks twitched with the hint of a heartless smile. "We both know that only Selene and Eos working together can break the curse. And we both know that only a queen in her full power—with a complete harem of seven—can appeal to Selene, just as only an elemental of the original bloodline can beseech Eos."

I exchanged a wary glance with Javier over my shoulder. That certainly hadn't been *my* experience with Selene, but I wasn't about to tell Veris that. The more I let him talk, the more he revealed, so I wasn't about to cut him short if he was winding up to villain monologue.

"And we *also* both know you are a couple of consorts shy of the complete set. It just so happens I have a guest from the original Star line on his way here right now, who I'm sure would be quite willing to be bound to the High Queen of the House of the Moon. You'll need him to break the curse anyway, so it's very convenient."

"Actually," I cut in. "I have my own—"

"*And* while I could order one of my people to fill your other *hole*, what kind of leader would I be if I asked my people to do something I'm unwilling to do myself?" His eyes hardened to chips of amber. "Your mother refused, and see how that turned out. I was good enough for her bed, but not for her bond."

The revelation hit like a slap. My mom—and *Veris*?

"You're lying," I said automatically, even as doubt crawled up my spine.

"Am I?" Veris's smile turned vicious, scenting weakness. "Ask your guardian. He was there, watching from the shadows. Diana's faithful dog, yearning for scraps while I feasted."

Javier's rage surged through our bond like wildfire, nearly overwhelming in its intensity. His fingers tightened on my shoulder, his silence confirming Veris's claim more effectively than words ever could.

"My mom would never—"

"Never *what*? Stray outside her harem?" Veris laughed, hollow and cold. "Oh, but she would. She came back, again and again. Power seeks out power."

A silver shimmer caught my eye behind Veris's throne—stronger this time. A faintly humanoid shape. Not distinct enough to make out any discerning features.

"*Lies...*" The voice that accompanied the half-formed specter, however, was clearly identifiable. "*Half-truths...*"

My mom. She was here. Not in the middle of a ritual. Not summoned by divine power. She was *here*. Anchored here. Trapped here. I scanned the room. This sick psycho must have saved part of her body, holding her ghost captive, intentional or not.

"*I used his weakness for flesh...*"

I swallowed repeatedly, attempting to regain my voice. "Where is she?" I asked, my voice low and laced with cold rage.

Veris cocked his head slightly. "One of the queens?"

"My *mother*, you sick fuck," I hissed. "You kept part of her body. Where is it?"

Veris straightened, his eyes opening wide. He looked around, suddenly very much on edge. "She can't manifest here. The wards—it's impossible. He assured me—"

"You will release Gavin," I ground out. "You will release the queens. And you will hand over whatever piece of my mom you kept as a trophy. Then, and only then, will I remove your curse." I spat at his feet. "Take the deal or leave it. But know that if you reject my offer, I *will* use my *will* on you, and we'll all find out once and for all if you're stronger than a *little girl*. And if you're not—if I can command you—then I will get everything I want, and you and your people will get nothing. Not so long as you're king."

Veris curled his lip in distaste. "Deal," he growled. His glare moved past me to the guards standing over Gavin. "Retrieve the queens." Veris stood abruptly. "I'll return shortly with the other item. *Then* you'll uphold your end of the deal." Without another word, he stalked away, leaving Javier, Gavin, and me alone in his war room with his stunned commanders.

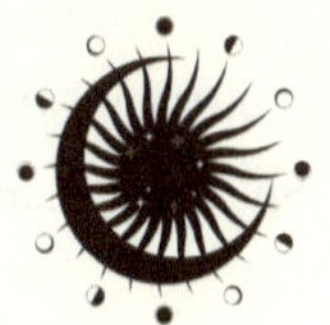

# 31

THE MOMENT VERIS DISAPPEARED through the doorway, I rushed to Gavin, my heart hammering against my ribcage, and fell to my knees beside him. His body was a wreck—skin ashen where it wasn't coated in dried blood, his usually immaculate appearance shattered by weeks of captivity. The cruel mask had left angry red gouges across his face, open wounds where corrupted manganese had rubbed his skin raw, and in his depleted state, he hadn't had the energy to heal.

I wanted to touch him, to hold him, but I hesitated, afraid of causing him more pain.

His eyes found mine, those distinctive silver irises now dull and clouded with exhaustion, but recognition sparked in their depths. "Sophie," he whispered, his voice like sandpaper against stone.

Just my name. Nothing else. But the relief in that single word was everything.

"I'm here," I said, finally reaching for him. My hands hovered over his face, tracing the air above his wounds without touching them. "I'm sorry it took so long." I whimpered. "I'm so sorry."

Javier positioned himself between us and the shifter commanders, his back to us, his body coiled with lethal tension. Through our bond, I sensed his focused vigilance, his eyes tracking every movement in the room while giving Gavin and me this moment.

Gavin attempted to push himself upright, but his arms were too weak. "You shouldn't have come," he rasped, collapsing back onto the hard floor with a grunt. "It's too dangerous."

"I wasn't going to leave you here." I slid my hand into his, careful of the raw wounds around his wrist. His skin was like ice. "I couldn't."

His fingers weakly curled around mine, the gesture speaking volumes about his depleted state. The Shadow King's corruption clung to him like an oily film, seeping from the wounds left by the manganese restraints.

"How bad is it?" I asked, though I could see the answer in the hollows of his cheeks, the labored rise and fall of his chest. Could sense it in the shadow taint wafting off him.

A ghost of his familiar, self-assured smile crossed his lips. "I've had worse."

The attempt at humor broke something loose in my chest. I laughed, a sound closer to a sob. "Liar."

The Sun commanders shifted uncomfortably, looking away from our reunion, perhaps finding something too relatable in the display.

"I need to feed you," I said, keeping my voice low. My eyes cut to the watching shifters, then back to Gavin. "Now. Before Veris returns."

Gavin's eyes widened slightly. "Sophie—"

"No arguments." I helped him sit up part way, settling his head on my lap. "You need blood to heal...at least to cleanse away that awful shadow taint."

His lips parted, protest forming, but I saw the hunger flare in his eyes. The darkened veins beneath his skin, telltale signs of severe blood deprivation. How long had it been since they'd allowed him to feed? Days? Weeks? Had they been starving him the entire time he'd been their captive?

I glanced at Javier, who gave me a terse nod without breaking his vigilant stance. Silent permission. Understanding.

I held my wrist in front of Gavin's mouth. "Take what you need," I whispered. "Hurry."

He shook his head, though it was a weak gesture. "I don't know if I'll be able to stop."

"If I have to bite my own wrist, I will, and that'll hurt a hell of a lot more than if you do it." I pressed my wrist to his lips. "Do it, Gavin. We don't have much time."

His eyes held mine for a long moment, silver depths still clouded with pain but now burning with something else. Hunger. Need. Desire. With agonizing slowness, his lips parted, and I felt his cool breath against my skin.

"I'll stop when you tell me," he promised, his voice steadier than it had been moments ago.

I nodded, bracing myself. When his fangs pierced my skin, the initial sting made me bite back a gasp, but it quickly transformed into a wave of warmth that rushed through my veins, straight to my core. Not the overwhelming, desperate hunger of our first *communion*, but something deeper—a connection reawakening after too long apart.

Through our bond, I felt the shadow taint recoiling from the moonlight in my blood. My power moved through him like a cleansing fire, burning away corruption, closing wounds, restoring what had been damaged. With each pull of his mouth against my wrist, his presence in my mind grew stronger, a flicker becoming a steady flame.

The intensity caught me off guard. Pleasure built low in my belly as his feeding continued. My head tipped back slightly, eyelids half-closing. I fought to keep my breathing steady, aware of the shifters watching from across the room, their expressions a mixture of fascination and disgust.

I glanced down to see color returning to Gavin's skin. The wounds around his wrists and face looked less angry, parts even beginning to close.

"Not yet," I whispered, pushing my wrist more firmly against his mouth. "Take more."

Gavin made a sound low in his throat, half-protest, half-surrender. He gripped my arm tighter, holding me closer as he drank deeper. Power flowed between us, awakening something primal and possessive. I felt his hunger shifting, transforming into a different kind of need.

My free hand tangled in his hair, my nails scraping lightly against his scalp. The gesture was meant to be soothing, but the way his body tensed told me it was anything but. The pleasure building between us was spiraling toward something we couldn't surrender to—not here, not now. Not with hostile eyes upon us.

"Enough," I said, breathless, and with tremendous effort, I pulled my wrist away from his mouth.

Gavin caught my hand, bringing my wrist back to his lips. Not to drink, but to seal the wound with a slow, deliberate caress of his tongue. His silver eyes never left mine, a promise in their depths that sent heat pooling low in my belly.

"Thank you," he murmured against my skin.

Through our renewed bond, I sensed Gavin's strength returning, the shadow taint banished. He was far from healed—that would take much more than a quick feeding—but the corruption had been cleansed from his body, and the worst of his injuries were less severe than before.

The shifter commanders whispered among themselves, clearly disturbed by the display.

Gavin sat up, easing himself from my lap with newfound steadiness. "What have you promised him?" he asked, his voice low and urgent. His fingers remained interlaced with mine, as if he couldn't bear to break the physical connection.

"The curse," I said simply. "I'm going to break it."

His expression darkened, silver eyes sharpening with alarm. "Sophie, no!" he said. "You can't. The curse—"

"—protects the shifters from the Shadow King's corruption," I finished for him, keeping my voice low enough that the commanders couldn't hear. "I know. I figured it out."

"Then why would you agree to remove it?" The confusion in his eyes mirrored the tension in his body.

I leaned closer, our foreheads nearly touching. "Because the barrier between worlds is already failing. The Shadow King is breaking through. I've *seen* it." I glanced toward the chamber walls, where corrupted manganese veins pulsed with subtle shadow taint. "The corruption is already spreading."

"More visions?" he asked, understanding dawning in his eyes, followed by strategic calculation.

I nodded.

"And what does Veris offer in return?"

"You. The queens. And…" I hesitated, searching his face. "A piece of my mom he kept all these years."

Fury flashed across Gavin's features, his fingers tightening around mine until they nearly hurt. "After all this time, he had a part of her?"

I nodded, swallowing against the knot in my throat. "Her ghost is here, Gavin. I can sense her, just barely, but the suppression wards are too strong. She's trying to warn us about *something*, but I can't make it out."

A flicker of alarm passed through our bond, but before Gavin could say more, the atmosphere in the room shifted suddenly, a cold draft sweeping through the chamber. Javier's tension spiked through our bond, his stance widening as he prepared for a threat. I knew without looking that Veris was returning.

Gavin released my hand and pushed himself upright, wavering only slightly before finding his balance. I rose alongside him, positioning myself between him and the door as it swung open.

Veris strode in, carrying a tiny lacquered box. His keen eyes assessed us, lingering on the fresh marks on my wrist, then on Gavin's healing wounds and improved coloring.

"How touching," Veris drawled, his smile lacking sentiment. "Feeding your pet already? I hope you've left enough for our ritual." His gaze traveled over me with deliberate lewdness. "You'll need your strength when we're done."

The suggestion in his tone made my skin crawl, but I kept my expression neutral as I extended my hand. "My mother's remains."

Veris placed the box in my palm with exaggerated care, his fingertips lingering against my skin a moment too long. "A lock of her hair," he said, his voice softening with what might have been mistaken for genuine emotion if it had come from anyone else. "It was all I could salvage before the fire consumed her."

The box felt impossibly heavy in my hand for something as light as hair. I curled my fingers around the box and held it against my chest, resisting the urge to open it immediately.

"And the queens?" I asked, my voice steadier than I felt.

"Being brought to the ritual chamber as we speak," Veris replied, his composure returning. "Along with our guest from the House of the Stars." His eyes glittered with calculation. "Everything as agreed. Now, it's time for you to fulfill your part of our bargain."

I slipped the box into my pocket, feeling its weight against my hip like a hunk of lead. With one hand, I reached back for Gavin, who stepped forward on steadier legs than before. With my other hand, I reached for Javier, who moved to my side without taking his eyes off Veris.

I raised my chin and met Veris's hard stare. "Lead the way."

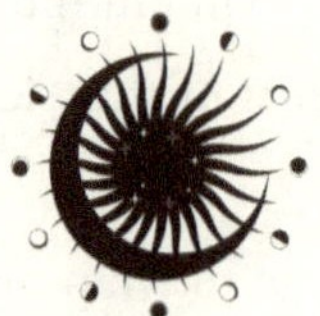

# 32

T HE RITUAL CHAMBER SPRAWLED beneath the earth like a forgotten cathedral to a dark faith. Massive stone columns soared upward, disappearing into shadows that even my *communion*-enhanced vision couldn't penetrate. The ceiling remained hidden in that artificial night, giving the unsettling impression that the chamber opened directly to some void beyond our world.

Veins of manganese ore threaded through the walls like tarnished silver arteries, pulsing with subtle, sickly light that made my skin crawl. The shadow taint had spread through this place like a slow cancer, corrupting even the stone itself.

At the center of the chamber, a circular altar rose from the ground, ancient and worn smooth by centuries of use. Symbols that tickled the edges of understanding had been carved into its surface, their shapes softened by time but still potent with old power. Half-melted black candles ringed the perimeter, their flames unnaturally still in the heavy air. Veris lounged in a massive throne off to one side of the chamber, the seat appearing carved from the bedrock itself.

"You feel it, don't you?" Gavin murmured beside me, his silver eyes tracking the subtle movements of that sickly light through the walls. "The wrongness."

I nodded, fighting the urge to wrap my arms around myself. The shadows in the corners stirred occasionally, as if responding to unheard commands. Everything about this place whispered of violation. This was a sacred space corrupted by profane intention.

"This was once a holy site," Javier explained softly, his voice barely audible. "The first shifters performed their transformation rituals here, drinking in the sun's power." His lip curled in distaste. "Veris had the whole thing disassembled and transported here."

I opened my mouth to ask more, but the heavy doors at the far end of the chamber groaned open, cutting me off.

A line of queens shuffled into the chamber, hands covered in what looked like leather oven mitts, wrists shackled, and mouths gagged, their weakness palpable in the staggered rhythm of their steps. My chest tightened at the sight of these women who had endured darkness and degradation while I'd built a life in the human world, oblivious to their suffering. Their skin was ashen, their hair dull and lifeless, but their eyes burned with an ancient dignity that decades of imprisonment couldn't extinguish.

I counted six of them, each supported by a pair of shifter guards who handled them with the careful precision one might use for volatile substances rather than living beings. The fear in the guards' movements would have been almost comical if it hadn't highlighted just how dangerous even half-starved vampire queens could be, though they couldn't do much of anything without their hands or mouths.

One queen in particular caught my attention—her frail body barely able to hold itself upright, yet her eyes gleamed with startling clarity when they met mine. Laelia, I recalled from Javier's descriptions. The oldest among the captives.

"As promised," Veris said, gesturing toward the queens with that familiar, calculated smugness. "This is half of the queens. The rest are being prepared."

Javier stood at my other side, his body strumming with tension, his eyes tracking every movement in the room. I felt his struggle through our bond, the battle between his need to protect me and his duty to the other queens, whom he'd spent two decades of his life keeping alive.

I reached for his hand, curling my fingers around his palm. "You should go with them," I said softly. "Make sure they get home."

His eyes widened, disbelief crashing through our bond. We had agreed that I would never ask him to leave me again, and now I was suggesting he do exactly that.

"Luna..." My birth name on his lips felt like both plea and prayer.

"I need someone I trust to get them safely back to the Moon Sanctuary," I continued, meeting his gaze despite the tremor in my voice. "And Gavin's not in any state to protect them. It has to be you."

He grasped my hand with sudden fierceness. "I don't want to leave you," he said, his voice rough with emotion. "When we were reunited—"

"I know." I pressed my palm against his cheek, the crescent sigil warm beneath my touch. "But this is what I need from you now. They need a protector who understands what they've survived. Who can lead them home."

Something shifted in Javier's expression, grief giving way to understanding, then to reluctant acceptance. He lifted my hand to his lips, turning it over to press a kiss against my palm. "I will return for you," he said, his voice vibrating with centuries of careful promise. "As soon as I've delivered the queens. I will return."

The certainty in his voice made my eyes burn with unshed tears. This man who had rescued me as a terrified child, who had taught me to survive, who had endured captivity rather than reveal my location—he was trusting me to face this curse-breaking ritual alone.

"I know you will," I whispered, fighting back tears.

We stood there for one heartbeat, then another, our hands linked as moonlight danced between us. So many words caught in my throat, but none seemed adequate for this moment.

Finally, he nodded, decision made. He stepped back, his fingers lingering against mine until distance forced our separation. As he moved toward the waiting queens, his posture shifted, centuries of guardian training asserting itself. He positioned himself at the optimal vantage point, his predatory stillness a stark contrast to the queens' weakened movements.

Laelia watched our exchange with ancient understanding in her eyes, her frail form straightening as my Prime Consort joined their ranks.

When he reached them, he didn't look back, a mercy I hadn't expected but desperately needed. If he *had* turned, if I had seen the struggle in his eyes one more time, my resolve might have crumbled.

The ceremonial chamber fell quiet as the queens filed out.

Gavin shifted closer, until his shoulder touched mine, a gentle reassurance.

Veris clapped his hands with theatrical flare. "Your attention, please," he announced, his voice echoing through the chamber. "Our final guest has arrived."

The hair on the back of my neck rose as a familiar figure strode through the arched doorway—tall and elegant, his long black hair pulled back to reveal sharp features. Reiji's dark eyes met mine across the chamber, and the calculation in his expression made my blood run cold.

"I apologize for my tardiness, Your Majesty," he said with formality. He bowed deeply to Veris, and when he straightened, his eyes found mine. "I got held up."

Veris's smile widened. "No matter. You've arrived just in time."

Dread clenched my gut as I watched Reiji move to Veris's side.

"Reiji?" I whispered, surprise catching in my throat. He was supposed to be spelled into unconsciousness, safe and secure in *my* dungeon. "What are you doing here?"

His dark eyes met mine again, and for a moment—so brief I might have imagined it—I thought I saw genuine regret flicker across his features before shielding his expression.

"I'm sorry it had to be this way, Sophie. Truly." He clasped his hands together before his chest. "If only you'd been more amenable... Well, we'd still end up here, but as allies, not as—" He gestured to me, then to himself. "This."

"You've been working with him all along," I said. The words tasted bitter.

A cold smile touched Reiji's lips. "I've been working toward this moment for far longer than you realize."

The silver shimmer at the edge of my vision grew stronger—my mother's ghost fighting desperately against the suppression wards. I shook off my absolute confusion about Reiji's role in all of this. Some things were more important, like figuring out what my mom was so desperately trying to tell me.

I straightened my spine, channeling every ounce of queenly authority I possessed. "Before we proceed, I require a private audience with the representative of the House of the Stars." My voice rang with unexpected power, silver light pulsing beneath my skin.

Veris's eyes narrowed suspiciously. "Why?"

"As you yourself claimed, the ritual to appeal to Selene and to Eos to break the curse requires a representative of the House of the Moon and the House of the Stars to work together in perfect unity. If I'm going to bind Reiji to guarantee unity, then I'd like to do so in private. The binding ritual is quite intimate," I said, hiding the lie behind the truth.

Gavin tensed beside me at the mention of binding someone I clearly didn't like, but I felt his understanding through our bond. He knew I was planning something.

Veris seemed to consider my request, his distrustful gaze flicking between Reiji and me. Finally, he inclined his head. "As you wish, *Your Majesty*." The mockery in his tone couldn't quite mask his curiosity. "There's an antechamber through there." He gestured to a small archway set into the far wall. "We'll await your...completion."

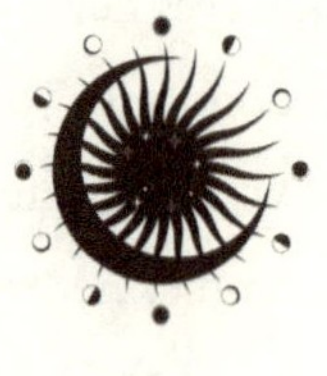

# 33

I MOVED TOWARD THE archway, Gavin a shadow behind me, and glanced back at Reiji, inviting him to follow with a nod of my head. The elemental's expression betrayed nothing as he crossed the chamber, but tension radiated from him like heat from an impending supernova.

The antechamber was small but ornate, dominated by an altar carved from the same stone as the chamber beyond. Ancient symbols were etched into its surface, and the walls bore faded murals depicting what appeared to be shifter mythology—Helios bestowing his gifts upon the first of their kind.

As soon as the door closed behind us, Reiji's careful mask slipped. "I know what you're thinking," he said hurriedly, "but you're wrong. I'm not an agent of the Shadow King."

Gavin positioned himself between us, his body straining with protective tension. "Then explain," he said, his voice deadly soft. "Quickly."

"It was a ploy," Reiji rushed to say, raising his hands defensively. "Illusion magic to trick Sophie into coming here."

I stepped around Gavin, my eyes never leaving Reiji's face. "Ren," I said simply. "What have you done with your sister?" She had been her brother's captor, and I feared what it meant for her that he was here.

Something like genuine pain flickered across Reiji's features. "She's safely contained in my cozy cell at the Moon Sanctuary—under a disguise illusion that makes her look like me." He flashed us a weak smile and held out his arms like he was saying, *what can I say?* "Illusion is my specialty."

"No shit," I breathed.

"She's fine," Reiji added. "I would never hurt her...permanently. She's my sister. I love her. She's part of why I'm doing this. She hates politicking, and she lives under a constant barrage of death threats from lower elementals. Our people aren't like your vampires. Elementals don't blindly follow; they plot and scheme and seek power." His shoulders slumped. "She doesn't *want* to be High Priestess." The words sounded sincere, but I'd learned not to trust surface impressions.

"I didn't want to be High Queen, yet here I am," I snapped. "We step up, filling the roles as required, whether we like it or not." I gritted my teeth and drew in a deep breath, attempting to cool my outrage. "Did Ren *ask* you to help her shirk her duty, or did you so generously take that upon yourself?"

Reiji paced the small space, running a hand through his dark hair. "You don't understand the larger picture," he said, frustration evident in the tightness of his jaw. So, *no*, she didn't ask him for help. At least I knew Ren wasn't complicit, as much a victim of her brother's manipulation as me. More, even, considering their close relationship. "For millennia, the Houses have been at war," Reiji explained. "This endless cycle of fighting and false reconciliation, while the real threat grows stronger beyond the veil."

"And your solution to prepare for war with the Shadow King is to betray your sister and to ally with Veris?" I challenged. "A shifter king who nearly destroyed the House of the Moon and keeps vampire queens imprisoned for shits and giggles?" I scoffed. "*That's* the guy you threw your lot in with to promote unity among the Houses?"

"We have an arrangement," Reiji said, his voice rising as he grew defensive. "I help him reclaim the shifters' rightful strength by breaking the curse, and in return—"

"He helps you become the first High Priest of the House of the Stars," I finished for him, remembering his earlier boasts to Ren. "A new era where the Houses work in harmony under your guidance."

Reiji nodded, a flicker of ambition burning in his eyes. "Precisely. No more petty conflicts, no more divided loyalties."

"I suppose being bound to the High Queen of the House of the Moon is integral to your plot. Like once you were my consort, the vampires would magically fall in line?" I laughed, the sound harsh and ugly and stepped closer to him. "What do you think your magic dick can do that my guys don't already do for me? What makes you so exceptional?" I sniffed, my gaze moving down his body and back up. "Nothing other than your exceptional lack of scruples. Manipulation and emotional abuse. Lies. *Illusion*. That's what you're good at, right? Your own words..."

The color had drained from his face as I spoke, and he swallowed roughly but said nothing. His first wise move since we met. I studied his face, his eyes, searching for the truth beneath his carefully constructed reality. "My mom's ghost is here. She's trying desperately to manifest, but the suppression wards are too strong."

I stepped closer, tilting my head back to maintain eye contact, my voice softening. "What do you think she's trying to tell me, Reiji? And *why* are the suppression wards so strong here? Veris should have no reason to fear invisible spies. Ghosts aren't free roaming. They're anchored. Like my mom, who's anchored here." I pulled the small enameled box out of my pocket and held it up on my open palm. "Because Veris kept a piece of her before he burned her remains and scattered her ashes."

I shifted my focus from the box back up to Reiji's face, furrowing my brows dramatically. "Why would he do that? Why would he trap her here, then suppress her into near oblivion?"

Uncertainty crept into Reiji's expression. "I don't know," he admitted reluctantly. "The wards were Veris's idea. He claimed they were standard protection against interference. She must—" He shook his head, struggling to voice the truth. "She must know something that would destroy him."

"Something worse than the world knowing he committed genocide upon vampires?" I asked. "Because he certainly doesn't try to hide that, does he?"

Again, Reiji shook his head. "I don't know," he said, sounding truly lost.

"Lower the suppression wards," I demanded. "Now, here, and I'll make my mom visible so you can hear what she has to say. No more secrets, Reiji. No more *illusions*. Unless you really do want to be my enemy."

Reiji hesitated, calculation flickering behind his eyes.

Gavin moved closer to my side, his hand brushing mine in silent support.

After a long moment, Reiji nodded. "Very well." He raised his hands, power gathering around his fingertips like crystallized starlight. With a series of fluid gestures, he traced complex patterns in the air. The antechamber shuddered as the wards began to dissolve, ancient magic unraveling like threads pulled from a tapestry.

The effect was immediate. My mother's ghost materialized fully beside us, her form more substantial than I'd ever seen it. Her eyes—just like mine—blazed with urgency.

"Daughter," she said, her voice carrying that peculiar echo of the dead. "At last."

"Mom," I whispered, emotion closing my throat. I reached for her, and she curled her fingers around mine, the contact pulling her partially into the physical world, making her visible to Reiji and Gavin.

Gavin dropped to one knee and bowed his head in deference.

My mom smiled down at him approvingly but quickly returned her attention to me. "Listen carefully, daughter," she said, her form flickering as she struggled to maintain her manifestation even with the suppression wards down. "Veris isn't just the Sun King. He's an agent of the Shadow King—has been for centuries."

I sucked in a breath.

"I maintained a relationship with him to justify frequent trips here so I could identify the shadow-bound among the shifters," my mother continued, her gaze never leaving mine. "But I never imagined he was the lead culprit. I learned the truth only after he killed me."

"Is this why he kept a piece of you?" I asked, grief and anger tangling in my chest at the thought of him possessing even a lock of her hair after what he'd done. "To prevent you from revealing the truth?"

She nodded, her form wavering. "He thought burning my body would silence me forever, but he kept my hair, just in case. He couldn't risk that I would attach to an object in the absence of my remains."

Reiji had grown pale as he listened, suspicion crystallizing into horror. "The Shadow King," he whispered, like he was testing the weight of those words. "Is this true?" He directed the question to my mother's ghost, apparently forgetting I was in the room.

"You've been played, Star Prince," she replied, her voice carrying a trace of pity. "Your ambition made you an easy target—just as my pride made me one."

Reiji staggered back, hand braced against the altar. "I didn't know," he insisted, his eyes finding mine. "Sophie, you have to believe me. I wouldn't align with that."

"The curse," I said, turning back to my mom's ghost. "Is it even safe to break it now? Won't that just make the Shadow King's hold over the shifters stronger?"

She nodded, her form growing more translucent. "Yes, but now it must be broken."

I frowned, confusion swirling. "But if it shields them—"

"The curse *was* meant as a shield—from the shadow taint corrupting their magic, not from the Shadow King directly," she explained. "But it's hamstringing their magic now, making them more vulnerable to direct influence. With it broken, the shadow taint will be obvious to all immortals." Her gaze shifted to the chamber door, beyond which Veris waited. "His power comes from secrecy, from slow corruption that goes undetected."

She looked from me to Reiji and back. "Work together. Break the curse, and he'll be exposed."

# 34

I RELEASED MY MOM'S hand, letting her fade away, and squared off against Reiji. I studied the internal struggle evident in his features—ambition warring with fear, calculation with horror at the huge mistake he had made in trusting Veris.

But Reiji was a manipulator. A self-proclaimed master of illusion. How could I trust a single thing he said or did?

There was only one way...

"Did you know?" I asked him directly, the faintest thread of my *will* resonating through my words. "About Veris and the Shadow King?"

Reiji hesitated, just long enough for doubt to flicker through me.

"Answer me," I commanded through gritted teeth, the strength of my *will* rising. "Tell me the truth, Reiji. Did. You. Know?"

"No," he said. The word dragged from him like it had been hooked and pulled up his throat. "I suspected Veris wasn't being entirely transparent, but—" He seemed genuinely shaken. "The Shadow King—no. I wouldn't align with that."

I was quiet for a long moment. "I need to break the curse," I finally said. "Will you help me?"

Reiji's calculating expression returned, but something had shifted beneath it. "If you bind me as a consort."

I stepped back, gesturing to the antechamber around me. "Isn't that why we're in here? For you, Prince Reiji of the House of the Stars, to become the first elemental consort to a High Queen in centuries?" I said, meeting his gaze steadily. I swallowed the guilt I felt at choosing Reiji over Ren, who I actually felt a genuine connection with. "A place of honor and power. Exactly what you wanted."

I stepped closer, moonlight pulsing from my skin, and peered up at him through my lashes. "But let me be perfectly clear—as my consort, you will serve me. Your blood will feed me. Your power will be my power. Not the other way around." I held out my hand, palm up, like I was waiting for him to give me a gift. I supposed, in a sense, I was. "So, what do you say?"

Reiji glanced down at my hand, like he wasn't quite sure why it was there. "What do I have to do?"

"Give me your wrist," I said, wiggling my fingers. "The binding requires blood." My heart beat faster, my nerves getting the better of me. "An exchange between queen and consort," I clarified.

Reiji's dark eyes studied me, calculation giving way to something more primal. "I understand."

I glanced at Gavin, who gave me a nearly imperceptible nod. He trusted me to do what was necessary.

Reiji placed his hand in mine, and I turned it over, revealing the paler skin on the inside of his wrist. I pulled the hairpin knife from my bun and unsheathed it, quickly dragging it across Reiji's wrist. He hissed as deep crimson welled in the wound, his blood almost seeming to glitter, like captured stars flowed through his veins along with the magic Eos had gifted his people.

I hesitated for only a moment before handing Gavin the knife and raising Reiji's wrist to my lips. The first taste of his blood was unlike anything I'd experienced before—not the dark richness of my vampire consorts, nor the wild sweetness of Bastian. This was somehow cold despite the heat of his body, toasty and tangy and just a little sweet, like the finest champagne.

I moaned as his essence flowed into me, my eyelids fluttering shut.

"Dear goddess," he hissed, the magic in my saliva doing its job, turning what had been a painful wound into something unexpectedly pleasurable. His other hand curled around the side of my neck, his thumb caressing my jaw line. "Sophie, please..."

I opened my eyes, locking gazes with him, and pulled away from his wrist. His thumb traced my lips, smearing his blood.

"That was..." He shook his head. "I don't know what that was."

I took a step back, and his hand fell away. "You heal quickly, yes?" I asked, licking my lips.

He nodded, holding his hand over his oozing wrist and clutching it to his chest.

"Good." I held my hand out toward Gavin, and he placed the slim dagger on my palm. With a quick flick of the blade across my wrist, my own blood was freed.

Reiji's eyes widened at the sight, a mixture of hunger and fear flickering across his features. I held out my dripping wrist, and he gripped my forearm on one side of the wound and my hand on the other, raising my wrist to his lips. I sucked in a breath at the sting of his tongue sweeping over the cut. But the moment he swallowed, threads of magic wove together between us, forming the foundation of our bond, and the sharp pain flipped to pulsing pleasure.

Power surged between us, moonlight meeting starlight in an ancient dance of cosmic forces. My vision blurred as ecstasy built within me, sharp and sudden, traveling from his mouth on my wrist to my core with breathtaking speed. I clutched his shoulder, barely registering the small sound that escaped my throat, somewhere between a gasp and a moan.

Reiji's hands tightened, his body tensing as the same euphoria coursed through him. Through our rapidly strengthening bond, I felt his surprise, his wonder, his reluctant surrender to something larger than himself.

The pleasure crested suddenly, a white-hot explosion that radiated outward from my center to every extremity, and moonlight burst out of me, washing the room in silver. My knees weakened, and I might have ended up on the floor if not for Reiji's steadying arm sliding around my waist. He held me close, our bodies flush, and I felt his hard length throbbing as, through the bond, I sensed his own release mirroring mine.

As the waves of pleasure subsided, leaving my skin hypersensitive and my breathing unsteady, I became aware of a new presence settling among the others in my consciousness.

I pulled my wrist away from his mouth, watching as Reiji traced his tongue over his lips, catching the last drops of my blood. His eyes had changed, starlight flaring in their depths, and he held his hand up, admiring the faint silver bonding sigil now marking his wrist with the phases of the moon.

"I had no idea," he whispered. "The old texts spoke of the bond, but they never…" He trailed off, words failing him for perhaps the first time since I'd met him.

"Now you understand," I said softly, steadying myself.

His expression shifted, the mask of ambition falling away completely for one unguarded moment, revealing something almost childlike in its wonder. Then, slowly, his composure returned, and he cleared his throat. "Veris will be waiting."

I nodded, my mind clearing as the aftershocks of the binding faded.

"He's going to try to force you to bind him as well." Reiji adjusted his clothing, a new determination in his eyes. "He says you need a full harem to speak with Selene."

I snorted. "I'd rather bind a slug. But no, I don't need a full harem of seven. I was able to channel her divine power with only five. If she was willing to grant me that, I'm sure she'll be happy to merely listen to me with six."

"And if he pushes the matter?" Reiji asked.

A cruel smile curved my lips. "Let him." I was itching to try out my *will* on Veris anyway.

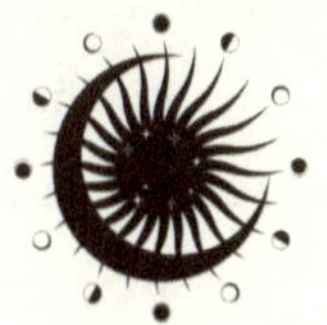

# 35

THE RITUAL CHAMBER FELL silent as Reiji and I returned, Gavin trailing behind us. My wrist still tingled from where Gavin had smeared his immortal blood. Undead vampires—especially those who'd received guardian status via the Second Rite—had much more potent healing capabilities than any other immortal.

The bond between Reiji and me pulsed with newness, shallow and uncertain, nothing like the deep roots I shared with my other consorts. But it was enough—a lifeline connecting the House of the Moon and the House of the Stars. An alliance born of necessity rather than desire.

Veris remained on his stone throne, his keen eyes tracking us as we entered, his gaze lingering on the silver bonding mark encircling Reiji's wrist like a phantom bracelet. His nostrils flared, no doubt catching the scent of our mingled blood, the telltale evidence of our *communion*.

"I see the binding was successful," he said, his voice carrying an edge that hadn't been there before. Jealousy, perhaps. Or disappointment that Reiji had claimed what Veris believed should be his.

I straightened my spine, the box containing my mom's hair weighing heavy in my pocket. My mom, trapped here for decades by this monster. Veris, serving the Shadow King while pretending to be a champion of his own people. The knowledge burned through me like acid.

"It was," I replied, stepping forward. Gavin moved with me, a shadow at my back. "Let's get this over with." The wrongness tainting this place set my teeth on edge, and I didn't want to be here one second longer than was necessary.

Veris stood, and his smile reminded me of a shark—all teeth, all hunger. "Not quite yet." He descended from his elevated position, each step measured and deliberate. "You still require one more consort to complete your harem."

I laughed, the sound harsh even to my own ears. "Not a chance."

"The ancient texts are quite clear," Veris insisted, moving closer. "A High Queen requires seven consorts to channel the full power of Selene." He gestured to himself, straightening the cuffs of his tailored suit. "And as I mentioned earlier, I am uniquely qualified to fill that role."

My stomach turned at the suggestion, revulsion crawling up my spine. "Absolutely not."

"Let me be blunt," Veris continued, undeterred. "*You* need me. Without a full harem, you cannot appeal to Selene with sufficient strength to break the curse." His eyes hardened. "Unless you wish to return empty-handed? To abandon your precious consort and those remaining queens to indefinite imprisonment?"

The blatant manipulation might have worked if I hadn't already channeled Selene's power.

I felt Reiji's uncertainty through our new bond, my awareness of him growing stronger with each passing minute. He projected calm certainty for Veris's benefit, but beneath it swirled a hurricane of emotions—doubt, fear, determination. Learning his trusted ally was a servant of the Shadow King had shaken him to his core.

"No," I said, my voice steady despite my racing heart.

Veris's expression darkened, calculation giving way to cold fury. "Then our deal is void."

"The deal was that I would break the curse in exchange for Gavin and the queens," I reminded him. "Nothing was said about binding you."

"The technicality was implied." Veris moved closer, his presence oppressive. "Let me explain something, girl. This is my domain. My rules. *I* am the highest power in this room, and *I* have final say on the terms of our arrangement." His amber eyes burned with ancient hunger. "Bind me, or watch your consort suffer for your childish refusal."

At his words, the shifter commanders stepped forward, swinging the assault rifles strapped to their backs around and aiming the weapons at Gavin. It was far enough from the full moon that they couldn't shift, but they wouldn't need to with all those guns.

I felt power stirring within me, moonlight pulsing beneath my skin. My consorts' essence flowed through me—Javier's steadfast protection, Bastian's primal wildness, Gavin's calculating precision, Ash's immovable strength, Thane's depthless patience, and now Reiji's cosmic clarity. The magic from their blood charged mine.

"Enough," I said, my voice resonating with the full force of my *will*. "Sit down, Veris."

The command struck him like a physical blow. He staggered, his eyes widening with shock as my *will* wrapped around him like invisible chains. For a moment, he fought against it, centuries of power battling my command.

Then, to the visible shock of every shifter in the chamber, he sat heavily on the stairs leading up to his throne.

"How dare—"

"Shut up, Veris," I commanded.

His mouth snapped shut, his teeth clacking together audibly.

Silence descended as the immortal king was cut down to size by my words. By my *will*. His commanders stood frozen, uncertainty and fear replacing their earlier confidence. They had likely never seen their king dominated, never witnessed his indomitable *will* broken. It took all my self-control not to betray my surprise at how easily I had subdued him.

"You are *not* the highest power in this room," I told him. "*I* am."

I felt Gavin's approval through our bond, his pride in my strength washing over me like a warm wave. He positioned himself between me and the shifter commanders, ready to defend despite his weakened state.

I turned to Reiji. "Ready?"

Reiji hesitated, seeming torn where he had been resolute moments ago. All other emotions had faded into the background through our bond, and now all I sensed was fear. He took a deep breath and, finally, nodded, moving toward the altar at the center of the chamber. "We'll need to work quickly," he murmured. "Your command won't hold him indefinitely."

I glanced at Veris, uneasy.

Reiji and I approached the ancient altar, its stone surface cool beneath my fingertips. The manganese veins pulsed with sickening corruption. This sacred place had been desecrated, just as the shifters themselves had been corrupted from within. Yet, the shifters seemed completely unaware. How they couldn't sense it was beyond me. I supposed that was the true curse—how the shifters had been blinded to their own poison.

"The ritual is complex," Reiji explained, his voice low and urgent. "We'll need to combine our magic—starlight and moonlight—to appeal to Selene and Eos simultaneously." He traced patterns on the altar's surface, his fingers leaving trails of crystallized starlight. "Follow my lead."

I placed my hands on the altar beside his, feeling the weight of centuries pressing down on me. Of millennia. This ritual had been performed only once before, when the curse was first laid. Now, we would undo what our ancestors had done, for better *and* for worse. But it had to be done.

"I'll reach out to Eos," Reiji continued, his shoulder brushing mine, "while you call upon Selene." His dark eyes met mine, raw honesty bleeding through our bond. "Whatever happens, Sophie, know that I truly believed I was doing what was right. For all immortals."

There was something in his tone that sent a chill down my spine, a finality I couldn't identify. "Reiji—"

"We need to begin," he interrupted, glancing at Veris and placing his palms flat on the altar. "Place your hands atop mine."

I hesitated, thrown off by what I was feeling through our bond, but only for a moment. I slid between his body and the altar until his arms caged me in. Pressing my lips together, I laid my hands over his, our fingers interlacing. Power surged between us, our newborn bond flaring with sudden intensity. His starlight met my moonlight, dancing together over the altar in spirals of ancient magic.

Reiji began to chant in a language I didn't recognize but instinctively understood—godspeak, the divine tongue—spoken before humans walked the earth and developed languages of their own. The words resonated within my bones, awakening something primal and otherworldly. Without thinking, I joined him, the syllables falling from my lips as though I'd known them all my life.

Power built between us, swirling around the altar like liquid light. The manganese veins in the walls brightened, then darkened, as though something within them was fighting against our magic. Cancer fighting chemo. Shadow corruption battling cosmic forces.

Our voices rose together, the chant becoming a song that echoed through the vast chamber. The candles surrounding the altar flared higher, their flames turning silver and white.

Through our bond, I felt Reiji's determination harden into something immovable. His part of the ritual grew more intense, his starlight flames burning brighter, hotter.

"For three powers divided by the same darkness," he intoned, switching to English.

"For three powers meant to stand as one," I continued, the words flowing through me from some ancient memory.

"For the magic that must never fade," we said together, our voices harmonizing with unearthly resonance.

The altar beneath our hands started to vibrate, symbols etched into its surface illuminating one by one. I recognized them now—runes of power, godspeak given form.

"I call upon Selene, goddess of the night sky," I chanted, silver light cascading from my skin.

"I call upon Eos, goddess of the dawn," Reiji answered, effervescent starlight building around him like a corona.

"We seek to undo what was wrought in necessity," we said together.

The air grew thick with power, making it difficult to breathe. The shadows in the corners of the chamber writhed as though disturbed by our invocation.

"Show us the path to liberation," Reiji continued, his voice strained.

"Show us the price that must be paid," I finished.

The words had barely left my lips when the altar blazed with blinding light. A voice that wasn't Reiji's, wasn't mine, and wasn't just one voice but many, resonated through the chamber.

"All magic demands sacrifice," it intoned. "To bind requires blood freely given. To unbind requires life freely surrendered."

Ice flooded my veins as understanding dawned. The curse had been sealed with blood—powerful, magical blood. Breaking it would require something more.

"A life?" I breathed, horror twisting my stomach. I craned my neck, peering over my shoulder at Reiji.

The truth was written in his expression. He had known. Perhaps not the specifics, but he had suspected the price would be steep. His life, or mine.

"No," I said, trying to pull my hands away. "We'll find another way."

His fingers tightened around mine and he pressed forward, pinning me against the altar, holding me in place. "There's no other way," he said softly, his lips brushing my ear. "The elemental texts were clear. Breaking the curse requires sacrifice."

My heart pounded. He was going to sacrifice me. This was just another manipulation. Another illusion.

"Then we don't break it," I insisted, squirming in his hold. "We'll find another way to—"

"No." Reiji sliced his chin to the side and closed his eyes, like he was gathering the resolve to do something distasteful. Like kill me. "The Shadow King is already breaking through. We can't stop him without united Houses, and the shifters will never truly unite with us while cursed." His dark eyes held mine, steady and resolved. "This was always how it had to end."

"Reiji, wait—"

"The curse weakens all of us," he continued, opening his eyes to stare at Veris, straining against my commands. "It's a bandage on a festering wound, useful once but now hindering true healing." He looked at me, finally, but there was no apology in his stare. There was only boundless sadness. "I've made so many mistakes." He bent his neck, claiming my lips before I could pull away. His kiss was fierce and harsh and painful, and when he pulled away, we were both breathing hard. "Let me do this one thing right."

And then I understood. He wasn't going to sacrifice me. He was going to sacrifice *himself*.

Before I could stop him, he released my hands and placed his palms directly on the central symbol of the altar—a sun, moon, and stars. "I, Reiji of the House of the Stars, descendant of the first children of Eos, offer myself as sacrifice." His voice rang with authority, with conviction. "I surrender my essence freely to break the bonds laid upon the children of Helios."

# 36

"**N**O!" I REACHED FOR his hands to drag them off the altar, but an invisible barrier prevented me from crossing the line of the central symbol. "Don't do this!" Frantic, I spun within the circle of his arms.

But it was already too late.

The altar accepted his offering with brutal efficiency. Starlight erupted from his skin, not just surrounding him but pouring from him. His eyes locked with mine as his form began to dissolve into thousands of twinkling points of light, like a constellation coming undone.

"Tell Ren I'm sorry," he said, his voice a whisper in my mind.

And then he was gone, his essence absorbed into the ritual.

I spun back to the altar, and watched it blaze with combined moonlight and starlight, with Reiji's life force, the power building to a blinding crescendo that made the very foundations of the Sun Keep tremble.

I clutched my chest and fell to my knees, tears streaming down my face. Our bond—new and barely formed—snapped with an audible sound, the emptiness it left behind a hollow ache after such a brief connection, an echo of what might have been.

The many-voice spoke again, but now it seemed to come from within me as well, resonating in my very marrow.

"The sacrifice is accepted," it intoned, using my lips and my tongue and my teeth to form the sounds. "The curse shall be broken."

The words echoed through the chamber, through my mind, through my soul.

And in their wake came a silence so profound, it felt like the universe itself had paused to witness what would follow.

The many-voice spoke again, this time repeating the words directly inside my head, a secret whispered between ancient souls.

"The sacrifice is accepted. The curse shall be broken."

Something inside me cracked open. Not pain, exactly, but the feeling of a wall inside my being splitting apart—a wall I'd never known existed until the moment it began to crumble. My vision went silver white as moonlight erupted from my skin, not streaming outward as it had before, but inward, illuminating something hidden in the deepest, darkest corners of my soul.

I was no longer in the ritual chamber.

I stood on the edge of a cliff, a cosmic precipice, stars scattered below me like a sea of spilled diamonds. My body felt both impossibly vast and achingly mortal, stretched between two realities. Before me hovered a woman—no, not a woman—a being of pure luminescence with features that mirrored my own, yet weren't quite mine. Her bottomless eyes held the wisdom of eons, her skin translucent as moonlight across water.

She reached for me, her palm against mine, our fingers perfectly aligned. Where we touched, the boundaries between us blurred.

"I've waited so long," she whispered, her voice the rustle of night winds and the silence between heartbeats. "You've carried me without knowing, from the moment of your creation."

"Who are you?" I asked, though I already knew the answer, had always known it somehow, like a forgotten word clinging to the tip of my tongue suddenly remembered.

"I am Selene," she said, her form beginning to dissolve into motes of silver light that streamed toward me. "And I am you. We were separated, bound apart for protection. As the shifters' curse breaks beyond these walls, so too does the veil that has kept us from knowing each other."

The particles of her being sank into my skin, not painful but profound, like puzzle pieces locking into place, like coming home after a lifetime of wandering. Memories that weren't mine yet belonged to me flooded through my consciousness—the birth of stars, humans turning their faces toward the night sky in worship, the first vampires fighting the shadow.

A deep, boundless love shared between three beings harnessing the power of the moon, the sun, and the stars. Selene, Helios, and Eos—lovers eternal.

"Remember," her voice echoed, now coming from within my own chest as the last of her form merged with mine. "The truth lives within you. Remember. Two bindings fall this night—one ancient, one older still."

The vision collapsed, and I found myself back in the ritual chamber, on my knees before the altar. But I was not the same. The revelation didn't strike me like lightning; it bloomed within me like a flower that had always been there, waiting for the right moment to unfurl its petals.

I wasn't just connected to Selene through the ancient bloodline of vampire queens. I was Selene incarnate, the goddess reborn in mortal form, separated from my true nature by an enchantment as old as the shifters' curse itself.

The understanding settled into my bones with quiet certainty. This wasn't new information. It was recognition, remembrance of what had always been true. My ability to channel divine power without a full harem, my connection to spirits, the way my *will* could overpower even Veris, the shifter king—these weren't gifts bestowed upon me by the goddess; they were expressions of my true nature, fragments of a goddess finding her way back to herself through the vessel of my mortal body.

The last of Reiji's starlight surged upward, carrying the binding magic of the curse with it. The manganese veins in the walls pulsed once, twice, then flared with bright, pure golden light as the shadow corruption was exposed to the surface.

A shock wave of power exploded outward, knocking everyone in the chamber off their feet. I sensed the curse breaking fully, its ancient bonds within the shifters shattering as Reiji's sacrifice tore them apart. The air itself seemed to sigh in relief, not just for the shifters, but for me, as the last of my own binding fell away.

And then, silence.

The chamber fell eerily still, the only movement the rising wisps of smoke from the extinguished candles.

I remained on my knees, too drained to stand. The revelation of my true nature echoed through my mind, too enormous to process in the wake of Reiji's death.

A low groan from across the chamber broke through my daze. Veris was rising from the floor, my *will's* hold on him one more thing shattered by the ritual. His amber eyes blazed with fury as he took in the scene—the glowing altar, the empty space where Reiji had stood, the manganese veins now pulsing with healthy golden light instead of shadow corruption.

"What have you done?" he snarled, his voice rough with rage.

I struggled to my feet, using the altar for support, silver light flickering weakly around me. The ritual had drained nearly everything I had, leaving me hollow and spent. "Exactly what I promised," I managed. "I broke your curse."

His composure shattered completely, and for the first time, I glimpsed what lurked behind his eyes—a darkness that had nothing to do with shifter magic and everything to do with the ancient and malevolent being pulling his strings.

"You've ruined everything!" Veris roared.

He lunged toward me, but Gavin intercepted him, moving with preternatural speed despite his weakened state. They collided with bone-crushing force, the impact echoing through the chamber.

The shifter commanders sprang into action, surrounding Gavin in seconds. He fought them off with desperate ferocity, his silver eyes wild. Even in his depleted state, he was magnificent, all coiled muscle and deadly precision, buying me precious seconds I couldn't use.

"Sophie, run!" he shouted, wrestling with two commanders at once.

But I couldn't run. I couldn't take a single step away from the altar, the only thing keeping me upright. The ritual had taken too much. My legs gave out, and I collapsed to my knees again, my power a mere flicker where it had once been an inferno. Through my bond with Gavin, I felt his desperate strength, his determination to protect me at all costs, even with the odds stacked impossibly against him.

"Please," I whispered, the word falling useless in the chaos, a plea to deities who had already shown their hand. I was one of them, and yet I couldn't even save myself.

A commander caught Gavin with a blow to the temple that would have killed a mortal man. He staggered, blood streaming from the wound, but continued fighting. For each shifter he dispatched, two more took their place, an endless wave of bodies overwhelming him through sheer numbers.

"Enough," Veris barked, his voice cutting through the commotion. "Take him to the portal. Throw him through. Somewhere remote." A slow, wicked grin spread across his face. "Atlantis. The queens, too."

"NO!" The scream tore from my throat, raw and primal. Atlantis—the sunken city where Veris sent his enemies. Where he'd exiled Bastian's mom, effectively executing her. It was a death sentence for the queens, possibly one for Gavin as well in his weakened state. I tried to crawl toward Gavin, dragging myself across cold stone, fingers bloody from the effort. My connection to him pulsed with his fury, his fear—not for himself, but for me.

Eight shifters finally overpowered him, forcing him to the ground with brutal efficiency. His silver eyes found mine across the chamber, luminous with a promise that transcended our circumstances.

"Sophie," he called, blood trickling down his face, his voice steady despite everything. "I will return to you." The same vow he'd made when he chose to stay behind during our first rescue mission. The same words that had sustained me through our separation.

I reached for him, my fingers curling around empty air as they dragged him away. Our bond stretched like a silver cord between us, straining but unbroken.

As they pulled him through the doorway, his struggles intensified, desperation replacing calculated resistance. The last glimpse I had of him was his face, twisted with anguish, not for the pain they inflicted nor for the inevitable fate of the queens who would accompany him through the portal to their underwater graves, but for leaving me behind.

# 37

THE SILENCE THAT FOLLOWED Gavin being dragged from the chamber crashed over me like a physical weight. I slumped to the floor, my forehead pressed against cold stone, a deep exhaustion settling into my bones. Not just bodily fatigue from the ritual, but a soul-deep weariness that made each breath an effort.

Veris's footsteps echoed as he approached, measured and unhurried. He crouched before me, bringing his face level with mine. He stayed just beyond my reach, caution evident in his posture despite my obvious weakness.

"Never say I'm not a man of my word," he said, his voice soft with mock gentleness. "Your consort and the queens are free, as we agreed."

Horror and rage sliced through my exhaustion like a blade. "Atlantis isn't freedom! It's a death sentence! You're going to drown the queens!" My voice broke, raw with fury and desperation.

Veris tutted, his expression a mockery of regret. "You should have been more specific in your terms. You asked for their release." His lips curled into a cruel smile. "You never specified where I should release them."

"You're a monster," I whispered, tears leaving hot trails down my cheeks. "You've served the Shadow King all this time. Did you ever care about your people at all?"

Something flickered in his amber eyes—a shadow passing over sunlight. "I've always done what was necessary for their survival." He reached out, his fingers hovering near my cheek but not quite touching, as though I were a dangerous animal that might still bite. "As have you. We are not so different, you and I."

I recoiled from his nearness, disgust giving me strength enough for that small defiance. The way he studied me made my skin crawl, his calculation mixed with a hunger that had nothing to do with desire and everything to do with power.

"What you've done is unforgivable," I said, each word pushing through the exhaustion.

A slow smile spread across his face, revealing too many teeth. "You're stronger than your mother was. More resilient." His eyes glinted with something that might have been respect if it hadn't been so poisoned by cruelty. "Diana would be proud, I think."

I gathered what meager energy remained in my depleted body. "I'm going to kill you," I promised, each word distinct and measured.

Veris laughed, the sound echoing in the cavernous chamber. "Perhaps someday." He stood, towering over my prone form, casting me in shadow. "But not *this* day."

He turned to his commanders, those who remained after the others had dragged Gavin away. "Take her down to the dungeon, to the cell we prepared for her." A cruel smile curved his lips as he added, "She's going to be here a while."

Strong hands gripped my arms, hauling me upright. My head spun with the sudden movement, black spots dancing across my vision. The ritual chamber blurred as they dragged me forward, my feet scraping uselessly against stone.

My mother's ghost appeared one last time as we passed through the doorway, her form flickering like a candle flame caught in a draft. She looked unbearably sad.

"You won't be able to see or hear me down there," she said, her voice reaching me through the growing darkness. "But I'll be with you. Be brave, my shining girl."

We descended into the bowels of the Sun Keep, each step taking me deeper into the earth, farther from sky and moon and stars. The air grew stale, tainted with old blood and despair.

The cell they brought me to was unlike the ones where they'd kept the queens or Javier, which had been simple stone chambers. This one was designed for containment of a different magnitude. Heavy manganese bands embedded in the floor and ceiling channeled corrupted magic in a circular pattern. Foul sigils etched into the walls pulsed like living ink, ward patterns I'd never seen before, likely because they had no place in this world.

My captors threw me into the cell with casual brutality, my body hitting the stone floor with enough force to drive whatever breath remained from my lungs. The cell door slammed shut with a finality that echoed through my bones, and their retreating footsteps let me know I was truly alone.

I lay there, my cheek pressed against unforgiving stone, too exhausted to move. Through my bonds, I reached outward, seeking the familiar presences of my consorts. I sensed unease and expectation from Javier, Bastian, Ash, and Thane. But Gavin was pure rage and chaos. That I could feel him at all meant he'd survived his trip through the portal to Atlantis. If I were looking for bright sides, I would have started there, but there was no room for hope or optimism in me at the moment.

I curled onto my side, drawing my knees to my chest. Slowly, my tears dried, leaving salty tracks on my skin. In their place grew something harder, something that even exhaustion and isolation couldn't extinguish. Not despair, not surrender. Resolve.

*Remember who you are*, my mother had said, her words echoed by Selene moments ago.

*I am a survivor.*

*I am a mother.*

*I am a queen.*

*I am the High Queen.*

*I am Selene incarnate.*

*I am a goddess.*

I closed my eyes, saving what little strength remained. They had made a fatal mistake, these shifters. These servants of shadow. They had left me alive. They had given me time.

And when my power returned—when my consorts came for me, as I knew they would—I would show Veris exactly what it meant to imprison a goddess.

I pulled the tiny box containing my mom's hair from my pocket and clutched it in both hands, holding it tight against my chest. As my mom had forewarned, I couldn't see her, not down here where the suppression wards were still active, but I knew she was with me. I wasn't alone.

Darkness claimed me, consciousness finally slipping away, but not before I whispered into the shadows,

"You can hold me for now, but not forever."

To be continued...

Another cliffhanger, I know. I'm sorry! I promise it will all be worth it in the end! If you haven't already subscribed to my newsletter, you definitely should – and you'll get another little story from Bas's POV when you do!

Scan the QR code or go to the URL below to read Bas's POV

https://bit.ly/BastianPOV

# ABOUT LINDSEY SPARKS

Lindsey Sparks lives her life with one foot in a book—so long as that book transports her to a magical world or bends the rules of science. Her novels, from Post-apocalyptic (writing as Lindsey Fairleigh) to Paranormal Romance, always provide a hearty dose of unreality, along with plenty of history, intrigue, adventure, mythology, and romance.

When she's not working on her next novel, Lindsey spends her time hanging out with her three little boys, working in her garden, or making bookish crafts. She lives in the Pacific Northwest with her family and their small pack of cats and dogs.

www.authorlindseysparks.com

## SIGNED COPIES & MERCH:

lindseysparksbookshop.com

## MAIN SOCIAL MEDIA

Instagram: @authorlindseysparks

Threads: @authorlindseysparks

YouTube: Author Lindsey Sparks

Discord: discord.gg/smTeDHQBhT

**www.authorlindseysparks.com/join-newsletter**